Without Enid and Other Tales:

Seventeen Short Stories

Stephen Constance

CP
THE CHOIR PRESS

First published in the United Kingdom in 2023 by
The Choir Press

ISBN 978-1-78963-348-1

Without Enid and Other Tales is a work of fiction. Names, characters, businesses, events and incidents are the products of the author's imagination. Any resemblance to actual persons, living or dead, or actual events and places is unintentional and purely coincidental. Some long-standing institutions, agencies and public offices may be mentioned to create scenery for the purposes of the story but the characters and events involved are wholly imaginary.

Contents

Acknowledgements

Although I have made acknowledgements before and after some of the tales, I must reiterate my thanks to Sophie, without whom it would have not been possible to breach the complexities of life with a laptop and Bethany, who has been a staunch reader and constructive critic. Di reads everything I submit and James may not realise his sense of humour has aided me more than he imagines! Thanks to Miles and The Choir Press – they must sometimes despair of callow internet users like me – and a big thank you to all who may purchase, perhaps savour and recommend the tales to their friends.

Just a final word on the Forest dialect. I have read various writers on the subject and since they vary considerably in their interpretation of what is not a written 'language', I felt free to write what I've heard phonetically over the years, although there are some words that have become generally accepted as authentic. For example, 'ship' (sheep); 'thee, thou' and the delightful 'zurrey o!' (Good heavens!).

Stephen Constance

Introduction

Now somewhat venerable, the author has spent most of his life tuning pianos, playing in jazz bands and somehow trying to find the time to put pen to paper in between. He received little encouragement from his family – music was all – and apart from this varied collection of short stories, there are novels, children's tales, poetry and even a radio play that have never seen the light of day.

From the poignant 'Without Enid' to the vulgar, yet hilarious 'A Hat for all Seasons', readers will surely find something that will appeal to them, and the six stories set in the Forest of Dean are a product of the author having worked in the area most of his life, also spending five years as a resident there in the seventies. There are no prizes offered for realising that a certain city in the Marches is the scenario for some tales, and further afield, 'Child of the Harvest' is a tear-jerker set in New Zealand. Too many ill-spent trips to Ireland resulted in 'D' boots', a completely illogical farce and 'The Rubber Tree Plant' dips a tentative toe into the realms of science fiction.

An autobiography is currently in the making and meanwhile it is hoped readers will derive a good deal of enjoyment from what is on offer in this book.

Without Enid

A novella for Sophie

Wendell had lived in Sutton all his life. Formerly known as the Royal Borough of Sutton Coldfield, in 1974 it became absorbed into the omnivorous sprawl that is Birmingham: a happening that did not impress the majority of the town's inhabitants, but Wendell was not amongst them. A mild-mannered soul, he remained indifferent to the change and deemed it not a matter to be overly concerned about. He'd retired at the right time with a more than adequate pension and still inhabited the several-hundred-year-old property he'd inherited from his parents in Coleshill Street. Situated near John Veasy Gardens, Coleshill Street was considered part of Sutton's designated conservation area which included High Street, King Edward's Square, Upper Clifton and Mill Street.

Of more significance was the fact that Wendell's abode stood no distance from the Three Tuns hostelry: another historic building where he frequently met a long-established friend, Denver, in order to partake of a pint and to 'chew over the fat'.

Unlike Wendell, Denver had not aspired to management at the Longbridge behemoth where they had both worked. Back in the day he'd been a culpable member of the notorious night shift, some of whom had been caught bedded down for the night; Denver had just managed to awaken before discovery and narrowly escaped instant dismissal. That Wendell had achieved management level and Denver had not, was no mystery. Wendell just got on with people and with the job, whilst Denver hated his place of employment and only exerted his indolent self long enough to claim his pay packet at the end of the week. Some years previously they'd chanced to meet on the short daily train trip to

1

town and the fact that Denver lived in a council house in a less salubrious area, did not impede the burgeoning friendship that quickly developed between them.

They could not have been more of a contrast physically. The eccentric Denver sported a handlebar moustache, possessed a prominent nose and probably confused the population at large as to his station in life. He wore jeans to work, his footwear took the form of Dr Martens and his various sweaters quite blatantly proclaimed semi-pornographic messages. He'd read the left-wing *Daily Worker* one day and the *Daily Telegraph* the next (he could do the crossword in fifteen minutes) and his attachment to Wendell derived from the fact that Wendell was one of the most amicable, amenable dudes anyone could wish to encounter.

Both parties shared similar interests. They fished in one of Sutton Park's pools, supported one or other of the two local rugby teams and often went with their nearest and dearest to a meal and night out at the Tuns. Sometimes they would visit one of the two theatres to take in a play and another option was to simply picnic in the park itself.

It is not a particularly well-known fact that Sutton Park is one of the largest urban parks in Europe and it was largely preserved by the eminent philanthropist and benefactor, Bishop Vesey. In the turbulent reign of Henry VIII, Bishop Vesey was surely a shining light. He was a beacon of compassion in an era of turmoil, corruption and squalor and, among other things, he founded the Bishop Vesey Grammar School; a seminary that still exists and thrives to this day.

No more than five foot five in height, Wendell could be very effusive when the mood took him. His mild features were deceptive and if roused he could become quite animated. But he had understandably receded into his shell of late and this was the first time for a month that he'd consented to visit his favourite watering hole. This was scarcely surprising, for only three weeks had elapsed since the funeral and he'd not wanted to see anyone. A hit-and-run driver, subsequently proved to have been on drugs, had struck Enid when she'd simply been crossing the road.

Now her deprived and inconsolable husband was sitting opposite Denver in the pub. Solemn and haunted, he occasionally acknowledged gestures of sympathy from the locals and struggled to lower the level of the liquid contents of his personalised pewter beer mug.

Suddenly he leant forward and said to Denver, "I've got the tickets."

"The tickets?"

"Yes, I did it online." Wendell was computer literate and Denver was not; simply because Denver couldn't be arsed and his friend's out of the blue statement disconcerted him.

"And what did yow get the tickets for?" Despite, like Wendell, having been educated at King Edward's, Denver made no attempt to disguise his obvious local accent.

"The ballet, of course. We always go this time of year."

Denver knew of the late Enid's passion for ballet. It had been one of the delights of her life when the Royal Ballet had come to the Hippodrome and formed a sister company to perform regularly in Birmingham. They'd seen *Swan Lake*, *The Nutcracker*, *Romeo and Juliet* and other works, and according to the deluded Wendell, they would be seeing *The Nutcracker* again.

"Yes," he reiterated, "we go to see it every year."

He sat back and waited for his friend to respond.

Denver took a large swig of ale, at the same time wondering how he was going to reply to this enigmatic statement.

"You taking your niece, then?" He was well aware Wendell had no children, but often talked about his sister's girl, towards whom they had always been very generous.

Without any change of expression, Wendell simply said, "No, it'll be just Enid and me. We have seats in the circle, you know, just like we always have ..."

ONE

Lydia lived round the corner from her grandparents in leafy Edgbaston and owed much to their keen interest in her welfare. Grandpa Prosser was pretty loaded. He'd been a big noise in the Bird's Custard factory before it closed and humoured both his wife and his granddaughter via his well-stocked bank balance.

He didn't care what their demands were, providing he could visit the golf course when he chose or, as a member at Warwickshire, nod off whilst watching the cricket.

Grandma Prosser had been a factory girl when Grandpa had first met her, but with polished and careful enunciation, she had become – in her own eyes – a pillar of posh Edgbaston society. She played bridge regularly, attended the Anglican church and met friends for coffee in the stylish modern bistro that someone had not long opened by the station. In stark contrast, she also helped with the local food bank (was there a need for one in this affluent part of the city, or were a goodly number of its regulars either mean or realised they were on to a good thing?).

Perhaps more importantly, she shared an overriding interest in Lydia. Lydia lived for ballet and like all seven-year-olds was fully convinced she would one day dance the Sugar Plum Fairy in the fantastic *Nutcracker*. With this in mind, she religiously attended the nearby ballet school's weekend programme. She and Grandma Prosser had been to see *The Nutcracker* two years running and much against her mother's will, who thought it outrageously extravagant, Lydia had persuaded Grandma to take her again. Her mum Sharon didn't have much truck with culture. Aged thirtyish, she preferred the pop music of the noughties. She'd been to Glastonbury more than once and gone to sleep in Symphony Hall when persuaded by hubby Jeremy to attend a performance of some interminable work by Bruckner. She had more in common with Lydia's renegade brother Jason, aged ten and a fanatical Villa supporter. Grandma had succeeded in largely eradicating her granddaughter's local accent but had despaired of Jason. The boy obstinately refused to refine his speech and although he knew it irritated Grandma greatly, he persisted in his determination to be dead Brummie. This secretly delighted Grandpa. He'd never forgotten his roots and though an ardent cricket lover who found football anathema, he was quite happy to treat Jason to matchdays at Villa Park throughout the season. True, it did antagonise his snobbish spouse, but it went a long way to appease his artistically brain-dead daughter-in-law and did not seem to concern his rather aloof and pretentious son Jeremy.

Right now, Lydia was deliriously excited. She and Grandma

were readying themselves to go to the ballet, though it was really just Grandma who was fussing in front of the mirror. Lydia had donned her party dress and been whisked round to the grandparents' with something akin to impatience by Sharon, who was anxious to visit the city's Bullring for some retail therapy.

It was taking Grandma the usual long time to apply her make-up and quite innocently, Lydia had once asked her why this was so. This induced a tart reply from Grandpa, who happened to enter the room at the wrong moment.

"There's more to do nowadays than there used to be," he said cheerfully and somehow succeeded in evading the hairbrush that Grandma threw at him.

*

The station wasn't far away, and it didn't take long for the suburban train carrying Lydia and a now smart-looking Grandma (Grandpa had to admit 'she scrubbed up well') to arrive at New Street, and for them to find the easiest exit for the theatre. They were used to it by now, but if you hadn't been before, it was easy to head off in the wrong direction.

With a modern section added on, the Hippodrome had become the home of the Birmingham Royal Ballet, sister company to its counterpart in London and you could more or less see any production here that you could see in the capital.

Back in the summer Lydia had been further indulged in going to see Prokofiev's fabulous *Romeo and Juliet* and parts of it had been inclined to scare her. She was quite alarmed during the 'Dance of the Knights' when the warring families had fought with swords and a pile of supposedly dead bodies had taken centre stage. Grandma had been quick to reassure her. They weren't really dead, she said, and the small girl was torn between excitement and alarm at the awesome music and what the dancers appeared to be doing to one another. She knew a fight would take place between the evil rats and the toy soldiers in *The Nutcracker*, but as the rodents would lose and the ballet eventually have a happy ending, all would be well, and she preferred it to the Shakespearean spectacle for that reason.

Two

There was always a buzz of anticipation as the audience filed in and, with an extraordinary cacophony of sounds, the orchestra warmed up. Grandma explained to Lydia that they were probably practising scales and tricky bits and the girl accepted this as she nodded and stood up for the third time to let people along the row.

Sitting next to Lydia was a nice old man in a smart suit who offered her a sweet. Normally she would obey the strict rule that you never took sweets from strangers, but as he invited Grandma to take one too, she gave him her best smile – a gap-toothed effort – and politely accepted. She noticed he had no one sitting next to him and thought it almost certain that someone would come to claim the seat at the last minute. They'd have to be quick, for the orchestral noise had subsided, the hum from the audience ceased and, to considerable applause, the conductor appeared. He raised his baton and the glorious music began. After her first visit, Lydia had tried to describe the spectacle to her teacher who the following year suggested she try and write about it. This was an ambitious project for someone merely six years old, who couldn't spell Tchaikovsky and was not allowed a smartphone with which to look it all up. Notwithstanding, she'd still received high marks for her effort and, feeling inspired, resolved she would do even better this year.

The first act passed in a whirl of music and a panoply of mesmerising dance. The costumes were wonderful, the scenery and effects exotic and a backstage choir sang ethereally in the 'Waltz of the Snowflakes'.

The interval arrived too soon, and they made their way downstairs to the bar where drinks were awaiting them. Lydia had a normally forbidden Coca-Cola, and the usually abstemious Grandma had something which her streetwise granddaughter suspected was a gin and tonic. That was one of the advantages of being with Grandma rather than Mummy. With very little protest from the former, you could eat and drink what you liked and did not have to consume what was allegedly good for you.

The genial old man had come down the stairway from the

balcony behind them and it did not take long for effusive Grandma to engage him in conversation. A formidable inquisitor when intrigued, she could give anyone the 'third degree'. This did not intimidate her current victim, who answered her somewhat invasive questioning with a surprising amount of tolerance. Nevertheless, Grandma found his use of the words 'us' and 'we' disturbing when he quite clearly remained unaccompanied; especially as the vacant seat next to him had still not been filled.

Lydia looked forward to the moment in the second act when all Clara's toy dolls became animated and her particular favourite, the Sugar Plum Fairy danced to the accompaniment of that lovely low instrument. Grandpa, who knew about such things, said it was a bass clarinet which added its lugubrious tones to the dulcet, tinkling sounds of the celeste.

Sadly, it all seemed to be over very quickly and being ushered out of a different exit onto a street, which fortunately Grandma knew, they hastily made their way to the station. They were accompanied by the same old gentleman they'd befriended in the theatre.

Smiling engagingly at them, he produced a card and expressed a wish that he and his 'wife' might see them again. To Grandma's bewilderment he said that he thought 'Enid' had thoroughly enjoyed the ballet and it was a pity the 'couple' had to catch a train. He hoped to make Grandma and Lydia's further acquaintance and, sadly loitering, seemed reluctant to part company.

Although it had been a matinee performance, the time of year meant that darkness was visibly encroaching and bidding the old gentleman goodbye, they hurriedly left him, scurrying down into the bowels of New Street to catch their train to Edgbaston.

Sitting opposite her granddaughter in the rather scruffy suburban carriage, Grandma puzzled over the old man's use of the plural when referring to he and his wife or partner.

How had this mysterious Enid supposedly enjoyed the ballet?

Whoever she was, had she been sitting elsewhere in the auditorium? Surely this could not be the case when the seat next to the old man was vacant?

On the other hand, did she exist and if so, had they had a quarrel and she declined to come at the last minute? This also didn't make sense and alternatively, could Enid have been that lady sitting two seats to the right of him? A relative, maybe, but if so, why would she show no sign of recognition and he of her? Besides, the lady had appeared to be very attached to the man on her right. They'd exchanged enthusiastic glances at climaxes during the performance and did not avail themselves of the interval to claim any ordered drinks. They were almost certainly nothing to do with the old man and the more Grandma contemplated the whole matter, the more she found herself unable to comprehend it.

Utterly reliable Grandpa was there to meet them at the station. When he wasn't practising his golf swing or bemoaning England's inability to overcome its former colonies at cricket, he could be quite useful. Grandma thought she might put the conundrum of the 'old man at the ballet' before him. Though timorous over the countless small jobs that required doing about the house, he had quite a brain and when motivated, often came up with the answer to things.

Who was Enid? In the train Grandma had idly perused the old man's card. Spurning frills and with an absence of garish colour, it simply stated him to be: 'W. BARNARD, COLESHILL VILLA, ROYAL BOROUGH OF SUTTON COLDFIELD.' Other information included a phone number and one concession to modern living, an e-mail address. No further information was given, but he was ostensibly not computer illiterate like herself.

Perhaps Grandma could find an excuse to get in touch with this 'W. Barnard', though it might not be a good idea. One old codger in her life was enough and anyway, Grandpa might not like it.

THREE

A whole line of chattering small girls stood at the barre in the junior room at Ashleigh Ballet School. They mostly didn't wear tutus at their weekend classes, but as some of them were to take part in the full-time students' latest production, they were dressed to perform in the rehearsal that came later.

Since the success of the film *Billy Elliot* quite a few boys had come to mingle amongst them, and these showed no trace of self-consciousness. As the junior ballet mistress called for order, a hush descended. A French lady, Madame Valois made no concessions where their extreme youth was concerned, taking no prisoners and insisting on good behaviour. Ballet requires absolute discipline and woe betide those who were not prepared to comply. They did not last long and all premature dreams of fame with the Birmingham Royal Ballet or any other company would quickly evaporate.

Upon reaching the age of eleven, pupils could apply to attend the main school and providing they possessed the required skill, had a fair chance of being accepted. The school also provided an excellent all-round education and was definitely the route to follow in order to achieve higher things.

Lydia and her friend Rosalind could hardly wait for these formative years to pass and Grandpa, who sometimes came to collect Lydia, reckoned they should be sprinkled with garden manure in the hope it would make them grow up sooner. Brother Jason, who still thought ballet prissy, promptly volunteered to administer the excreta. He was hastily prevented from visiting the garden shed to raid one of the sacks of the stuff and threatened with exclusion from Villa's next home match if he dared to try and carry out the foul deed. This threat did suffice to ensure that an uneasy truce broke out between him and his sister who were not far apart in age and forever falling out with each other.

Lydia had been very surprised when one Saturday, Rosalind's Great Uncle Wendell had picked her up from the ballet school and there had been instant recognition between Lydia and Wendell. When informed of this by her granddaughter, Grandma had no hesitation in inviting him round to visit. She hoped that by doing so she would kill two birds with one stone by encouraging the girls' friendship and finding out more about this mysterious 'old man' they'd met at *The Nutcracker*. He talked of his deceased wife as if she were still alive and Grandma remarked to a disinterested Grandpa that Rosalind's Great Uncle might well benefit from seeing someone she termed 'a shrink'.

But to Grandma's surprise, Grandpa woke up and demurred. He opined that if the man chose, he should be left to live with his delusions. Why, Grandpa queried, should not those who chose to live in the past be left unhindered; particularly if their former existence had been more palatable than their present one? Her eyebrows ascending with slight disbelief at Grandpa's unusual viewpoint, Grandma still thought Wendell's unwillingness to concede his wife's death a strange aberration. And with this unexpected statement, Grandpa had proved once again that he could stray from his usual casual and conventional attitude to life. With the wisdom garnered from umpteen years of marital sparring and knowing him so well, she decided to drop the subject. If she persisted, he would surely elaborate at length and the whole discussion would become too deep for her: anything for a peaceful life. She just hoped Wendell would eventually recover and emerge from his current delusions unscathed.

The rehearsal went well and in an almost unprecedented pep talk, Madame Valois intimated that she was looking forward to the evening performance. This made a change from her customary tendency to pick holes and resulted in Rosalind being on a high, going home to have tea with Lydia at Grandma's house; with both girls almost too excited to eat.

FOUR

The kitchen at Coleshill had a charm in that it had retained most of its original features. This reluctance to implement anything too drastic in the way of kitchen equipment or modernisation did not wholly meet with the approval of niece Helen. She patiently stood, brow creased, whilst Wendell struggled with the ageing stove and utensils in order to provide them with a meal. To give him his due, since his retirement, he'd always done his fair share in the house. Whilst not exactly being a 'new-age man', he stoically stuck to his task and was also not shy where such aids as the vacuum cleaner were concerned.

Since her aunt had so tragically died, Helen had subtly contributed meals to his freezer and to help keep him occupied, on some Saturdays sent him into town, where he changed for Edgbaston and picked up Rosalind from the ballet. From there he either conducted her to Lydia's home, where she sometimes stopped the weekend or brought her back on the train. Otherwise, it was a bind to drive into Brum twice on a Saturday and she sensed Wendell's willingness to help probably provided a respite from what must be an aching and unremitting loneliness.

Her frown increased as she surveyed the kitchen table. Four places were laid, and it seemed nothing on earth would persuade Wendell from providing a plateful of food for his beloved Enid. Fortunately, Rosalind appeared less disconcerted about it than her mother. They'd discussed it with Dad and even Lydia's folks, and both little girls were still adamant that they didn't think it was a lot to worry about. They often lived in a fantasy world themselves and if it comforted him, why shouldn't Uncle Wendell do the same?

When Helen's family came to tea, any surplus food usually ended up inside their doleful and voracious basset hound, Nureyev; an inappropriately named canine whose increasing obesity obviously hampered any resemblance he might have to his once extremely agile and illustrious namesake. Helen could not envisage where Enid's food went when they were not present, but she was pretty sure poor Wendell laid two places when alone and her initial attempt at questioning this practice had met with what could be termed stout resistance.

The next step might have to be to seek medical advice, though on this, opinion differed. Her husband was all for it, as was Lydia's mum, the forthright Sharon: not that that prosaic lady's views on the matter were ones that Helen particularly sought or valued. On the other hand, Lydia's grandma was lauding the expertise of a consultant she knew of in Lichfield and Lydia's grandpa stuck to his guns and avowed Wendell should be left to get on with life without too much interference.

The eggs, chips, and bacon left the stove in reasonably edible condition and Helen fervently hoped that when alone, Wendell's culinary efforts did not result in the chip pan catching fire.

Waiting for a moment when he answered the call of nature and with Rosalind assigned the wiping up cloth, Helen commenced to do the dishes. The contents of the fourth plate were scraped into the bowl Uncle Wendell had kindly provided for Nureyev's visits and without hesitation or refined table manners, the basset hound consumed it with undisguised relish.

Friday night meant an after-meal visit with Wendell to the Three Tuns, where Dad would meet them, and Rosalind would revel in the company of 'cool' Denver. He spoilt her rotten and if not discouraged, bought her endless soft drinks and unhealthy packets of crisps. The glass of water masquerading as a gin and tonic for Enid remained untouched, as it would do, and did not attract comment from any of the regulars who were fully aware of the situation.

Although the pub was busy, attracting its usual weekend clientele, Helen considered it fortunate they'd not decided to come on a Tuesday night. Tuesday night was karaoke night and that hangover from the sixties, Denver, would most likely have embarrassed them by insisting on doing his execrable Elvis impression! Rosalind had resorted to hiding under the table during this tortuous exhibition, until he had been usurped by another talentless individual, whose attempt at a Cliff Richard number was hardly much of an improvement.

Helen had always liked the Tuns but thought some of its renovations had destroyed the aura of timelessness that had once prevailed within it. The impressive, fronted building was redolent with history, and she thought it a pity that the original carriageway had been glazed and enclosed in to make more room. There were sundry myths and stories, including the one about the poor drummer boy who was alleged to haunt the cellar. He'd been murdered whilst in the stocks and unceremoniously dumped amongst the beer barrels by Roundhead troops. The Civil War was rooted in the history of the pub and Helen wondered if that sober and merciless puritan, Oliver Cromwell, had celebrated his victory here after the Battle of Worcester with something stronger than non-alcoholic mead. Another intriguing thought was that the Bard himself had graced the tavern with his presence and just suppose she was sitting in the very ancient place where Shakespeare had placed his exalted derrière.

But everyone had to make a living in the very different and almost surrealist twenty-first century. The food was excellent, and the beer well kept. The invasive TV screens were a bind, but a dartboard remained prominent and Rosalind's dad, Frank, and Denver were currently taking advantage of the pub's snooker table.

She noticed Wendell's receptacle had at last become empty and she offered to replenish it, but he seemed too distracted, sitting there restlessly and muttering to himself. The bogus gin and tonic remained untouched and with a despairing sigh, she thought that it really had become a matter of some urgency. Something would have to be done about Wendell before it became too late.

FIVE

Lydia and Rosalind only became friends after Lydia had been to see this Christmas's performance of *The Nutcracker*. It was a 'girl' thing. Rosalind had fallen out with one of their number who was inclined to be spiteful, this possibly caused by the slightly obnoxious child's inability to keep abreast and her ultimate exclusion from the Saturday morning class.

Rosalind had been upset that Great Uncle Wendell had not taken her to the performance as usual, and his explanation that he just wished to take Great Aunt Enid she naturally found inexplicable, but she was resigned to it far more than the adults in her family. The situation had made Helen despair. Without success, she attempted to convince Wendell that Enid was no longer around. This met with little response. He would instantly clam up and could give no good reason for excluding Rosalind, other than commenting that he and Enid wanted to go 'on their own'. Previous visits had been happy, exciting occasions, and Helen could only conclude that his present morose and bizarre mood would not enable him to cope with the ebullient Rosalind. His great niece's presence was apparently perfectly acceptable and, indeed, very welcome normally, but he somehow could not countenance her coming to the ballet with 'them' this time. He reckoned Great Aunt Enid was poorly and if Rosalind didn't mind, she'd just have to let them go on their own.

Somewhat wearied by the whole business, Helen was currently discussing the state of play with distracted Frank. At the time of the pre-Christmas *Nutcracker* money had been tight, and they couldn't raise the necessary to take Rosalind to a performance themselves. But the little girl had been bravely reconciled to it and had contented herself by discussing it with her new friend, whose grandma had been very sympathetic and hinted she might take both girls to the Birmingham Royal Ballet's summer production. She said it would be 'on her', a generous gesture which Helen's pride might not allow her to accept.

At present the two girls were visiting the vast Sutton Park with the two fishermen, Wendell and Denver. This was a perfectly acceptable circumstance for Wendell. Enid had never come to the park when they were spending hours with rod and line 'catching helpless underwater creatures,' only to return them from whence they had come: she much preferred to stay at home. She would happily visit the park for summer picnics or go there with Wendell to sample its varied attractions; in her case, this included the study of its plentiful and often rare Lepidoptera.

Lydia was making her first visit to Rosalind's home, reciprocating a couple of weekends at Edgbaston, and now accompanied by a distrusting Helen. Wendell had picked them up from ballet and taken them on the train to Sutton. This was an expensive business, involving getting Rosalind there in the first place, shopping and having lunch in town with a bewildered Wendell and returning in time to fetch them from the school.

On the Sunday they humoured Wendell by coming to see Enid and himself and afterwards he and Denver had taken them to the park.

March had taken over the year in a mild manner. The daffodils were burgeoning and with it being lighter at night, they would have plenty of time to explore. They'd both become used to Wendell's references to his no longer existing wife and it was just something which, to their respective mothers' consternation, they still fully accepted.

Helen thought it unhealthy and noticed there were other changes beginning to show in Wendell's behaviour and his normally presentable appearance. She did his washing, but his change of clothing did not occur that frequently and with Frank's connivance, she had taken the bull by the horns and contacted Wendell's surgery. A battleaxe of a receptionist maintained that if

Wendell was indisposed, he should make an appointment in person and, not sure of her ground, Helen rang off and they were now considering the alternatives.

"Have they taken that cumbersome idiot of a hound with them?"

In referring to Nureyev, Frank nearly always deprecated the creature. He hadn't wanted Rosalind to have the basset hound in the first place, but in a very short time, had come to love him.

"Of course."

"Good thing."

It hadn't taken long for the dog to become one of the family and he soon realised that Rosalind and her friends were vulnerable members of the human species. He adored her and strangers who in his eyes had dubious intentions, were treated to a subterranean growl until they were deemed acceptable to him and everyone else.

An absolute clown where children were concerned, Denver quickly gained canine approval and had even attained status as the primary stick thrower. This was an activity at which, fortunately, the not particularly nimble Nureyev soon grew tired. Sniffing the park's proliferating butterflies was more in his line, though he could hardly be termed a success at this. At his lumbering approach, most of these elegant creatures would flee rapidly and he was frequently left inhaling the aroma of the floral head from which they had hastily departed!

Water was another compelling attraction. With joyous alacrity, Nureyev would gambol into one of the park's several pools. His exit, which involved shaking half its contents from himself and over anyone else who happened to be near, caused the two little girls to quickly absent themselves from the scene in hasty flight, accompanied by shrieks of unrestrained laughter.

The dog's unsavoury habit of inspecting people's crotches was promptly quashed by a sharp tap on the nose, but nothing could be done about his perfectly natural habit of doing the same to the hindquarters of friendly animals of the same species. A vulgar, but harmless bachelor who often frequented the less salubrious alehouses; Denver had once speculated that if Nureyev's ambitions in that direction had been fulfilled, what would the feasible progeny of such an unlikely liaison look like? He declared that whilst a cross between a poodle and a basset hound might be acceptable, what if (with difficulty!) Nureyev had chosen to mate with a Great Dane? The mind boggled at the prospect!

A somewhat disinterested Wendell had smiled wanly at his friend's attempt at humour and anxiously looked about him to make sure the girls were out of earshot. He studiously ignored the question and said, "Are you coming back to tea then, Denver?"

Not for the first time, Denver seemed nonplussed. He wondered what tea his friend would provide, and if the pretence of Enid's presence would be perpetuated.

"You sure?"

Despite his ostensibly deteriorating mental condition, Wendell could sometimes be resolute.

"Of course I am. Enid enjoys your company. She said what a good night out it was at the Tuns last weekend."

Denver sighed inwardly. He'd noticed that his friend's shirt wasn't the cleanest and he wondered how Helen was managing to cope with the situation. There'd been the incident midweek, when Wendell had apparently gone down to the local store in the middle of the night for some milk and came back very distressed upon finding the store closed. A bit of an insomniac, a neighbour had spotted Wendell on the doorstep and keeping an eye, had gently ushered him inside, ringing Helen, who promptly came with Frank, both distinctly wearied and in a lather of concern.

According to Helen's befuddled uncle, it was Enid who had run short of milk, and nothing they did to explain why the local store wasn't open at midnight would pacify him.

Attending to his rod, Denver still had a protective eye on the girls who, contrary to the rules, were a little distance away feeding two of the park's eager and avaricious ponies. Ponies had been residents of the park for centuries and were there as of right. An interested spectator, the ubiquitous Nureyev treated these equine curiosities to the odd woof, which they contemptuously disregarded. Taking umbrage, he retraced his steps to seek solace in the company of the two fishermen, who absorbed in their own silent piscatorial reverie, were inclined to treat him in a similarly disinterested fashion.

With clouds gathering to further darken the fading light, the two fishermen decided to pack their rods away, at the same time, rounding up the girls and dog in order to take advantage of the park's Wyndley Leisure Centre. Here could be purchased diverse milkshakes or smoothies for the junior element and a free bowl of water and a doggy biscuit for the faithful Nureyev. This would have been perfectly satisfactory had Denver not nearly always bemoaned the fact that the place didn't sell alcohol. He intimated that coffee would pollute his 'Guinness stream', an observation that before Enid's demise, would have provoked an appreciative guffaw from his friend, but on this occasion scarcely induced a fleeting smile.

SIX

As the spring advanced, Wendell's mental condition deteriorated further and only a chance visit with Rosalind to the local surgery, gave Helen the opportunity to talk to a sympathetic young locum. Wendell now had no concept of time and, unless supervised, had become too much of a responsibility. He still seemed able to feed himself, although his meals were irregular and on the domestic front, if it had not been for Helen's intervention, the house would have become a tip. Trying to balance a job, look after her own household and cope with Wendell's erratic behaviour had become a nightmare. Things could not be allowed to continue as they were, and the young lady locum soon set the wheels in motion.

Wendell was to have an assessment. He'd somehow agreed to have something that masqueraded as a 'general physical', but the purpose of this was to examine his mental condition. Frank had persuaded him to comply by asserting that all menfolk should have this check-up on a regular basis. With blatant mendacity he stated that he had it done most years and in so doing averted health problems before they began. This ensured that the capable young doctor could, with dexterous subterfuge, learn enough to make an accurate prognosis.

With spring morphing into summer, Wendell went downhill fast and after a lot of agonising, Helen was given power of attorney. He was not short of cash and with him hardly knowing what day it was, they reluctantly put him into a care home and hoped the money wouldn't run out. Helen was aware that she'd ultimately inherit the property in Coleshill Street, but not a covetous person, she considered that if needs must, it would have to be sold to pay the care home fees. Supporting her in this, Frank nevertheless thought the amount required was outrageous and, as a bit of a socialist, resolved to instigate some sort of an enquiry, perhaps aided by the local MP.

Wendell did not take much notice of his fellow residents and persisted with his illusion that Enid was still extant: not a belief that the home's staff in any way discouraged. They were used to such aberrations and just let him keep up the pretence aided by a certain amount of complicity on their part. When visiting, Rosalind and Lydia were sometimes recognised and sometimes not, but their visits were very much enjoyed by the other residents, some of whom had never experienced the vivacity of children even before they had become old and tragically, cruelly forgotten.

One old lady played the battered old upright piano, an instrument not quite ruined by the overwhelming central heating. Even on coldish summer days, the heating could be on. The care home proprietor informed Helen that this was the only thing the lady could still do. Millicent had been a BBC accompanist most of her life and she had lost none of her powers where music was concerned. Everything else had gone. She never knew where she was and went to a day centre twice a week where she offered to pay her dues several times over and generally lived in a world containing no worries, having a gentle nature that endeared her to all the care workers.

To the delight of Lydia and Rosalind, she had some transcriptions of ballet music and on several occasions, they'd treated an ancient but enraptured audience to their own impromptu versions of scenes from *Swan Lake* and *The*

Nutcracker. This was to generous applause and the liberal dispersal of confectionery.

EIGHT

As it does, time remorselessly elapsed. Without anyone harbouring any doubts, at the age of eleven, both the not-so-little girls made it to the Ashleigh Ballet School.

Not only did they thrive, but without them being aware of it, they were already being viewed as potential candidates for the Birmingham Royal Ballet and a bright future. They knew that competition would be intense. A good number of the high-flying stars came from abroad, from countries like Cuba, an island that was still a Communist state and had gained its proficiency at ballet through an association with the former Soviet Union.

One day, after they had been at the school some four years, quite amazingly, a leading soloist from the Birmingham Royal Ballet came to talk to them. Not only did he talk; he demonstrated the great leaps that male dancers seem to spend most of their time doing and in something she would never forget, performed a *pas de deux* with the head girl!

That particular summer, Grandma Prosser was coming to see *Romeo and Juliet* and, now fifteen-year-olds, Lydia and Rosalind were to be allowed backstage to watch the performance she attended. Becoming somewhat advanced in years, it took Grandma considerably more time to prepare herself, but this did not deter Grandpa from commenting that she 'scrubbed up well' and Sharon's sotto voce remark that he obviously hadn't been to Specsavers lately fell mostly on semi-deaf ears. It was only picked up by eighteen-year-old Jason, who was currently doing things with a female Villa supporter that perhaps he shouldn't, and he couldn't help falling about with unrestrained laughter.

Now more mature, in some ways Lydia preferred Prokofiev's Shakespearean tragedy to the works of Tchaikovsky. Tchaikovsky's were glorious, but the music was a bit like chocolate: you could have too much of it. To her, Prokofiev succeeded in breaking the rules, yet managed to remain remarkably emotional in his composition. She loved the opening of the current production when the first thing you witnessed on the stage was a pile of dead bodies! Lydia had not revealed her preference to Rosalind, a diehard Tchaikovsky fan, and contented herself with her new ambition to play Juliet as well as the Sugar Plum Fairy; especially if Romeo turned out to be as fit as the one taking the lead tonight!

The sword fighting was breathtaking and unlike a lot of ballets, *Romeo and Juliet* allows the male dancers to display their prowess to a greater degree. They are not just confined to leaping around the stage in subsidiary roles. In Lydia's opinion, Prokofiev's slightly dissonant and ravishing score, added to some startling choreography, made *Romeo and Juliet* the best ballet of them all.

They met a delighted Grandma Prosser in the interval who, to their surprise, wanted to know which member of the horn section the prima ballerina was 'obliging'. She thought all four of them were good-looking; except one was a girl, who she understood from both a musical and sexual point of view, was perfectly acceptable.

Grandma enquired after Rosalind's Great Uncle Wendell, but the girl could not be induced to say too much. It upset her to visit him, for sometimes he recognised her and sometimes he didn't. Things had always been more difficult for Rosalind than Lydia in that she didn't have any supporting grandparents.

Frank had been a Dr Barnardo's boy and didn't know who his parents were, and Helen's had passed away young. They had shown little interest in Rosalind from the spartan island in the Hebrides to which they had strangely chosen to retire about the time she was born, and perhaps this showed that Great Aunt Edith's demise and Great Uncle Wendell's virtual incarceration proved that some of us draw decidedly shorter straws than others. Fortuitously, Grandma Prosser had sagaciously comprehended this and in an entirely unobtrusive way, had taken Rosalind under her wing and included her in all the treats and attention that Lydia enjoyed, for which Helen was eternally grateful.

Grandma Prosser had also become attached to Helen. They occasionally met in the Bullring and now able to travel on their own, the girls did likewise, usually with a waddling Nureyev tagging along as a probably totally ineffective bodyguard.

It helped that without being asked, Denver had become chief dog walker. He liked the canine company and missed Wendell. He still took his fishing rod and the dog to Sutton Park where, more sedentary nowadays, Nureyev sat beside him wondering what it was all about. Nureyev frequently accompanied Denver to the pub where he had the status of local celebrity; a circumstance which perhaps explained his ever-expanding girth: crisps and leftovers do not a slim doggy make. Despite all his efforts to discourage the punters in their desire to feed the beast, Denver eventually gave in, noting the dog's contented demeanour, which could largely be attributed to his gluttonous tendencies. With some misgivings, the dog walker reluctantly ceded defeat and just hoped that the over indulged creature would not expire from premature obesity.

Lydia suggested it might enliven Great Uncle Wendell if they brought him to the ballet. This was a proposition about which Grandma Prosser expressed grave doubts. Frustratingly, Wendell continued to insist that Great Aunt Enid was still alive and in the opinion of the care home's matron, there was still no reason to refute his belief in her continued existence. Sometimes he recognised his family and at others he didn't, and the doctors were of the same opinion as the matron. He enjoyed good physical health, and they could well cope with his mental difficulties: Wendell was just one they had to deal with and no more of a problem than other residents.

Stricken with second thoughts, Grandma didn't entirely disparage the notion of taking Wendell to a ballet performance and wasn't disturbed by the prospect of having to purchase several tickets. It looked increasingly likely that Rosalind's parents would have to sell the house in Coleshill to pay the care home fees. She knew money was tight, so she'd get Grandpa to cough up, knowing that it would be peanuts to her rich spouse. His generosity she knew would prevail and overcome any objections he might have. She didn't know exactly how much he'd got stashed away and didn't particularly want to but knew it must be a vast amount.

He still played the Stock Exchange, they nearly always attended both Ascot and Cheltenham races, but to give him his due, he usually won large amounts on the 'nags'. This suggested he was privy to inside information not granted to other poor mortals. Far from being enlightening, this only served to hornswoggle her weak and tenuous grasp of fiscal matters, to the extent that she had long since ceased to worry. She was confident in her man's innate ability to handle it all. Grandpa was extremely benevolent and trying to keep her in the picture, donated a lot of his wealth to charity.

And suddenly, right here in the interval of this glorious ballet, she had an inspirational idea, and knowing her husband as she did, if he could, she was positive he would help her to realise it.

NINE

Frank and Helen were having a tiff, something they tried not to do in front of Rosalind. Not that it happened very often. They got on well most of the time, but Helen's pride would not allow her to accept this latest proposal. A more pragmatic and less sensitive individual, her husband was all for it.

"How do we know he won't want to turn us out sometime in the future to put it on the market?"

"Oh, come on Hel, he's become a great friend. Why would he do that?"

"But why is he offering to do it anyway? In this day and age people don't do things like that. Philanthropy is not something you encounter much in the twenty-first century."

Helen was a deceptively well-educated girl and often surprised him with her extensive vocabulary. A little exasperated, Frank emitted a deep sigh and drummed with his fingers on the kitchen table.

"He just does and from what I gather on the grapevine, quite a number of people in Brum have reason to be grateful for his generosity."

Helen wasn't convinced. "So he buys it and rents it to us. There must be a snag. What is it?"

"As far as I can see, there isn't one."

"Why can't we just put it on the open market?"

"That would take time and there's no guarantee it would sell quickly, and we need the money soon."

Frank thumped the table. "There's more than your pride at stake and I for one would like to get out of this stifling social housing place, away from some of the dodgy neighbours and their dubious lifestyles!"

Helen pulled a face. "Could be out of the frying pan into the fire. What sort of rent's he going to charge? He could get a lot for a place in Coleshill."

Frank felt it was time to come clean. "Well-uh-well," he said, his speech stumbling. "With that in mind, he's coming here on Thursday at seven to discuss it." He cast his eyes down, waiting for her response which was not slow in coming. Not normally a person of extreme reactions, she was nevertheless outraged.

"You mean to say he approached you over it, rather than me? In case you've forgotten, Wendell is my uncle, I stand to inherit the property and it should be my decision what happens to it. I have the power of attorney!"

Her neck had gone red, and her face had a type of disapproving animation he didn't often see and raising his hands in a protective gesture, he wondered what was coming next.

"I didn't think you and Grandpa Prosser were male chauvinists, but it would appear you are!"

Managing to interject, he riposted, "D' you want me to cancel it or re-arrange it? ... I'm sorry, it seemed such a good solution. I jumped at it ..."

She couldn't be mad at him for long, and with an engaging smile, stood up, and sauntering round the table, put an arm round him. This only served to bemuse him. Like man since the dawn of time, he'd never understand women, but as every wise male knows, the secret is not to try. Quite inexplicably, she started to cry; another thing that experience taught him could happen at any time, often for no apparent reason. He produced a tissue and attempted to dab away the tears.

"I'm sorry," she managed between sobs. "It's just that I remember how happy Aunt Enid and Uncle Wendell were at

Coleshill and looking at him now, I despair."

He pulled her on to his lap.

"Tell you what," he said, "why don't we consult Rosalind about it?"

"Rosalind?"

"Why not? She's old enough now. Where is she, by the way?"

Helen pointed to the ceiling.

"Up in her room listening to Stravinsky."

"Stravinsky?"

Helen shrugged. "It's her and Lydia's latest passion."

Frank still did not comprehend, and his wife endeavoured to explain.

"It's *The Firebird*. Rosalind almost forced me to watch it on YouTube. Not sure I could fathom it first time round, but the Brum Ballet is doing it in the not-too-distant future, she says, so I expect we'll have to go and see it somehow."

"OK," said Frank somewhat wryly and rose to his feet. "I'll go and disturb her, though it's a shame having to interrupt the music of a fifteen-year-old who's listening to something decent, rather than the usual crap they inflict on their long-suffering parents."

TEN

All in favour, Rosalind looked forward to inviting Lydia to the lovely old property that was Coleshill Villa. (Centuries ago, archery butts were situated in Coleshill and with sites like it throughout England, it is not surprising that the deadly longbow reigned supreme over the French at Agincourt and Crécy.)

Grandpa Prosser had arrived as promised and had insisted on sitting in the kitchen to discuss things. He offered Frank a cigar, which the latter declined, and further enhanced his genial persona in Rosalind's eyes by taking three sugars in his tea. She'd already twigged that in the ballet world not everyone approved of the 'woke' world you were supposed to live in. A lot of them smoked and drank on the quiet and she was grateful that both Lydia's and her parents allowed the odd glass of wine at mealtimes. Sadly, the use of substances by one or two dancers was not unknown and rumour had it that only just recently, a couple of them had left – another term for 'dismissal' – due to their unacceptable 'habits'.

The nearest Rosalind and Lydia had got to this undesirable underworld was when a senior boy at Ashleigh had offered them a cigarette and feeling sick halfway through smoking it, they resolved never to do it again. The boy had subsequently disappeared: presumably, they thought, because you can't become a principal or even a soloist on thirty a day. A goodly amount of under-age imbibing and other undesirable traits caused his parents to hastily withdraw him. There has to be the odd bad egg in any demanding environment but generally speaking, the Ashleigh School was remarkably free of them.

It didn't take long for Grandpa Prosser to stump up for the house and then there was all the business of giving notice and moving; an uprooting Helen had contemplated with entirely unwarranted feelings of guilt. Where their respective abodes were concerned, her current neighbours were a mixed bunch. Some looked after their houses meticulously and others blatantly neglected them, and overall, she would be glad to move on. But it all seemed too good to be true and she could not help thinking of Uncle Wendell languishing in the care home, his property relinquished and his relatives usurping him. Frank declared that her feelings were nonsense. What better solution could they and Wendell hope for? Wendell had long since forgotten his former existence at Coleshill Villa and he'd become secure in the care home for life.

And was it not better that 'family' should occupy his old house, even if only rented? This was surely better than some complete stranger taking it over and renovating it in perhaps a wholly tasteless and unacceptable way?

The one thing that disturbed Helen was that Grandpa Prosser insisted he only required a peppercorn rent. They had to argue the point in favour of raising the amount. A compromise was reached, and this allied to Frank's willingness to tackle one or two jobs for Grandma at Edgbaston, sealed the deal.

As it transpired, neither Lydia nor Rosalind took their first professional steps with the Birmingham Royal Ballet. Lydia took up an offer from Scottish Ballet and to her parents' partial dismay, Rosalind flew off from Heathrow one day to start her career with the Royal New Zealand Ballet.

By this time, the slightly ageing Nureyev was noticeably waning and even Grandma Prosser had recourse to a walking stick. She would never reveal her age: a subject of constant speculation amongst the vociferous matrons who patronised the bistro near the station. However, the advancing years had not hampered her mind, which remained as agile and acute as ever.

Thanks to modern technology, both girls could Zoom one another and their folks, and not completely devoid of his marbles, Nureyev would pitifully wander behind the laptop desk in his attempts to find them!

Neither girl stayed in the corps de ballet for long. After a couple of years with the New Zealand ballet, Rosalind moved to San Francisco and not long after, landed the part of Clara in that prestigious company's production of *The Nutcracker*. Not to be outdone, Lydia who'd remained in Scotland and also made rapid progress, fulfilled one of her ambitions when dancing the title role in *Romeo and Juliet*.

Both their families still went to visit the slowly deteriorating Wendell in the care home (Grandma Prosser had long since adopted him as another of her good works) and though his mental capacity was certainly not improving, his physical health remained reasonable. With supervision, he could still be taken to see the folks at Edgbaston or for an outing to the Bullring. About the only thing he recognised were the pictures of the girls, mostly in their ballet costumes. Helen had shown more forethought than most twenty-first century citizens by actually printing the photos from her smartphone! It concerned her and acute Grandpa Prosser that future generations would not have old photo albums to peruse and that at the rate technology was forging a surrealist world, historians would have more knowledge of the twentieth century than the twenty-first.

Wendell's surprising recognition of the girls – he even named them – served to change both families' stance on the idea of taking him to the ballet. It would be totally impractical to fly him to San Francisco: heaven knows how he would react to going all that way on a jumbo jet. Even though Grandpa Prosser had been willing to dip into his seemingly inexhaustible pocket, the doctors had firmly vetoed it and also thought a visit to see the intensely dramatic and emotional *Romeo and Juliet* in Scotland not an option for someone suffering from mental illness. For ambivalent reasons, Helen agreed with them. She'd discussed it with Frank, and they'd decided that even if the medics had OK'd the trip, they could not possibly accept Grandpa Prosser's generosity yet again.

But miracles still tend to happen.

After a couple more years and short spells guesting with other illustrious companies in such diverse places as Cuba and South Africa, both girls came home. The Birmingham Royal Ballet did not hesitate when it came to engaging them and after scintillating summer debuts in *The Firebird* and *Sylvia*, they waited with bated breath to see what roles they might be given in the annual Christmas production of *The Nutcracker*.

Much discussion took place amongst the dancers concerning what some considered the premature elevation of the two 'local girls'; but now somewhat hardened by their achievements elsewhere, Lydia and Rosalind did not let it worry them. There were always two principals allotted to the main roles and despite the happy-go-lucky Denver's observation that 'life was just a lottery', it didn't seem so when Rosalind was picked to dance Clara and Lydia, the Sugar Plum Fairy.

Where the purchase of tickets was concerned, Grandpa too, would brook no dissent. It had been decided that Wendell would be allowed to attend the performance and Grandpa would let no-one else pay. With virtually all members of both families wanting to come, except for Jason, pragmatic Sharon drily commented to aesthetic husband Jeremy that her father-in-law must keep his wealth in a bottomless pit.

Now a muscular hunk with a more sensitive, non-football-loving girlfriend, Jason was secretively very proud of his little sister. But lest his mates found out, he could not possibly go to the ballet, and with the lecherous intent of most healthy young males, saw it as a good opportunity for Lucinda and himself to have the Edgbaston 'mansion' to themselves.

A fly in the ointment was Grandma Prosser's insistence that Grandpa bought an extra ticket to show Wendell that Enid had not been forgotten. Grandpa thought this ludicrous, but with Grandma having a firm ally in the care home matron, he gave way, shaking his head at the idea of appropriating an empty seat which some other ballet buff would have been glad to occupy.

The only other notable absentee from the performance, of course, would be the venerable Nureyev. Denver still had a big share in him and latently realised the dog's gluttony could cause premature departure from life. Helen had bought him a doggy coat with a stark message emblazoned on it, which implored the 'inmates' of the Three Tuns not to feed him. This had been effective in that he could now accompany Denver to the park again. Albeit at an almost funereal pace, but as Frank asserted, he now 'looked good for another year or two'.

TWELVE

Wishing to further her education where ballet was concerned, Grandma Prosser had delved into its history. She was particularly intrigued by the way the dancers enacted their roles as choreographed; an achievement she thought extraordinarily difficult, and one which to the layman seemed to involve phenomenal dedication and a flawless memory. She discovered that all the great works were preserved by a system of 'notation' depicted in parallel lines passing through the body from the head to the feet. This was the preserve of an important personage called the choreologist, who committed the steps to paper. This enabled the classic ballets of such great choreographers like Diaghilev to be preserved, modified, and even changed. This was particularly useful when a contemporary ballet was being produced: the choreographer being still extant and possibly wanting to make great cuts or re-invent the whole thing. An added bonus was that a system of 'bar lines' similar to those found in a musical score, made for an easier marriage between the two art forms.

A prominent figure, the conductor performs a particularly vital role in this and must plough on with the music regardless of what is happening on stage. The dancers are expected to recover from any mishaps by recognising where the music has progressed to and must hopefully resume from that point. Such moments are rare and even less likely, wrong entries by instrumentalists can cause problems. Grandma Prosser had once been at a performance of Swan Lake when the errant French horns had entered four bars too early and caused panic both on stage and in the pit.

All this made Grandma immensely proud of Lydia and at present engaged in the almost Herculean task of readying herself for the performance, she prayed that all would go well. Her still plentiful hair meant that a comb-over was totally unnecessary and in a surprisingly complimentary manner, Grandpa had declared her to still be 'a splendid filly'. He declined to call her a 'mare', which could well be interpreted as a left-handed compliment and discretion being the better part of valour, his sagacity might well have avoided the necessity to duck in order to evade the progress of another missile as it sailed through the air, with the object of doing him considerable physical harm!

Lydia and Rosalind's initial performance would be a matinee, and this involved Frank driving to the care home to fetch Wendell for lunch. This was always a precarious business, for Wendell had no recollection of Coleshill and if not watched very closely, was apt to wander off. It would also mean going to the Hippodrome by car, rather than taking the train; not an ideal circumstance and one Frank normally liked to avoid if at all possible. Birmingham on a Saturday afternoon was a nightmare and finding somewhere near the theatre to park, was a bit of a lottery. But needs must and although he might not go to the ballet out of choice, he was still a proud dad and hoped when Rosalind appeared as Clara, he'd not have to ask Helen for a tissue.

Another slightly reluctant ticket holder, Sharon, didn't like the idea of attending the ballet. David Bowie was more in her line, but as a proud mum, she could well end up being captivated by the sense of occasion and sheer brilliance of it all. Then there was that self-abnegating dissenter from all the mounting anticipation, brother Jason. He could not risk the derision of fellow footie fans by going to the ballet but knew that his mind would not be on the game when making his usual pilgrimage to Villa Park. He and Lydia had become good mates and he'd missed her when she went away for what seemed an age, though he'd never admit it.

THIRTEEN

A t eleven that morning, Lydia and Rosalind were taking a break and talking to two young men in the cafeteria. One of these admirers was Petroc Mulholland, a finely chiselled artiste from the Celtic county and the other, Alan Ramsbottom, the bluff new principal trombone player of the Royal Ballet Sinfonia. Petroc resembled someone from a Greek tragedy and would be taking part in the Russian Dance; a role he'd not had before and looked forward to performing, though not without a certain amount of trepidation. Petroc had not long joined the company after a spell with the New York Ballet and – a hearty and reassuring lad – the brilliant Alan had arrived via Yorkshire's Brighouse and Rastrick Championship Band and the Royal Northern College of Music. He'd also had a spell deputising with the City of Birmingham Symphony Orchestra and like most brass players, his confidence matched his playing. He was the quintessential Yorkshireman, who had no qualms over saying exactly what he thought and had no trouble in making complimentary remarks to Rosalind. She pretended to mind, but really enjoyed his brusque manner. In common with most of those who blow down a piece of tubing, Alan could sink more than a few pints, but he never drank to excess and situated where he was in the pit, he had a good view of the stage. This enabled him to take more than a few glances at the 'new' Clara during rehearsal and his unsolicited inspection had deemed her not exactly unattractive. As a result, he'd resolved to make her acquaintance as soon as an opportunity presented itself.

Of the two young men, Petroc was the more self-effacing. He still retained his Cornish lilt and whenever Lydia addressed him, was inclined to flush and lower his eyes; an occurrence that, if he only realised it, made him even more alluring to her.

Although confident from having danced leading roles with companies abroad, both girls were understandably nervous and for the indomitable tyke Alan, this was not something to which they should give a second thought. With not the slightest knowledge pertaining to how the whole onstage performance worked, he assured them they had nothing to worry about and with Petroc gently nodding in agreement and casting upon them his charming half smile, who were they to assert that the blunt lad from Ripon was not right? More to the point, both Rosalind and Lydia had received nothing other than encouragement from both of the company's prima ballerinas who were to alternately share the roles with them. Far from engendering any remote hint of jealousy, they were told that their elevation was thoroughly deserved, and they were to completely ignore any dissenting voices; going out on stage and dancing the roles as if they'd performed them a hundred times before.

FOURTEEN

Fetching Wendell from the care home had not been a problem. Frank would have liked Helen to accompany him, but she hadn't been able to as she was busy preparing an early lunch. Thanks to the assurances of the matron, who had evidently become the leading confidante in Wendell's narrow existence, the patient raised no objection to going with Frank who, as usual, he'd not recognised. The only thing he seemed to recognise nowadays were the photos of the girls and sometimes, niece Helen. Frank did attempt to engage him in conversation en route to Sutton, but eliciting no response whatsoever, gave up and was glad when they pulled into the driveway of Coleshill Villa.

Helen had prepared what amounted to a light brunch in the form of an inviting and colourful salad which proved very acceptable to Wendell who, despite his other difficulties, had not lost his appetite. But the fourth place his wife had laid for Enid caused Frank to raise his eyebrows.

They were done by noon and well on their way by quarter past. Helen had insisted they'd arrive in good time to meet the others at the Hippodrome. The traffic was not quite so bad as Frank anticipated and he was pleased to find a car park nearby. Walking into the foyer, they found they had an hour to spare. Coming down off his cloud of intellectual daydreaming for once, Sharon's Jeremy had done the whole ticket booking online for Grandpa. But to Helen's slight disapproval, the elderly benefactor had insisted on providing them all with a programme at the not inconsiderable price of £2 a copy. This done, they all wandered into the bar for drinks and not choosing to breathe unwanted alcoholic fumes down the neck of whomsoever might sit in front of her, Helen opted for a J2O. She was glad to note that the gentlemen present – including normally non-abstemious Grandpa – were restricting themselves to effluvia-less vodka, though she suspected Grandma's glass contained a suspicious looking double something-or-other.

The corridor to the auditorium lacked what Frank thought adequate lighting and he took Wendell's arm until they entered the door to the circle. They were seated in the near end of the third row, with the seat next to Wendell near the stairs left vacant. To the right of him sat Helen and she felt relieved that it would just look as if one of their number had not turned up: a seemingly expensive case of amnesia or misfortune at £60 a ticket! Glancing at her uncle, she could not help noticing that he seemed more animated than he'd been for some time and was startled when out of the blue he said, "Where's Rosalind?"

Pleasantly taken aback, Helen pointed at the stage, and even in the midst of the atonal racket emanating from the pit and the anticipatory buzz of the audience, she managed to reply.

"Rosalind is on stage. She is to dance."

This didn't appear to register and unresponsive, Wendell lapsed back into his usual vacuous state. But Frank had heard the exchange and squeezed his wife's hand as she rummaged in her bag for an elusive packet of tissues. And whatever ailments Grandma Prosser suffered from, being hard of hearing was not one of them, and sitting on the other side of Frank, gave Helen a knowing, wide-eyed smile.

Sharon wanted to know when the Birmingham Sinfonia would cease making the same cacophony she'd experienced before the interminable concert in Symphony Hall. Jeremy informed her that there wasn't long to wait. The conductor would soon appear and the whole performance, as their absent and down-to-earth son would say, would 'kick-off' bang on time.

Sure enough, the baton wielder entered to spontaneous applause; the curtains parted and not long after a short oration by a well-known actor, Helen had to keep a strict hold on her emotions. There on stage was her baby Rosalind as Clara! Attired in a long, decorous flowing gown, her hair beautifully coiffured, she danced with ease and amazing confidence.

Her appearance caused a startling change in Wendell. Highly excited, he'd grabbed the opera glasses, turned sideways to face Helen and with an expression of sheer exuberance, held the glasses to his eyes with one hand whilst pointing at the scene on stage with the other. Then quite loudly, he uttered just one word.

"Rosalind," he said jubilantly and not content to let it go at that, he said it again. "Rosalind," he repeated, and the supposedly macho Frank had to ask his wife for a tissue.

*

Their drinks were ready for them in the interval and now it was Sharon's turn to feel nervous. She'd been seduced by the whole scenario and had watched the whole of the first half in a state of semi-hypnosis. She had not realised how superior ballet could be to a lot of the alleged musical events she'd attended. Although asserting that anyone had a right to 'like' and listen to what they preferred, she had to admit that no one who was not a thorough musician or dancer should be permitted to disparage the remarkable creation she was currently witnessing.

The toys came to life and the national dances were performed: Petroc was prominent in the Russian one and with mounting tension, Grandma Prosser knew it would soon be time for the Sugar Plum Fairy. Jeremy pointed out to Grandpa that the second clarinet, who they could just make out in the pit, was abandoning his normal instrument for the bass of the species and Grandpa, who was equally knowledgeable, noted that a member of the percussion section had moved to the celeste, where she was studying the music.

Biased they might have been, but both Grandma and Grandpa later declared that they had not seen a more exquisite Sugar Plum Fairy and during the faultless *pas de deux*, Sharon quickly had to raid her own packet of tissues. During all this, Helen had grasped Wendell's arm, wondering if he'd recognise Lydia in the same way he had Rosalind. She handed him the opera glasses and said, "Uncle Wendell, d' you know who that is?"

She hardly needed to ask. The same smile encased his features, he was nodding his head and extending his arms, said without hesitation, "Yes, that's Lydia."

*

As family, they were allowed backstage and after hugs all round and tearful congratulations, the new boyfriends made themselves known. At least Alan, whose dominant instrument had been prominent in the finale did and made it his business to introduce himself and the reticent and somewhat reserved Petroc. Other members of the company, including the male partners, were equally friendly. One of the prima ballerinas who would take Rosalind's role in the evening performance, made a point of seeking her out, conveying her admiration and inhaling the aroma of the two sumptuous bouquets the girls had been presented with during the curtain calls. Even the great maestro, conductor William Montreaux, an American of French origin and one-time assistant director of the illustrious Chicago Symphony, came to add his congratulations. He amused Sharon with his habit of constantly brushing his vast locks out of his eyes. She wondered how he followed the music – was it called a score? – and thought that divested of his penguin suit and dressed as he now was in extraordinarily colourful mufti, he could be equally at home in the pop world. Rosalind was trying to penetrate the normally vacant world of Great Uncle Wendell and in line with his recent awakening from verbal hibernation, she appeared to be having some success.

A lull came in the babble of conversation, and they all heard what she said and with astonished reactions, what he replied.

"Did you enjoy it, Uncle Wendell?"

There was a moment's hesitation before, with some difficulty, he said, "Ah-ah-well, yes," and stuttering he went on, "Au-au-Aunt Enid en-en-joyed it as well."

Complete silence descended, but this did not deter Rosalind. She simply gave her great uncle a long and extended hug, the like of which he hadn't had since his wife was alive.

EPILOGUE

Was it called a predicament, a dilemma or what? Denver didn't know. All he knew was that Nureyev had collapsed in the bar and a mate had transported him and the distressed dog to the vet who handily, lived nearby. He had enough savvy to realise that no one would leave their mobile switched on at the ballet and tried to directly ring the theatre. He soon became fed up when told to contact them online or alternatively, press the right buttons. Deciding he didn't want to 'murder his mother-in-law' or 'have it off with the sexy barmaid in the foyer', he ended up where he started and had to listen to the hideous 'music' they played to appease frustrated and despised non-technical mortals like him.

As it transpired, he was too late. He'd done his best, but the vet had to inform him that Nureyev had ascended to that great canine paradise in the sky: perhaps a place of proliferating juicy bones, mouth-watering doggy treats, the ability to chase and actually catch rabbits, and to cap it all, a goodly selection of come-hithering bitches with, in his case, a revived ability to sort them out.

The 'funeral' was an upsetting affair. They interred Nureyev in the back garden and thereafter, Frank often wondered what any future tenants or owners might make of the inscription on the mound where he lay:

HERE LIES NUREYEV. MUCH LOVED AND CHERISHED
BY HIS FAMILY.

People might well get it wrong. After all, how could this conceivably be the last resting place of the world-renowned ballet dancer? Why on earth would they bury him here?

*

A footnote from the Bard himself:
> 'My hounds are bred out of the Spartan kind,
> So flewed, so sanded, and their heads are hung
> With ears that sweep away the morning dew.'
> *A Midsummer Night's Dream*

Author's Note

From what I recall, I think the Hippodrome no longer has opera glasses and I may have taken a liberty here, but it does help tell the story. Also, dog owners visiting Sutton Park are asked to keep their pets on a lead and not to feed the Exmoor ponies: two other strictures I broke and for which I expect to be roundly chastised! As usual, the characters are entirely fictional and any resemblance to actual persons living or dead is purely coincidental. Although real places and organisations, including the Birmingham Royal Ballet are mentioned, Ashleigh Ballet School is fictional as are the events depicted in the story.

Acknowledgements – Many thanks to my daughter Sophie, who has helped me edit this story and accompanied me on very rewarding trips to the Birmingham Royal Ballet. Also, thanks to Cheryl Watkins, Great Niece Bethany and all those who have read it and provided feedback.

Metamorphosis

2021

From my rocker I can see the pigeons prancing on the long-gable roof. It is more the pumped-up cock bird that is strutting and the females submitting without too much preamble. I can also see the proliferating cobwebs festooned outside the windows and a wonder it is that the spider can climb to such an altitude The gallant creature is not alone in displaying this aptitude for heights. Bees visit me and once discovering they can venture inside, it distresses me that it takes them a long while to realise that they can exit in the same way they gained ingress.

It all must have something to do with the hot air currents, but this does not suffice to explain another visitor. It is an inquisitive magpie who, were there sufficient opening, might fly right in: perhaps attracted by some bright object; though I cannot imagine what that could possibly be.

Fronting our residence is a favoured haunt of the pigeons. Here, two gargantuan cedars cast cones into the yard where people park their cars and from this excellent vantage point the birds drop their white calling cards; indiscriminately besmirching and desecrating, and not caring a jot about doing so.

Next to our car park, a garage plies its trade. In times gone by it had housed early black and red omnibuses in an era when clippies issued your ticket and practically every soul had been obliged to travel on public transport. The garage has a benevolent and amenable owner and unlike most establishments that employ such artisans; his mechanics are not the gleeful prophets of doom to be found elsewhere in the motor trade. This inclination to be well disposed to all clients also embraces 'blackie', a stray, who now belies that description. He is now well fed and obviously knows which side his fawning feline bread is buttered. Blackie constantly patrols the neighbourhood and during these peregrinations, visits us quite often. Not that we particularly have need of his visitations, for we possess one of his kind of our own. Strangely, our version is all-white and thanks to the manager's aversion to the species, we are instructed not to feed it. To do so, the management maintains, would attract rats. The management cannot see that the aptly named Snowball survives mainly on rodents, and themselves obsessed with health and safety and strictly adhering to the book, have lost sight of the fact that it was once the tenants' welfare that mattered and not that of the management.

Perhaps I could persuade you to sample the view from my kitchen: the window of which looks south towards Ross-on-Wye. From here I can see the front garden's highly perfumed roses displaying themselves round the front lawn; whereupon just at this moment I am witnessing a curious happening. Contrary to what might be the natural order of things, there is the bizarre sight of Snowball scurrying across the grass pursued by an aggressive magpie. If a cat can glance behind, apprehensive, with ears flattened, then this is what he is doing, and I feel it incumbent on me to come to the rescue. Is this the same bird, I wonder, that alights on my window ledge to visit and why doesn't the object of its undoubted harassment turn to confront it? Sometimes ours not to reason why and clapping my hands, I cause the pursuer to take flight and the pursued to take refuge underneath the nearby quince bush. I then briefly ruminate over the incident. I am not superstitious, but one for sorrow? Sheer nonsense and the worst that could happen is that the magpie (even if the same one) will not visit me again.

*

They usually met by the swimming pool. Two pairs of eyes gleaming in the half-light. A far cry from the daytime when the car park would play host to frequent coachloads of chattering children come to swim and hopefully bent on conquering the art of not disappearing without trace into depths they might indiscreetly explore in future.

"Are you getting enough?" Blackie felt guilty. He knew he was lucky enough to be well fed by the garage people and it concerned him that Snowball had to rely entirely for sustenance on the local rodent population. This part of the city wasn't exactly infested, and he just hoped that his friend was not hungry.

Snowball laughed. "Getting enough? There's Ming at the Chinese, she's an obliging Siamese and then there's Persephone at the 'Lich', you know, that Greek menu pub in Church Street. There's plenty of it around if you care to look for it! That's the advantage of being so-called feral. You don't have to have the operation."

"Don't be disgusting. You know perfectly well I don't mean that. Are you getting enough to eat?"

"Sure. Plenty of vermin around and I can even get the better of rats. I also polished off the garden robin the other day!"

The very thought of this repulsed Blackie, but it would never do for one of his kind to admit it. Birds maybe, but rodents no way. He'd been lucky to end up where he had. Whoever deigned to designate reincarnation had decreed he should return as a cat and thankfully he was content that it should be so. Occasionally, after a particularly heavy slumber, he would awaken perspiring and alarmed, convinced that what he dreamt was true. A pack animal heavily burdened, winding through the endless towering mountains. He'd told Snowball of this, and his friend had not questioned it. A positive character, the white cat reckoned that this is what Blackie had probably been in his previous existence. A yak in somewhere like the Asiatic regions. Blackie did not argue, and it suddenly occurred to him that he had never probed into Snowball's background.

When questioned about this, Snowball was not put out and without demur, proceeded to tell all.

"Therianthropy and ailuranthropy, dear boy."

"I beg your pardon?"

Snowball chuckled (if a cat can chuckle). "Therianthropy refers to turning humans into animals and ailuranthropy specifically means turning humans into cats. So that's what I did."

Blackie was impressed. "So you are saying you were human and came back as a cat? A strange happening if I may say so and what spiritual being arranged it for you and why?"

"No god had a hand in it. I did it myself."

Incredulous, the black cat did not comprehend. "And that's possible?"

"Course it is. That's what ailuranthropy is. You just take the form. It's all controlled by the mind."

"But why?"

"Why? I just got fed up with hauling a rickshaw in the fetid quagmire that is Delhi twelve hours a day and told one of my high caste clients where to go. His minions later beat me up in an equally squalid alley and I'd had enough, so I started to take the form and it worked and here I am."

Blackie considered this and came to a conclusion.

"So what are you asserting is that you are not actually reincarnated in the usual sense?"

In that imperious pose that only felines can assume, Snowball sat bolt upright, furled his tail round his paws and gave his friend a look that, again, only a cat could impose.

"I guess so."

Still bemused by this startling revelation, Blackie had had enough. A glint of flaming red had appeared in the sky, intimating that another fine day was in the offing and in his book, it was time for shut-eye.

Snowball agreed and bidding one another an amicable farewell, they made off for their respective resting places: Snowball's under the quince bush and Blackie to his appointed cushion in the MOT bay.

*

The plumage of a magpie is smartly black and white with a touch of colour, but what goes on in his mind is another matter and who is to say that birds are not reincarnated? He'd ordered the comeuppance of that upstart rickshaw driver, but some fancy god had decreed his own humiliation. Death had arrived sooner than expected and here he was, transported to this damp, inhospitable often winter bleak land, a bonus being that he had soon come to recognise and stalk the meandering and unsuspecting white cat.

Cats don't look both ways and in any case, Snowball is furtively looking back over his shoulder when the bus hits him. The number 33 from Gloucester. The driver and passengers are very upset, but the driver does stop and asks Mick at the garage to sort it out.

The magpie flies away just as Blackie, materialising from nowhere, appears to observe his friend's plight as he lies lifeless in the gutter.

I look out of the front window and observe the double-decker. Double-deckers come past every hour and are not an uncommon sight. I deduce that someone has been late pressing the bell, but even though I continue to look, the bus shows no signs of moving off.

And here is that malevolent magpie, alighting on my windowsill. It must surely not be right to label a bird malevolent, but I cannot help feeling antipathy towards it and I hammer on the window in order to make it take flight.

Later, I hear the sad news of Snowball on the grapevine, and I somehow know who is to blame. And that new rock dove on the gable roof: what stamina he must have!

The Rubber Tree Plant

1983

John Carberry brought his ageing typewriter to a halt, slung the results of his day's toil into the 'out' tray, lit a cigarette and sat gazing vacantly at the peeling wall of this, the firm's smallest office. A minor cog in a vast empire, John Carberry had spent fifteen years of his life bent over a typewriter in these seedy surroundings. To him, it felt more like fifteen-hundred. Dark eyed, he was greying rapidly, sallow in complexion, slightly hunched in posture and thoroughly disillusioned.

"Yes, Mr Carberry," they had said on the day that they had recruited him in the cause of spreading the gospel of their holy great commercial empire, "you are just the man we need!" It transpired that he was just the man they needed to vegetate in this claustrophobic parrot cage, along with three other similarly deluded colleagues, four ash trays, four typewriters, a bevy of intrusive filing cabinets and an ailing rubber tree plant. The rubber tree plant belonged to John Carberry and as his landlady had not wanted the thing in the house, he had bloody-mindedly transferred it to the office. His workmates had protested, but in his obstinate, yet slightly engaging way, he had refused to move it and this was probably one of the reasons why, in fifteen years, he had not managed to gain promotion. He was not a person who would crawl to the management and the rubber tree plant was somehow a weird symbol of this defiance.

Carberry arose from his desk, grunted a begrudging goodnight to the others and reached for his umbrella. He slammed the door heavily behind himself and was just in time to follow a swaying skirt down the stairs, through the entrance hall and into the street.

The girl and Carberry boarded a bus together and two stops later, disembarked in a less gracious part of town. Here the shops looked as though they could do with a lick of paint and the people had tired, harassed faces.

The Treehouse coffee bar was a bamboo and pine log monstrosity which had the one advantage of being off the beaten track. For this reason, John Carberry and Ellen Walters always used it in preference to any other watering hole. The coffee wasn't bad, and they could talk unmolested by inquisitive friends or Ellen's husband, who was pretty ingenuous and hadn't stumbled upon his wife's infidelity in twelve months.

"A good day?" Ellen Walters spooned three sugars into her cup. She preferred brown to white.

Carberry frowned and shrugged his shoulders.

"I had my sort of day," he replied. "You know, the sort of day littered with overwhelming ennui and trips to the toilet. A day devoid of advertising ideas calculated to prevent the omnivorous empire from collapsing."

Ellen laughed and felt for his hand which he'd placed firmly, palm down, on the table. She took it in hers and reciprocating, he asked her how her working hours had passed. Her reply convinced him that what he was about to embark upon where she was concerned, had a very good chance of succeeding.

*

Glittering with a green, translucent glow, the oval shaped craft dropped stealthily down on to the lake, purred across the surface and being also amphibious, slithered onto land. It came to a sudden halt, the light was extinguished, and it sat there, somewhat ominous, clicking and throbbing. A hatch opened and a tall, striking figure emerged. He was some six and a half feet in height and had on a tunic which, being a bright shade of indigo, boldly reflected the fullness of the moonlight. The newcomer paused, sensed the atmosphere, apparently found it satisfactory and reassured, alighted from the craft. Awaiting him, John Carberry stood a short distance up the bank, and they were soon in animated conversation.

"Well, my friend," said the traveller, "we meet again after almost a decade and from the small amount I could digest from the thought transmission, your proposal is intriguing. Doubtless the possible transaction is not without its pitfalls, but none of them I am sure, are such that we cannot overcome them." His English was impeccable; evidence that his advanced race could imbibe any language without any effort whatsoever.

Not without a small amount of apprehension, John Carberry placed his cards on the table.

"I gather, then, that you would be interested in meeting Ellen?"

The stranger elegantly put the ends of his elongated fingers together and allowed a momentary show of interest to pass across his finely sculptured face.

"Would that be possible?" he politely asked.

Taking a deep breath, Carberry outlined his plan.

"But of course it's possible. Ellen was somewhat taken aback when I asked her to travel down here for the weekend, but as her husband's away on duty in another part of the country, she complied and is waiting for us at present in the pub – that's an alehouse, you know. You are to be a Mark Brown, who will arrive in the pub by coincidence. You are down here selling double glazing. I left Ellen with the excuse that the atmosphere in the pub was too stifling – people still smoke tobacco here – and I shall not have to be too long away. I have supposedly gone to the village shop which opens all hours, and she will be suspicious if I have not returned by ten." He pointed to a small suitcase which he had placed in the grass behind them. "There are some clothes in that case which I hope fit you, though it wasn't easy to kit you out in your sizes. Otherwise, although slightly alien, your appearance should not arouse too much comment."

The traveller laughed; an unlovely metallic sound which wafted lingeringly across the surface of the lake. "And what on earth, may I ask, is double glazing?"

John explained and after initial incomprehension, his companion commented that Earth must indeed be an intemperate place if it required such elaborate measures to keep out the cold. Where he came from you pressed a button on a small unit within your suit and this warmed you or cooled you, taking into account the prevailing temperature. There was no need to reside in anything other than a lightly clad homestead. But since it served their purpose for him to become a double-glazing salesman, he would concur and do his best to act the part.

John Carberry made the stranger promise to give him ten minutes' start; explained the exact whereabouts of the pub which was to witness the contrived meeting, and quickly vanished into the night.

*

The Cherry Tree was one of those pseudo 'olde-worlde' inns that the misguided landlord from Birmingham had equipped with horse brasses and modern hunting prints. A mock log fire stood in the newly revealed stone fireplace and the landlord's personal collection of keyrings were suspended above the serried rows of real ale barrels which dominated the bar-come-cellar. A regulation crisp eating Labrador lay before the artificial fire and a veritable covey of town loving country dwellers sat around on uncomfortable bar stools and in cheap reproduction antique chairs; trying desperately to be rustic and treating one another to sometimes flat real ale at exorbitant prices.

Mr Brown's arrival in this bastion of false jollification caused an understandable flutter within the females present and in order to impress Ellen, John Carberry had to feign surprise at his new friend's sudden appearance. Introductions were quickly made, and Ellen asked Martin Brown how business was and whether he would be staying for a while. She was quite bowled over by this unusual looking hunk of male virility and her eyes kept meeting his as they sat for the rest of the evening conversing and mutually admiring one other, whilst maybe drinking too much alcohol. Noticing this more than adequate attraction between the two, John Carberry was well pleased. It was a potential agreement that should suit all concerned. A situation he had planned meticulously to achieve and one which would result in him telling the great Holy Commercial Advertising Empire to shove his job up their collective anal passage.

It was five forty-five in the office and Carberry sat alone, working late. This was something he rarely did, but this evening he had a good reason for it.

The door swung open, and Martin Brown walked in.

Carberry motioned him to a chair. "You found your way without much trouble?"

Martin Brown languorously fitted his lengthy frame into the proffered seat.

"It was easy. My satellite directive also works on Earth."

"Satellite directive?"

"Yes, have you not got such things here? It pinpoints places exactly, works out a route and guides you there either by voice or by displaying a map on your mobile device. I have it here, look." He took a small, oblong object from within his tunic and displayed it to the astonished John Carberry. "It seems your technology is miles behind ours, but I'm not going to give anything away, you'll probably catch up eventually."

Though bemused by this small wonder, Carberry had other things on his mind. He came quickly to the point. "So, is it a deal, then?"

Martin Brown smiled. "It is a deal if you approve the form of payment I sent for Ellen?"

John Carberry shrugged and expelled a slight whistle through his teeth. Although from an alien, distant world, the diamonds were real enough. George in the back streets had not asked any questions and the price had been paid without any quibble.

"So that's it in a nutshell," said John Carberry, sitting back in his easy chair, inhaling and blowing smoke rings rapidly upwards.

Ellen, who had been tolerating his dry, matter-of-fact voice for nearly ten minutes, thought she had never heard anything so fragrantly outrageous. Of course she liked Martin Brown, but she had only met him once and certainly did not wish to go and cohabit with him as John was suggesting. It was a monstrous idea and even the thought of sharing all that money with John did not tempt her. Why had this strange man parted with it; where did he live and why did John think he had the right to 'sell her off'.

With a sinking feeling, Carberry realised she wasn't going to play ball. Although half the money would be no use to her on the alien planet, she didn't know where he'd planned for her to be abducted to and would have only found out after Martin Brown had taken possession of her.

Obviously infuriated, she sprung athletically up from the couch from which she had been impatiently listening to this super pimp with increasing incredulity and indignation and landed a vicious blow to his face.

"What the hell did you do that for?"

Not even contemplating a reply, she then trod on John Carberry's foot and followed this by aiming a deliberate kick at his private parts.

"If you don't know after twelve months, you rotten bastard, then I'm not going to tell you!"

The door slammed behind her and John Carberry sat nursing himself and his recently acquired problems. After a few minutes he got up, went to the sideboard and took out a stray can of beer he'd removed from the fridge the previous night and forgotten about. He punctured the can, poured the contents into a patterned glass and meditated. He supposed he would have to try and retrieve the diamonds somehow. He hoped that George the Fence hadn't managed to shift them just yet.

*

On a dark, wild night, over a month later, the oval spacecraft skimmed rapidly across the lake and rested by the lakeside.

This time John Carberry was invited inside and was surprised to be offered a meal and a drink or two. He declined the meal, but quite liked the taste of unfamiliar alcohol and perhaps drank too much of it. Anyway, it seemed to calm his nerves and prepared him for what he had to say to Martin Brown; not something to which he looked forward.

The alien listened patiently, and his face displayed little trace of emotion. He waited until John Carberry had finished talking and plied him with a further drink.

"So what you are saying in your long-winded way, my friend, is that you were unable to recover the diamonds?"

Nervously, John Carberry stated that he'd brought the money instead. He knew precisely what was coming next.

"What use is Earth money to me?"

"You could buy some of our jewels and take them back to Plaetron?"

The alien gave him a frightening smile, full of rancour and menace. "You have a point," he said. "I will take your money and return very shortly. As you rightly say, there is sure to be something valuable I can acquire from Earth and sell at a profit on Plaetron and if you will allow me to retain those clothes I borrowed and did not return, then all things are possible. Will you have another drink before you depart? I am sorry things do not appear to have worked out for you. You seem to have gone to a lot of trouble for nothing. It is all most unfortunate, particularly as I quite relished your Earth woman."

The alien watched John Carberry walking unsteadily up the bank from the lake, the light from the spacecraft keeping him in view for quite some time. Resolute, he slowly and deliberately pulled the lightgun from his belt and took aim. He hated shooting anyone from behind, Earth man or Plaetorian, but John Carberry had reneged upon their agreement and besides, there was another perfectly valid reason for his disposal.

John Carberry was unaware of the impact. It was all over in a fraction of a second and where he'd been, there was now a small column of blue vapour.

*

They did not really miss John Carberry in the office for several days. He was a dry stick; dull and uninteresting and was probably only away with influenza, a virus which seemed to be attacking a number of the 'Empire's minions at the moment.

"What's the matter with his wretched rubber tree plant?"

questioned one of the office colleagues. "The damn thing's positively wilting since he hasn't been here."

Another of them examined the plant more closely. "I do believe the damn thing's died," he said. "All the leaves have gone yellow, and it looks as though it's going to topple over any moment! Do you think, Charles, we should have watered the poor creature, or something?"

"No, I expect he'll be back soon," replied his co-worker. "Funny he hasn't rung the firm though."

*

Still a mundane, but welcome oasis from the bustle of everyday life, The Treehouse coffee bar served a young lady wearing a short skirt. It was not unusual for the place to supply coffee to young ladies in short skirts and the consumption of three cups in half an hour was not something upon which to remark, for most young ladies could not survive without downing gallons of the beverage per day. But this one did take rather a lot of sugar; in fact, she took three spoonfuls per cup, which could not have been in any way good for her.

Ellen Walters sat at the table impatiently; drumming with her ten slender digits on the surface and waiting for her man to turn up. She had been waiting far too long and had already seen off the advances of at least three predatory males.

An unusually tall, distinguished man entered, ordered a coffee, walked over to Ellen Walters and sat down. His gleaming eyes projected a bright greeting.

"You're quite sure you want to do this?"

Ellen grinned wryly. "I'd rather come of my own free will," she said. "Hopefully white slaving is a thing of the past. Even before you appeared, I was fed up with John and I've left a note for my near alcoholic husband telling him I won't be back."

The alien looked over his coffee cup at her. He only forced himself to drink the stuff for the look of the thing. He hated the foul-tasting muck.

"I think," he said, "you are – how'd you say it – a wanton hussy. But if you are ready, I think it is time we were off. You'll like Plaetron, though I'm afraid you won't find any coffee bars on the planet."

*

A strange humming craft with a luminous glow skimmed across the cliffs watched by a solitary coastguard whose wife had just left him. It was raining and the coastguard turned up his collar to protect him from the wet, windswept blast. He was making his way laboriously over the rough terrain to his small lookout hut when he stumbled across something which did not look remotely like gorse or bracken.

I'm getting wet, he thought, and what's more, I'm bloody seeing things! "A rubber tree plant can't grow here," he muttered to himself, "and I didn't see that thing taking off into the sky ..."

The coastguard sat in his hut and consumed half a bottle of Scotch. Then he fell asleep dreaming of Ellen.

Author's Note

I would not wish readers to think the reference to mobile phone and sat-nav like devices were included in the manuscript when I first wrote this story in 1983. I'm not that clever but enjoyed writing them in when revising it in 2019. I wonder if there are other worlds where the beings are far in advance of us?

On the Mezzanine

2014

The manager called them the paper cartel. Three or four lonely males who ensconced themselves upstairs in the reference area of the library and if not checked, monopolised all the broadsheets. This disparate quartet often had recourse to pontificate about the reading matter they imbibed and inevitably, caused dissent and fierce argument to erupt within their ranks.

Not surprisingly, these vociferous disputes startled other library users who entered the place under the impression that they could assimilate what it had to offer in comparative peace. But they often found their reveries abruptly shattered by the noisome foursome, who seemed oblivious to the needs of others and were only cowed by one of the bright young assistants, who frowned and sometimes admonished them, before taking a couple of the papers back to ensure some sort of order was restored.

When they left their respective homes in the morning, no one bid these men farewell and upon returning, they had to endure a bleak and lonely existence. Two were widowers, one divorced and one a very short-sighted young bachelor, none of whom coped with their single state very well.

They did not appear to have relatives who particularly cared for them and what offspring they had varied in allegiance: some were spasmodic visitors, others conspicuous by their absence, and some obsequiously materialising only when they were in need.

The homes they occupied varied from the squalid to the passably habitable and whilst they all made some effort with their personal appearance, they all exuded an aura that stamped them as woefully 'womanless'.

Just now, Gareth from Llangua – a hamlet halfway between the city and Abergavenny – was treating the company to his experiences in trying to renew a lapsed passport. A keen country music fan, he had a mind to visit Nashville and for some reason this involved a visit to the passport office in Newport on three separate occasions. This information he imparted in his pleasant sing-song tenor whilst perusing the Daily Telegraph and for once his utterances did not provoke anything more than a smattering of good-natured banter from the others.

"Do I deduce you need this passport to legally cross the Monnow?"

Very dry, Warren had always maintained, tongue-in-cheek, that the Welsh should have to show their passports before entering the English border county and Gareth countered by claiming that it had once been an integral part of the Principality and in his opinion, still should be. An angular matter-of-fact personality, Warren could have been anything in life, but was, in fact, an ex-member of the crack elite special force that was stationed near the city. Unwittingly, he dressed in too short trousers, always wore the same faded mustard-coloured jacket and claimed to be the definitive authority on every conflict from Agincourt to the present troubles in Ukraine. He studiously ignored the library's golden rule – not to do the crosswords in the papers provided – and with his slightly dictatorial attitude it was easy to see why had had parted company with two wives and become another victim of debilitating loneliness.

"So this passport," said Milton, the euphemistically named 'farmer' and, therefore, agricultural authority of the group, "will it allow you to come and see me in Urishay?" Milton kept a few fowls and pigs in the Golden Valley, a glorious unspoilt landscape in the west of the county. This fertile and picturesque domain lay in the shadow of the towering Welsh mountains and Urishay, a settlement with a castle and a couple of houses, had changed its allegiance a number of times: a fact denied by the locals who would have it nowhere else but in England.

As soon as he had said it, Milton realised his mistake. You did not suggest socialising with people you met in the library or the pubs in this conservative city. It was not like that. The people here were perfectly friendly outside their own homes but did not encourage visiting. The city was a strange place. You acquired 'acquaintances' but could not classify them as friends. There was nowhere to go when the gut feeling of utter loneliness struck you, except perhaps the pub or you could join things, but you didn't make friends and for some, survival in this environment could be a very tenuous and insufferable thing. Missing the point, some happily settled people would occasionally offer a bolt-hole, but rarely or never came to see you.

Edward who was attempting to read the centrist Guardian with difficulty, lived in a studio flat in town and didn't have a lot going for him. In his thirties, he was seriously myopic and asthmatic and only managed to read the frequently anti-establishment journal with the aid of a strong magnifying glass. At the moment he could not seem to keep still, and this trait was not helped by the dilemma with which he was wrestling. A birthday was in the offing. His thirty-fourth and he thought it would be nice to invite his 'friends' at the library to meet him for a meal in town. He had his eye on one of those new restaurants in the Old Market and wondered if he could persuade them to come. Some people called the new development Colditz or Alcatraz, but since his myopic state did not enable him to take a normal view of it, he thought it might be as good a place as anywhere and anyway, why would people open eating houses there if they did not attract plentiful custom and make money?

There was a lull in the conversation as they all became immersed in their respective newspapers and 'girding his loins', Edward cleared his throat and carefully put what he had to say in order. Unfortunately, when it did emerge from his mouth, it came out in a blurred and partially incoherent rush.

"I just wondered – that is to say – it, it's m-m-y birthday next week and I – I wondered – not if you're too busy, like. That is – would you – all of you – you guys like to have a – a m-meal in town? You know, perhaps, well, like, in the new part?"

The reaction to this garbled invitation varied from raised eyebrows to a stern expression on Warren's leather-beaten face. He'd never been called a 'guy' before and was not sure he could cope with it. A birthday party? An uneasy presentiment prompted him to refuse, but a long dormant element of humanity caused him to pause and reconsider. An unfortunate lad was Edward and

Warren's disturbed mind switched to a flashback: the time he had encountered a poor Kurd rebel lying in a ditch in Northern Iraq. Common sense would have dictated you put him out of his misery. One shot would have done, but he hadn't been able to do it. Instead, he'd given the lad some of his rations, held the water bottle to his lips and with difficulty, carried him back to the nearby village, where the natives were surprised, but very grateful.

It would be difficult not to accept this other disadvantaged young man's invitation.

"OK," he said. "I'm game. Tell us where and when and I'll endeavour to turn up!" Slightly fazed by his acceptance, Warren resumed his reading, then broke off to address the equally disconcerted Edward again. "But you'd better let me have your mobile number just in case!"

To Edward's astonishment and furtive delight, the other two accepted the invitation quite readily and it was arranged that they should meet in the newly opened Beefbar the following Tuesday at 7.30 p.m. He gave all three of them his mobile number and hoped they would not be disposed to use it. His mission accomplished, he stood up awkwardly and made some lame excuse to leave. Never that effusive, they all gave him a nod in farewell and watched him with his white stick as he gingerly made his way down the flight of stairs to the lower level. Then they all paused for thought, wondering how they could get out of next Tuesday. Perhaps a family illness could be concocted, or the ageing cat needed to be taken to the vet? It shouldn't be too difficult to manufacture an excuse. Each of them kept their thoughts to themselves and hoped the other two would attend: local protocol did not encourage you to meet up with someone only acknowledged from visits to the library. The border people were decidedly conservative with a small 'c' and only indulged in friendship within strict parameters.

Settling down again after Edward's departure, they resumed their reading and later, Milton's non-laying Rhode Island Reds and Gareth's resurfacing passport problems re-emerged to quell the unrest generated by the dilemma of whether to attend Edward's birthday bash.

The Beefbar was perhaps not the best place to hold a birthday celebration, being mostly inhabited by the night-time younger generation: a circumstance that did little to re-assure Edward as he waited anxiously for his invited guests. He'd arrived half an hour early, fifteen minutes had elapsed and just then the strident tones of his mobile rang out. He answered it with consternation and learned that Gareth's old mother in Abergavenny had been taken ill and Gareth, with profuse apologies, would not be coming. He was sorry he had not rung before, but the illness had only struck a couple of hours ago and Gareth was the only relative available. Edward had never previously heard of any mother in Abergavenny and making what he thought were suitably sympathetic noises, he made to put his mobile away, only for it to ring again. Milton's new puppy had apparently escaped, making him distraught. He was out looking for it and very sorry, it meant he would not be able to attend the celebration.

This only left Warren and the time on Edward's highly illuminated watch was now showing twenty-five past seven. Upset, he stumbled to the long counter at the back of the establishment and acquired another Coke, wending his way back through the closely packed tables with difficulty and resuming his seat with growing despondency. Only Warren left and he somehow knew that the old soldier would not turn up.

By seven forty-five he had given up hope and convinced himself that the whole idea had been doomed from the start and the only thing to do was to retreat to the isolated studio flat where he belonged.

"Hi. D' you mind if I sit down? It's a bit crowded in here and dere aren't any spare tables."

He could just about discern the girl. Very obviously female and very chatty. He'd never had a girlfriend and women made him nervous.

"Are youse not eatin'?" Very direct, she was disarmingly friendly. "Would y' like me to attract the waitress and can I help youse with the menu?"

He could see her well enough to recognise that she might be

beautiful and since he was not the sort of cussed partially blind person that never accepted help, he feigned slight helplessness and said, "Yes, please!"

The girl had noticed his white stick and Edward could not believe she would have been attracted to him otherwise. He resigned himself to the fact that she was just being kind and tentatively listened to her soft, Irish lilt as she read the menu to him. It saved him trying to do it in his ponderous way with his magnifying glass and they were soon tucking into a giant pizza for two, complemented by a more than palatable bottle of red wine.

"Y' have a name?"

This took him aback and resulted in a fit of coughing which she quelled by procuring a glass of water from one of the harassed and overworked waitresses.

"You'd like to know my name?" He could not but think why and was surprised when her voice took on a mischievous timbre.

"Ah, sure. Are we not sharing an intimate meal together? I like to know who my men are when I eat with them!" The reference to 'males' plural did not augur well and Edward tried hard not to delude himself.

"Well, if you'd really like to know …"

"Sure, I would. Y' seem a nice, sensitive guy. Why would I not be wantin' t' know yer name? The name's Simone by the way an' I come from Cork."

To his further astonishment, he was dimly aware of her leaning forward and clasping his hand in hers. "Dere, does that make you feel more comfortable?"

He gulped out his name and felt his whole world had utterly changed. By the time they had finished the meal, she had captivated him, soothed him into becoming more forthcoming and persuaded him to accompany her for a drink in the nearby Bowling Green public house.

Some figures were only vague to him, but the man that passed their table on his way to acquire his second pint of Stowford Press from the bar was unmistakably Warren. And the unmistakably stentorian voice which he used to humorously harangue the barman confirmed this. Edward thought it almost certain he'd been recognised by his defaulting guest and that thinking himself now out of Edward's range of vision, Warren had chosen to ignore him. The ex-soldier sat on the bar stool and pulled a book out from somewhere within the recesses of his mustard jacket. Quite naturally, thought Edward, he wanted to avoid an awkward confrontation and was now far enough away for it not to happen.

"Y' know that man dat just walked by?" Simone was all-observant.

"Not really."

She was not satisfied. "It's just dat yer man looked hard at youse as he came by."

They were now sitting side by side holding hands. He'd not held hands with a girl before and the more it went on, the less inhibited he felt.

Finishing his pint, the furtive Warren scuttled through a side door to the left of the bar and Edward breathed a sigh of relief which did not escape the notice of Simone.

"Ah, y' did know dat man, then?"

Edward came clean. He explained and she was aghast.

"Dat's rotten and none of dem turned up?"

"It didn't matter ..."

"But I tell youse, it does ..." Simone was adamant.

"No, it doesn't," and here he paused, hesitant, fearing that at some point soon he would be on the receiving end of a rebuff from this enchanting Irish girl. But 'hung for a sheep', he took a deep breath and said, "It doesn't matter, because if they'd turned up I wouldn't have met you."

Disaster. What a fool he was. Simone almost certainly had another man and why had he been so rash as to come out with a corny declaration like that? If only he could retract it. Too late now the damage was almost certainly done. But astonishingly, she took off his overwhelmingly powerful glasses and gently kissed him, and the sweetness of it made him shudder.

*

The head librarian noted that there were only three of the cartel seated round the table on the mezzanine. The youngest one who struggled to read with the aid of a glass, was not present. He hadn't been seen for ages and the head librarian hoped nothing unfortunate had happened to him. The ramrod straight one with the too short trousers appeared exceptionally animated and the head librarian caught the words 'some girl or other' before the trio cast eyes down once more to indulge in their usual diurnal dose of heartbreaking escapism.

Author's Note

The reference to war and Ukraine does not refer to the current Russian invasion, but from what I can recall, is an allusion to that same country's aggressive act in annexing the Crimea. Also, the local library no longer has newspapers, another victim of the computer age.

To Music

2014

Ten years older than me, my sister possessed a glorious voice and great things were predicted for her. She travelled to Gloucester once a week to have lessons with an eccentric and lovable teacher with an inestimable reputation whose brother was the cathedral organist: a position the younger sibling did not get, many thought, through not having as many old-school-tie connections as his senior.

This is how the large volume of *Schubert Lieder* happened to be sitting on the music desk of the old burr walnut grand piano when the German prisoners came in for tea one day. There were two of them. Hans wore a different uniform to Ervine, but neither of them were the Third Reich two-headed monsters I had been led to expect. My slightly indoctrinated older friend, Graham, had been threatened with a visit by Germanic apparitions when he would not comply with strict bedtimes or otherwise misbehaved and puzzled, my six-year-old self could not see how these two seemingly ordinary soldiers of the Wehrmacht fitted that description.

With an appalling inclination to indulge in blatant jingoism, Graham's father often declared that 'the only good German was a dead German' and this only served to confuse me further, for I liked Hans and Ervine, who tended our formerly unruly garden and would often break off to join me in a game of football.

A pacifist by inclination, my own father worked in a munitions factory for a short while during the conflict and his recent decision to employ two prisoners from the nearby camp had not gone down well with most of the neighbours. I could not at the time understand why the Allen children who live up the lane were not allowed to fraternise with us and there were others who spitefully used their offspring as pawns in their shameful attempts to show their disapproval of my father and his principles. But he did not let their misbegotten vendetta deter him and my mother was fully acquiescent in his peaceful intentions. A Christian of the utmost sincerity, my father practised what he preached and derided those who gave the teachings of Christ lip service but would not attend to the practicalities of the doctrine. He avowed that it was no use giving out tracts and preaching at people who were half starving and would often give a meal to the down and outs who, having returned from serving their country, found it anything but 'a land fit for heroes'. His gentle nature was slowly having an effect on the two Germans and as their English improved, they began to assimilate his viewpoint and Ervine, a former member of the Hitler Youth and a convinced acolyte of the same megalomaniac who founded that invidious movement, gradually softened and was further befriended by my mother's cuisine: not part of the arrangement, but an offering that was eagerly accepted by the two young men.

When there were more than four of us – I also had an elder brother – the small table in the corner was not big enough and with consummate unflappability, my resourceful mother laid the Broadwood Grand, a desecration which would have probably made John H, the founder of that illustrious piano making firm, turn in his grave. But needs must and the lovely old instrument did not appear to suffer from its mealtime transformation in any way.

The family lived on the outskirts of a small town. The house overlooked common land and beyond was a single-track railway which carried passengers and goods down the scenically opulent Wye Valley to Chepstow and the waiting Severn. The house was also one in an avenue which had not been completed. The residences were all rented and had generous gardens, with some boasting the odd pigsty and a number, a bevy of cackling hens. My own place had a stone wall with a privet hedge trained to grow on top of it and inside this mini bastion, a semi-circle of rowan trees graced the garden and provided a colourful display on autumn days. Two other early memories were of happenings in this amicable setting. One concerned the bustle of troops and weaponry gathering for D-Day and the earliest, only dimly recollected, was of our old collie Crusoe; who stationing himself, a canine sentinel beneath my pram, would bare his teeth at the approach of any possible stranger and ensure that my mother would quickly emerge from the household to see if there was any cause for concern. To my knowledge this rarely occurred and if it did, it was usually only someone who required directions or some person disposed, to my annoyance, in 'chucking the sweet little fella' under the chin. Crusoe acknowledged my brother as his master and his walks were plenteous. I was often invited and took great delight in ambling along by the sandy banks of the broadmeadow brooks where, from the overhanging withies, we cut and later fashioned homespun bows and arrows. An even more deadly weapon was my brother's sling. Unintentionally, he broke a neighbour's window with the ammunition from this extremely effective weapon and this caused his retreat to a neighbouring farm for a period of twelve hours, until he was apprehended and hauled in for confession and an uncharacteristic 'clip round the ear' from his normally passive parent. The last walk in this idyllic netherworld with the ageing Crusoe happened when I was well on to double figures and was my first encounter with death. Obviously in great distress, the old dog suddenly keeled over and suffered a fatal heart attack before our very eyes. Hardly able to rouse myself, I was despatched to summon help and left my brother grim faced, heartbroken and in tears. Crusoe was duly buried at the bottom of the garden, a ceremony attended by most of the children in the avenue and I don't think he ever had a successor.

Tea finished and including Hans and Ervine, we all helped to clear away, and my father sat down at what had been the table to play. He had a penchant for jazz and during the war, had run concert parties, arranged dances and played the organ at the local Congregational Church. He despised and despaired of the Congregationalists who were the very people who handed out tracts and disapproved of the more worldly pleasures like dancing and frequenting public houses yet would not usually lift a finger to help those who had to battle against straitened circumstances.

From 'Ain't Misbehavin'' to 'Kitten on the Keys', there wasn't much he couldn't play and when Hans handed him the Schubert volume, he effortlessly launched into the hallowed introduction to the great songwriter's 'To Music'. Unable to resist, my big sister came in and unprompted, Hans joined her. They sang in unison, but in two languages. He had the purest lyrical tenor, did this two-headed Nazi who should not be alive, and he moved me and those about me to tears. Recalled in later life, this happening did not detract from the enormity of the war crimes perpetuated by Hitler and his colleagues and for that reason, I could never persuade myself to become a pacifist. But I often wondered what would have occurred if the ordinary troops on both sides had abandoned their weapons and refused to fight. Let the men of cant and heinous propaganda argue it out amongst themselves. I had the good fortune not to have to go to war and I often conjecture what I would have done if I'd had to. Since I am appalled and cannot conceive that mankind is the highest species in the universe, then I would have prayed to this mind that must be greater; this awesome being who must have the knowledge, the reason for the existence of not one, but many universes and with a heavy heart, shot myself.

Touché

2013

Quiet and untroubled on a weekday afternoon, the library was reckoned by some to be outmoded and lacking in modern facilities, but since e-books were now well on the way to being used by all and sundry, Guy could not quite see the necessity for its replacement.

He loved the atmosphere of the place and the sense of history engendered within, plus the presence of an art gallery and the unchanging city museum above. Contemporary, functional buildings were just that: contemporary and functional and usually, after a couple of decades, became dilapidated and outmoded themselves.

He did not resent the 'TOTS' HOUR' or even the 'TEENAGE WAR GAMES' which at times permeated and disturbed the overriding calm and he was not so hidebound in that he did not realise these boisterous sessions helped to keep the place viable.

Glancing absently about him, he slowly observed that the mezzanine currently contained up to seven of the ubiquitous computers, six human beings almost prostrate in obeisance before them and as a saving grace, the entire fascinating local history collection.

One of the computers' supplicants, an eager-looking young man with a thin, V-shaped face, closed the machine down and to Guy's consternation, came to sit right opposite. Guy silently resented his presence, and even more undesirable was the badge the newcomer displayed, which proclaimed him to be a member of the Church of the Latter-Day Saints: known otherwise as the Mormons.

Reluctantly, it seemed that a move would have to be made and – sensing the evangelical glint in the eye of the apostolic invader –

Guy began to gather up his loins, though trying not to do it in an obvious and perhaps, slightly churlish way. His *raison d'être* was fiction: a pen and an exercise book his only required appurtenances.

"Excuse me, sir, but-uh-well-would, uh-I guess you might be local?"

Too late, it looked as though it might be necessary to become embroiled. Maybe he should not be prematurely condemnatory. Talking to this young man might even be fun. Introducing himself as a certain Walter B. Manton Jnr, he offered a hand and then, as is the way with most uninhibited Americans, launched into a lengthy appraisal of himself and his antecedents.

Guy waited for what he assumed would be the inevitable evangelistic foray on his sensibilities and was mildly surprised when all that issued forth was an enquiry about possible accommodation.

Ah, what a chance to indulge his mischievous sense of humour! He pondered the moment for scarcely a minute and then took the plunge.

"Well, as a matter of fact, I do know of lady that takes in lodgers, though I don't know if she would have any vacancies at the present time." Evidently, Walter B. Manton wasn't the only soul who urgently required housing. His companion, another young blade rejoicing in the name of Jesse P. Winkleton, also of Salt Lake City, was ostensibly in the same boat. Mormons, of course, always assailed the populace in pairs.

But would it be fair, Guy mused, to expose these two gullible young tyros to the rigours and pitfalls of Meerschaum Wood, the city's least-desirable housing estate? Meerschaum Wood, where men grew hairs on the inside of their chests and the police spent a good deal of time chasing shadows. A place of drugs and dodgy deals, which reflected badly on the majority of the estate's peaceful inhabitants, most of whom were ordinary law-abiding citizens.

A crescent or avenue here could take on the appearance of a row of decimated, gapless molars. For every manicured lawn, a neglected patch next door; for every carefully painted portico; a shabby bare-wooded porch: these roughly corresponding to whether the domicile was bought or rented from the relevant housing association.

Coming to a decision, Guy wrote down an address on a brown paper bag, which in another life had contained a piece of moist, succulent, bread pudding; an unhealthy morsel to which he was severely addicted.

"Uh, I sure am grateful to y', uh Mr, Mr, uh ..."

"Guy Wilson."

"Well, I guess I could google this ..."

"It's south of the river, over the old bridge, not that difficult to find ..."

Guy closed his exercise book, stood up and smiled at the enthusiastic youngster from Utah. He apologised for having to keep an imminent, non-existent appointment and a little gracelessly, left him to his own devices. Guy would now repair to his second home, Mario's bistro to sample the proprietor's nostril-beguiling coffee. It would surely be quieter in there at this time of day.

*

Gladys Smith didn't enjoy being a widow. A widow encumbered with a large Victorian house known as Meerschaum Lodge, which now stood halfway down Acacia Avenue in the midst of a collection of variable and nondescript post-war houses. The lodge had been there long before the ill-considered development and was all that was left of a fertile farmstead, formerly owned by Gladys's husband's grandsire, an opportunist of the first order. He had sold out to the council who, determining that the lodge gave 'tone' to the building project, left it out of the purchase. They then proceeded to surround it indiscriminately with homes for the masses; ultimately causing the present owner to suffer from both aesthetic vandalism and impecunity: a result partly exacerbated by her former father-in-law's ability in losing the family fortune on questionable equine 'certainties' that failed to respond to the whip.

Tired of working twilight shifts at the local cider works, Gladys now did part-time bar work and took in lodgers; a precarious living, not helped by the presence in the house of her two teenage sons, Warren and Willie. This pair, apart from being classic examples of the non-earning, all-consuming, omnivorous Meerschaum Wood teenage underworld, were apt to have their father's inclination for practical jokes and surely would not resist the temptation to activate this trait upon the two gullible young Americans who now resided with them in the lodge.

Gladys had to admire the Americans' courage but thought their whole mission preposterous. That Joseph Smith had uncovered some gold plates, since lost, buried by a defaulting tribe of Israel – who had somehow navigated the Atlantic in something BC – just had, in her opinion, to be a real no-brainer: the sort of tall story which might have been concocted by an inhabitant of the local mental health unit. However, she had to admit that the two young Americans displayed a courtesy which her own offspring did not possess and that, to a certain degree, their missionary persistence was succeeding.

A pleasant American lady, currently visiting the well-attended city temple to which the missionary duo were attached, had called and confirmed their success and, despite her refusal of tea or coffee, Gladys concluded there were probably worst things to belong to than the Church of the Latter-Day Saints.

*

Guy entered the Bull's Head in the certain knowledge that he would encounter someone with whom he could while away a pleasant hour or so. The ancient watering hole needed thousands spent on it, a fact that the ageing landlord did not recognise or chose to ignore. Gloriously situated on the banks of the fast flowing, but treacherous Wye, the hostelry had unparalleled views overlooking the opulent Bishop's Palace and the grandiose cathedral and could well have been the most prosperous licensed premises in the city. Sadly, its flaking paintwork, structural defects, fading décor and dubious toilets did not attract the uninitiated and it was difficult to conjecture what would transpire if the present incumbent ever abdicated. This slightly run-down aspect of the place, paradoxically, did attract a leavening of intelligent persons who did not wish to patronise the soulless drinking places that dominated the city centre. Particularly at weekends, the city centre was a fractious maelstrom of incapable, often belligerent, late night 'clubbers'. With potential fracas liable to erupt anywhere, it sported obligatory bouncers and had an all too frequent necessity for a considerable police presence.

This being a warm evening, meant that the plastic chairs overlooking the river were fully occupied and some discussion ensued concerning the number of immigrants who were now coming to settle in the city. Jobs were an issue, though half the company present were unemployed, and some might have been in that state for a decade or more.

"Yes," commented one inspired regular, "they either comes 'ere an' takes are jobs or lives on the social!"

"Yes," interjected another equally misguided mortal, " 'n' wa's more, they can't even speak th' bloody language!"

Guy, who had unobtrusively joined the company, found he could not resist. He seized the moment.

"Then I would think Herefordshire's possibly a good place to come!" He pronounced this boldly, perhaps a little louder than he should have done but – to give them their due – some did laugh, though most just displayed bucolic incomprehension.

An off-duty police officer, an acute individual called Dan Heath, took the opportunity to accost Guy in a friendly manner.

"Written anything defamatory lately, Guy?"

"Not particularly. And you? What's the strong arm of the law been up to lately?" Guy noticed that the policeman's previously full pint had descended very rapidly to a state of being either half full or half empty, according to how you looked at it. The officer was heavily hire suited, not an option for one of his ilk in former days, but now acceptable. He had an intelligent disposition and from past dealings Guy had experienced with him, did not beat about the bush or suffer fools gladly. He put his pint down and calmly wiped the surplus froth from his moustache with the back of his hand.

"Had a funny old case the other day. This American lad got knocked off his bike. Not really hurt, but was told to wear L-plates and forgot we drive on the left-hand side in this country!"

Here he took another large quaff and Guy, suddenly aware of great feelings of culpability, tried to assume a nonchalance he did not feel.

"And since he's lodging with Gladys Smith and those two young buggers of hers, I know who told him to don the L-plates! The poor young sod! You know Gladys, don't you, Guy? I thought you had hopes in that direction one time?"

This was accompanied by a broad knowing wink and Guy, still immersed in unseen guilt thought it might be appropriate to divert the big man's persistent interest in such matters by offering him another libation, which was gladly accepted.

*

What had happened? Guy's cynicism, honed by years of unrelenting journalistic zeal, was now being slowly eroded.

The pleasant lady from the Church of the Latter-Day Saints rejoiced in the solidly biblical name of Miriam and Guy had found that the physical aspects of her, too, were both 'pleasant and alluring'. He had been persuaded by the lady to attend the temple and, hypocritically, feigned enthusiastic interest; a monstrous exercise in deception which did, however, cause his excessive consumption of alcohol to diminish quite rapidly.

Meanwhile, the two zealous lodgers found solace in a willing couple of local girls who were glad to oblige the all-American duo and did not stint with their favours. Whatever transpired between them, Gladys Smith turned a blind eye to, but she did not believe for a moment that her wayward sons were innocent parties in arranging this liaison.

*

Time passed. Two whole years of it and time for the two young Mormons, having served their tour of duty, to return to God's own country. There were a few feminine tears, though not from the same ducts of the original girls – the lads had learned quickly – so this made their departure not too much of a wrench for those left behind. The Church of the Latter-Day Saints, being situated in another part of the city, knew nothing of their 'sons' extra-mural amatory adventures; these same being mostly conducted in and around the alleyways of Meerschaum Wood and the now streetwise couple returned to the 'good old USA' still outwardly saved, but inwardly changed beyond all recognition.

*

Dan Heath sat one side of the fireplace in the Bull's Head and could not restrain a chuckle as he thought of the e-mail he had just received from Salt Lake City. One thing about old Don, the affable landlord, he did not resent having to supply his punters with this glowing, red-hot open fire. Jokes were made about the anthracite lumps being numbered and the clientele took it in turns to add logs to the blaze when required; all of which banter and duplicity mein host took in good part.

Fancy the 'great sceptic himself', condescending cynic and scourge of any well-intentioned advocates of any religion whatsoever, becoming a Mormon! This only confirmed Dan's solid belief in the superiority of the feminine sex. Guy, hopelessly outgunned by the charms of the alluring Miriam, had slavishly followed her back to Utah and was now a press officer for the Church in Salt Lake City. And this was all because he had, out of a sense of guilt over what happened to young Walter, visited the Smiths when the desirable Miriam had been there. Still, in Dan's opinion, Guy had not been the same since his first wife died and this Miriam seemed quite a girl.

There had, according to the e-mail, unfortunately been one blot in this otherwise blissful scenario for Guy. He'd gone out one day in a big Chevrolet and turned onto the left-hand side of a main highway from a side track. This resulted in him spending some time in the local hospital with minor injuries and slight whiplash. Fortunately, the oncoming car had slowed down to take the side track, so things could have been a lot worse and, bearing in mind what happened to the one missionary boy, there was a sort of poetic justice about it.

Dan emptied his tankard in the usual manner and arose, intent on replenishing it. Perhaps there is a God, he mused, one that occasionally sat up and took notice. Not a jealous or vengeful one; not a menacing Jehovah that brandished the abyss of Hades before the simple-minded; or even one that demanded impossible, onerous perfection. Not a hypocritical one or a sectarian one; an overly sanctimonious one, or even a cerebral one. Not a layer down of laws or one of questionable omnipotence, or one conspicuous mostly by his absence.

The policeman banged his empty receptacle on the bar in mock intolerance at the not particularly expeditious service.

"Shan't be long," riposted cheerful Carla, the portly on-duty barmaid, attempting to assuage the thirsts of several people at once and perhaps being the best of the staff raconteurs, she added "and any more of that cheek, Chief Constable, and I'll be givin' you a bit of knuckle 'round that kisser of yourn! I wouldn't mind a night in jail. Be a lot more peaceful than Meerschaum Wood!"

Of course, thought Dan, suddenly illuminated. Why not a humorous God? Surely only a humorous God would have put willies on such a vulnerable part of mankind and given women no sense of direction whatsoever? Then, taking a swig from his pristine pint, his thoughts strayed to the similar accidents experienced by young Walter and the lovelorn Guy. There was a word for it. One of those anglicised French words that had crept into the language. The French always had a word for it. Touché! That was it. He'd have to e-mail Guy in return and use it, just to show that policemen were not all dull and merely phlegmatic crime solvers.

Cataracts
January 1989, revised 2019

The mist unrelenting. The trees slattern grey, gripped by the remorseless hand of a premature winter. Crackling leaves scudding beneath the hooves of the gregarious sheep and summer now a millennium away. Harshly calling, a jay wings overhead like a feathered jet plane: grey and pink and scarcely discernible. Searching for a buried acorn, it flashes across the swollen Lyd and lands shivering within the withers of a mighty oak.

Brackish, the water still flows and though hampered by detritus, it is unremitting on its way to the Wye.

I nurse my Morris Minor up the steady slope and come to a clearing surrounded by what used to be called 'humble' dwellings. Most have smoke eddying from their chimneys. Here is the slightly isolated community known as The Pludds and I wonder which of these cottages contains the piano I have come to tune. I park the car and make to address the old man who regards me over the half-door of one of them. Surely an ex-pitman, his rancid briar emits a blue smoke into the prevalent Forest mist and the gnarled pipe is almost an extension of his wizened face. Perhaps traced by some celestial pit wagon, lines criss-cross his leathern visage, and his eyes match the tints of some long-forgotten autumn. Long suffering, changing and ever watchful, waiting in faith for eventual immortality. He coughs violently and is almost at a loss how to terminate it. The ague racks his whole being and he stays my hand as I try to help him.

"Thas what d' come vrum bein' fifty year down the pit," he says when he recovers from his affliction and ushers me inside with total disregard for his own discomfort.

"I take it thou 'az come t' screw up thick pianna?"

For answer I smile and start to dismantle the beast; one of

somewhat ancient lineage. Marauding moths fly out and knowing what is to come, startled woodlice burrow further and are thankful they have escaped retribution for such a long time.

"Is 'im worth doin', ol' butt?"

I nod and take out a crank. The tuning pins have obviously not been embraced by this tool for many years and as I turn, flake down into the subterranean regions of the trapwork or pedals.

"My gran'daughter, 'er's good on thick pianna. 'Er 'ave taken 'er graide vive and 'er got a sterstificate. Thaiy wunt let 'er 'ave thick pianna at wome. Thaiy d' zaiy it d' taike up too much room."

I take a brush to the action and the old man coughs at the clouds of neglect.

"Thou do'st want a damp rag vur that, ol' butt," he says and goes away to fetch one. Whilst he is gone, I glance and gasp at the barely decent calendar which hangs on the wall above the piano.

January is modest; February is pleasant; March is saucy; April inviting; May partially covered in blossom and little else; June more or less revealed; July blatantly displayed; August in the harvest field; September twin apples; October exposed by fallen fronds; November utterly indecent and December defiled beyond anything imaginable.

Returning suddenly, he hands me the rag and chuckles at my discomfiture.

"Sin all thou want, young 'un?," he says merrily. "I be zorry I did come back too zoon vur thee. Thou looked uz though theese wuz enjoyin' thyself!"

Burdened and surprised by the unaccustomed contraction, a string fractures and hangs limp, duty finished, but impeding further progress. I fetch a coil of wire from the car and taking the bottom door off the vintage instrument, set to work.

"Would'st like a drop o' this in a cup u' tea, ol' butt?" He flourishes a bottle of spirits before me which he has removed from the top of a corner cupboard.

"Just the tea, please," I say, and he goes away to make it.

Fifty per cent tea and fifty per cent Johnnie Walker's! He can't have understood what I requested. I try to control any contortions which might be evident and swallow the deadly mixture as best I can.

He offers an almost demonic grin and says, "I thought thou wou'n't mind a drop o' zummat good. Uz don' zee many people up 'ere theeze daiys. I yewsed t' know every 'un by naime an' most of uz were related when I wuz a byoy. Thaiy be nearly all retired 'uns vrum Birning'am an' London round 'ere now an' thaiy'll give we the time o' daiy, but not much else. Thaiy yunt very sociable!"

He sighs and his chest rattles in sympathy, malignant and out of accord with the tenor register I am tuning.

"Thick gran'daughter o' mine – 'er naime's Kirsty – 'er d' play the pianna zummat vairish (pretty well) an' 'er plaiys the carnet in Lydbrook band an' 'er's good; that is, when 'er yunt jumpin' thaiy bloody great 'osses over the sticks in them there gymkhanas."

He sits in the rocking chair, contemplates my actions for a while and finding the coal scuttle, leans forward to throw a few more black nuggets on the already blazing fire. "Oi," he says, removing his weather-besmirched cap and ignoring the fact that I was having a hard struggle without interruption. "Almost fifty year Oi spent consultin' wi' Lucifer down b'low. I never sin 'im, but 'im's there theese d' know! 'im cun be in a vall (fall) an' in th' axe that d' bring about thick vall. I remembers when we wuz trapped at Lydbruck. I did see th' fear on the vaices of me butties uz we zung 'yms till thaiy got uz out, y' zee. Although the ol' docter did 'iz best. Not all o' 'em got out, but 'im wuz worshipped in the village adder that, though even 'im couldn't beat the Devil!"

The bottom octave always gives difficulties. Fey harmonies spring from nowhere and are made hazier by the overriding cover of half a century's grime.

He takes a covert swig of the Scotch bottle and puts it back on the cupboard. He sits back in the rocking chair and his eyelids lower. His nose emits a porcine, startling snore and his chest heaves unhealthily in unison. If he will stay thus while I mount the treble, then the finishing post is in sight.

A grandmother clock ticks rhythmically on the wall and fragrantly, a true Aussie, the exotic budgie bursts into life as I ascend. Just as I finish, the old man awakens and asks me to play an old Victorian ballad called 'Bless This House'. I find it by rummaging through the parting-at-the-seams music stool and he carousels in a high, nasal, feeble tenor which still suggests he once had a voice. A verse or two and he is finished. The coughing grasps him again and he rasps and shakes, afflicted by the conflict within.

He recovers and says, " 'Ow about the ' 'oly City'?" another ballad sung in Victorian times. I demur, thinking it unwise for him to attempt it.

"Maybe thou be right," he says. "T'yunt too good fur a wheezy owld bugger like me t' be singin'. I dairzaiy I yunt be long vur this world, any road. But I tell thee what, ol' butt," – he leans forward with a hand on my shoulder, his rheumy eyes displaying a vestige of amusement in them – "I tell thee what," he reiterates, "I be goin' t' make the best of it while I'm 'ere! Oi d' 'ave me a bottle or two o' whisky ev'ry wik (week), an' when I d' gow, Oi intends to gow with a bang!"

A frail old lady who had not been evident until now, comes from the kitchen and settles herself in the rocking chair which her old man has obligingly vacated. She seems only vaguely aware of my presence and does not directly look at me. I hasten to eclipse the calendar with my broad back and the old man gives another of his falsetto chuckles.

"This be the owld 'oman," he says, " 'n' doesn't thee 'ide thick calendar, old butt, coz 'er 'ave got cataracts an' 'er can't zee it!"

During another fit of coughing, he pays me, and I awkwardly attempt to take my leave. But he presses upon me a clutch of newly laid eggs and I am dimly aware of the very fowls that have produced them as they scratch around my departure.

The mist has dispersed elsewhere and the naked trees stand revealed in serried ranks: defoliated, but unvanquished to live another day, given hope by the sun's latent struggle and lingering stoically, waiting for another awakening. This a slight respite before the harsh season of frugality: the time of biting bonewinds and often endless days of ceaseless precipitation. Perhaps a respite preceding the mantel of descending whiteness, and for some, a reprieve before descent into purgatory or hell or oblivion.

I wonder shall I see the old man again when the spring stream flows bountifully and people garner watercress from its pools and in the way of things, young people with 'fern tickets' copulate amongst the fronds? And will the great oaks play host to a million creatures and the squirrels dart through the boughs like quicksilver before the old man goes.

January is hostile; February little better; March virulently rampant and April … April? He doesn't feel the balm of April, but I am passing through the churchyard on my way to resurrect the church piano and I pause beside the proud daffodils on the newly dug grave.

I am not alone. The young girl is very pretty and she smiles wanly at me and I wonder if she still plays the piano and 'carnet', and if nirvana has as many fine brass bands as the Forest of Dean; for if it hasn't, it would surely not be the right place for an old miner to end his existence.

Once More Unto the Breach

1978

It was half past two, we'd just come down from the Forest, the sun was dominant, and Polly had gone off to the Market Hall to see about material for the children. As usual, the small market town of Monmouth was teeming with humanity and I had already decided that my most likely escape route would be the inviting bookshop in Church Street where, upon arrival – and to my mortification – a small boy swiftly opened the door for me to enter. I didn't think that at the normally prime age of thirty-seven I appeared that decrepit and felt mildly irritated by his gesture.

"Thanks," I said, pulling a face which must have seemed part approving and part grimace, "do I know you?"

The boy shrugged, looking nonplussed and almost embarrassed. He could not have been much more than twelve years old and to ease the situation, he resorted to disjointed and not uncommon juvenile irrelevance.

"No," he said abruptly, "I'm off to the fair. It's down at the Cattle Market." With very little hesitation, he scuttled out of the shop in his disheveled school uniform; wended his way down crowded Monnow Street and quickly disappeared.

But his chance remark had engendered an irrational fear in me. Mention of the word 'fair' had triggered a cold sweat to break out and although this was a surprising thing to occur on a hot day, it was perfectly understandable when you had a wife that loved the razzmatazz and the dubious offerings to be found at so-called travelling fairs. Without a doubt, my dear Polly would revel in the chance to knock over a few innocent plastic ducks and given the opportunity, patronise the dodgems without respite. She would place a pound's worth of pennies from my pocket into the maw of anything that would gratefully swallow them and in doing so, easily enhance the cause of ever encroaching impecunity upon our family in one mad bout of feckless fairground spending.

Needless to say, I'd never known Polly buy material so expeditiously. I met up with them all again outside the cinema and by the expression on her face, I knew that she knew.

"How about the pictures?" I said, desperate and disregarding the X-certificate and the poster which displayed a nubile young woman in a state of alarming undress. Though unlikely, we might just have managed to smuggle the kids in, and it would surely have been cheaper in the long run. But it was to no avail.

"There's a fair on," Polly said innocently and the children, her eager minions, cavorted in sheer anticipation.

I tried several restraining gambits. What about fish and chips all round for tea or the musical Robertson's jam figurines that Sophie desperately wanted from that nice man who kept the second-hand shop halfway down Monnow Street? Or would they care for a monster lolly each, or even a pre-Christmas present from that disgustingly expensive store in St Mary's Street?

Doleful expressions caused me to capitulate. We went to the fair and I consoled myself with the thought there could be one small, albeit pyrrhic compensation.

My Polly was a crack shot with an air rifle or, for that matter, with any sort of missile-aborting weapon. On one occasion I'd seen my young nephew place a bean can upon a bird table in his parents' large garden and standing back, expected to see dotty Aunt Polly miss the target by a large margin. To his possible chagrin and certain astonishment, her devastatingly accurate shot from some fifty yards caused the can to fly off the table, where it lay shattered and vanquished, in the middle of the burgeoning potato patch.

Most of the stallholders were sallow-faced individuals from somewhere in neighbouring Herefordshire. They did not take kindly to my Polly's undeniable expertise with a gun. But she just shot and smiled; dismembered her favourite ducks, carved miniscule cavities in less than prominently displayed playing cards and splayed pellets unerringly into a variety of, to her, easily violated targets.

I soon became a donkey. A beast of burden transformed from a questionable form of humanity. I carried a large, garishly apparelled doll, a cheap imitation-leather handbag, a few hairy coconuts, a packet of Singhalese tea, some junior hairslides and James's plastic mac. Finally, as a *coup de grâce*, Polly won three goldfish in a small water-filled polythene container and one of these creatures already looked as though he had caught the mange or scurvy or – maybe through lack of things citric – caught a related and terribly contagious Welsh affliction.

But things could have been worse. Thanks to Polly's obsession with her gun-toting act, only the children rode the dodgems and patronised the penny-gobbling attractions and then only under my restrictive supervision. We would have remained relatively solvent had I not, alas, been dragged into the pet shop. The poor goldfish were deigned to be too cramped in their transparent and slightly leaky homestead (which I had furtively nicked with my penknife en route) and a more capacious domicile for them was obviously needed to ensure their survival.

So the kind pet shop owner sold us all that was necessary and these piscatorial appurtenances included a large goldfish bowl, pondweed, fish food and various other 'essentials' that he avowed were indispensable to all underwater creatures. It was a pity, he said, that we'd not bought the creatures from him but, never mind, two of them didn't look too bad and the grey one might last a little longer than a fortnight and anyway, we could always come back for the purposes of replenishing dead stock. There was, he chortled, enough room for a 'blubbering blue whale' in the bowl and we, of course, now knew where his shop was situated, a magnet for unsuspecting, penniless parents.

"Something for the cat, madam?" I had to admit I had a soft spot for sixteen-year-old Brindle, our spoon-fed tabby; a mild and gracious creature who, when they were appropriately in season, spent most of his waking hours sniffing the spring flowers or lying asleep under the garden's solitary petunia bush. Sardonically, I suggested he might like an offering of a clouded goldfish and Polly intimated that it was time we went home. It would be indiscreet of her to accost me in the pet shop, and I made a stumbling exit, hopelessly overburdened and mollified by a glance which bore all the marks of her famous 'wait until I get you home' look: an expression normally reserved for recalcitrant children and those, for often irrational reasons, with whom she often wholly disagreed.

I was now encumbered by the multicoloured figurines, the hairslides, the handbag, two coconuts – the others I dropped unobserved on the way to the pet shop – the Singhalese tea, the goldfish (three sickly musketeers), the fish food and decorative bits, and for the feline that ruled the household, a catnip mouse.

Divesting myself of this vast and eclectic collection of goods, I drove unsteadily across the bridge into our sylvicultural wilderness in silence; a state of reticence which did not, however, affect either my excited offspring or their equally animated mother.

We arrived home and the fish were transferred unceremoniously by me into the goldfish bowl. With juvenile approval – my kids were quite cultured – I proceeded to name them Henry the Fifth, the Sixth and the Eighth, all the time surmising whether the latter looked like an obese Protestant. Whereas the fittest of the aquatic trio, Henry the Fifth, whose association with Monmouth inspired my choice of names, was looking reasonably well, the remaining member of the trio, Henry the Sixth, had about him the pallor of his allegedly poorly namesake. Our judgemental and nosey neighbour – who kept budgies and was therefore 'an expert on goldfish' – asserted that the 'thick grey 'un d' look uz if 'im yunt long vur this world', and eyeing Henry the Sixth, who had started floating instead of swimming or whatever it is that fish do to propel themselves when in good health, I was inclined to agree with him.

Panic ensued. Monday night at the vets was primarily dog night and accompanied by grief-stricken children, I transported the invalid to the surgery. All it required was an ambulance siren to shift the two cars, one bicycle and the few ethnic woolly creatures that normally inhabited our small town after half past five any evening and the drama would have been complete.

The surgery was full of fearsome dogs, and cats in cardboard boxes and their owners gave us odd looks as we entered with

Henry the Sixth. They proceeded to express in that straight-faced way of theirs, which frequently passes for humour, a variety of opinions.

" 'Ant zeen a grey goldfish, 'ave thou, Royston?"

"No, I yunt, are Mam. 'Im d' look a bit rough don' 'im? Waz thick 'un doin' vloatin' around on top u' thick wayter, are Mam?" The small boy was relentless. "Ex that mon, are Mam, why's 'im ..."

"Kip quiet, are Royston ..."

Someone else took up the thread. "Oi daime (imagine) 'im yunt a'gwowin t' 'ave much use vur a vern ticket by the look on 'im, iz 'u?"

This provoked unrestrained mirth, for a 'fern ticket' was something you supposedly acquired from the Forestry Commission in order to 'gambol' with your young lady anywhere within the forty-thousand acres of dense and obligingly unrevealing woodland.

It went on to the bitter end.

"Waz 'im's naime then, Jaws? 'Im yunt goin' t' jump outta thick bowl 'n' bight we, iz 'u? Thou d' wanna put zalt in 'iz wayter, ol' butt. That'll cure 'un. My Uncle Graham, 'im did kip some o' thaiy perhana vish in 'iz 'ouse until thaiy yut Auntie Maureen! Thich salt musta done thaiy vish good, mind, cus are Maureen wuz a tough owld bit o' ship mutton!"

When we eventually got around to seeing the vet, he awarded us a pitiable look, gave me a sort of white powder and as we were leaving, muttered something about not accepting emaciated piscatorial species from dubious sources in future.

Two days later, Henry the Sixth died and Henry the Eighth caught the grey mold. True to his heroic namesake, Henry the Fifth seemed unaffected and even showed signs of putting on weight.

We buried Henry the Sixth using an old sardine tin (a bit sick really) and heavy mourning commenced; especially as Henry the Eighth deteriorated some days later and gave all the signs of being destined for that same fishy Valhalla under the oak tree in our back garden. Inevitably, Henry the Eighth expired as I predicted he would. I found him upside down one morning and the children woke up just in time to stop me in my dastardly attempt to feed him to Brindle who, perhaps fortunately displayed a complete lack of interest and went on playing with his catnip mouse. Nobody had ever had the heart to tell Brindle it wasn't a real mouse and since he'd never caught and wouldn't recognise a live rodent if he saw one, we'd never enlightened him and he went on happily chewing his substitute and sniffing the wild flowers.

Anxious eyes were soon cast upon Henry the Fifth. At first it appeared he would not contract the dreaded affliction, but it was to no avail. It crept insidiously upon him; a grey cumulus of approaching doom and the only thing for it, the children averred sadly, was to have the valiant warrior 'put down' and so relieve him of his suffering.

Again it was a crowded post-weekend surgery. A couple of ship badgers (shepherds) were present with their collies and added interest to the proceedings.

"Be that the vish thick 'un thou 'ad 'ere last time, Mr C?"

"No," I replied shortly and a little ungraciously, as I sat holding a Pyrex mixing bowl with the measured markings on the sides which would ultimately end up serving as a hearse for the fated monarch. I was almost convinced we were too late to save him.

"Dost breed 'un or zummat, Mr C?" someone chipped in tactlessly. "I daime I did 'ave zummat like thick 'un in my taikaway tother night! I d' reckon thou d' never know what bist getting vrum thick Chinee in Clearwell Street these daiys!"

This ceaseless banter endured during all the time it took to treat three Alsatians, two Labradors, a bald chow, a finger-severing Jack Russell, a Siamese cat, a ginger tom, a Senegal parrot with long claws and an extremely obscene vocabulary, a venomous and decidedly un-British snake; the two collies and a 'ship' or sheep which someone had solicitously brought off the road and that – unusually after a collision – had the breath of life left in it.

I eventually emerged from a consultation with the exhausted vet, plus an empty mixing bowl and alas, minus Henry the Fifth. The vet, who had been born in Africa and therefore was used to eccentric Englishmen had, nevertheless, turned his back on me when he had committed the stricken Henry the Fifth to the unknown. He put the hapless patient into a small polythene bag and took it straight out again. It was quick and painless, and I left with the impression that all an adventurous fish needed for a foray on land was a polythene bag, into which airless zone he could secrete his person and roam at will.

It was James's birthday the next day and when I arrived home from work that evening, I was informed that Uncle William had been with a present. Uncle William, curse him, had learned of the demise of the three Henrys and had remembered it was his favourite nephew's birthday and misguidedly tried to soften the blow.

Later that night when everyone – including Polly – had retired to bed, I tried to get Brindle embroiled with the 'Duke of Gloucester'. But he showed little interest in the newcomer. He flicked his racoon-like tail, jumped down from the table and with a last disapproving backward look at me, made off in the direction of his three obligatory feeding bowls.

I decided the only thing to do, would be to buy James a junior fishing line and to inform him that fishing was an indoor sport.

Jem's Boots

1988

An owld 'un, Mother Harding lived somewhere below that sinuous road which descends from Cinderford to Blakeney. Her small, whitewashed cottage stood on a slight rise overlooking the stream which ran parallel to the road and bubbled away until it met the mighty Severn at the culmination of the peninsula beyond the small settlement.

For company she had her bachelor son, Bill, aged forty, several invasive cats and Jem's boots. But she didn't have Jem. Jem had been her pride and joy; an overtly amicable bundle of golden hair and mischievousness who had gone 'oodin' one day and failed to return and all she had of him now was his Sunday-best boots. Bravely proclaiming Mother Harding's unflagging optimism, they now hung forlornly above the black Victorian fireplace and below them, on the mantel, a sepia photograph was a constant reminder of the small boy's still unexplained disappearance. An extensive search had failed to find him, and the appalling conclusion reached was that, horrendously, he'd fallen down one of the Forest's disused mineshafts; a fate that did not bear too much thinking about.

Every evening for the past forty odd years, Mother Harding had gone slowly to the garden gate and whispered Jem's name into the night air in the hope that her entreaty would carry forth and reach wherever the child lay sleeping. Inevitably, this pitiable supplication had been to no avail. It had also been too much for her 'owld man'; a taciturn miner, who succumbed to silicosis and grief. This left her beholden to her second son, Bill, whose existence in Mother Harding's blinkered eyes, could never compensate for the loss of Jem. In the past, comparisons between the two sons had been made, unjustly and hurtfully. In his formative and as it turned out, only years, Jem had ostensibly been quicker, brighter and allegedly more proficient at everything he did. Jem could apparently tie his bootlaces earlier; knew his catechism at the age of eight, his spelling was faultless, and he was said to have excelled at arithmetic.

In the years that followed, Bill tilled the garden and tried to concern himself almost solely with things practical. He was a good son to his mother and found compensation for her lack of affection in his peaceful surroundings. At the age of fourteen he went to work in a soulless factory and sometime later went to war and upon his unscathed return, found that nothing had changed. The boots remained, freshly polished, above the mantelpiece and were kept company by the youthful photograph, which had cracked and warped in the heat from the fireplace.

Mother Harding had done her best with the garden, except that sweet peas, asters, primulas and wallflowers now flourished where vegetables had once reigned supreme. He had to admire the honeysuckle clinging in a blaze of saffron to the front porch, but resolved that stick beans and brassica would soon have their day again.

Time passed and Mother Harding's nightly walks to the garden gate became a test of endurance. Her sibilant beseeching into the wind for her lost one would mount to a crescendo and now ended in a stark, harsh cry which alarmed Bill and attracted the attention of those few neighbours who were living in similar cottages both below and on the bank above the road. Most of these declared that Mother Harding 'were tuppence short uv a shillin' and furthermore 'thick son of 'ern oughta 'ave 'er put awaiy!' Patiently, Bill listened to a lot of this largely unsolicited advice but being 'a chip off 'is owld faither's block', steadfastly ignored it and did not seek medical assistance.

Then one day at the end of a cruel March, when the suffocating hand of winter still lay upon the trees and very little in the way of fauna deigned to move from hibernation or arrived to herald the coming spring; Bill cautiously made his way down the slippery patch to the cottage. Here constantly swirling white emissions from the chimney stack gave evidence of an abundant and welcoming fire beneath. Despite her suspected mental shortcomings, Mother Harding could always be relied upon to provide a good dinner and as he opened the front door, Bill inhaled the pungent aroma of mutton stew. Briefly, he paused to savour the smell and upon entering, threw his work haversack into the vacant rocking chair, hitched up his coat and presented his buttocks to the blazing fire.

"Bist there, are Mam?"

"Be that you, Bill?"

"O' course. 'Oo else did thou think t'wuz?"

"Thee 'ad better come on in 'ere an' yut thee tea then, ol' butt."

Bill entered the kitchen and sat down at the old oak table; an heirloom inherited from some uncle or other. Two places were laid, complete with freshly laundered serviettes. The best silver condiment pots sat squat in the middle of a damask tablecloth and as if to cheat the last remnants of winter, an elegant vase of early narcissi completed the picture.

Mother Harding seemed more alert than she had been for some time and an unusual smile wreathed her features as she doled out the stew.

" 'Im's comin' back t'night," she stated flatly.

Caught in mid-mouthful, Bill started, and half a dumpling fell off his fork to sully the pristine tablecloth. He'd only just noticed the bottle of homemade Golden Rod wine which stood on the nearby sideboard; a rarity left over from his father's day and something that Mother Harding – being teetotal – under normal circumstances would never have countenanced.

" 'Im zaid 'im 'ood come vur zertain."

" 'Oo, Mam?"

"Are Jem."

"Are Jem?"

"Yes, tha's what 'un zaid, an' I aa still got 'iz little boots waiytin' for 'un."

"Oi d' know thou 'ast are Mam, but 'im byunt comin' wome t'daiy nor no other daiy. 'Im's up in 'eaven." Bill went on steadily eating and talked soothingly between mouthfuls. "You ant yut nothin' yet, are Mam. Come on now, get theeself stuck in. Oi don' wunt thee t' faide awaiy. Wunt do thee no good at all if thou doesn't yut!"

Mother Harding sighed and made some attempt at a repast which did not last long. She sat back and surveyed Bill with vacuous and strangely uncomprehending eyes. "Oi shall 'ave t' go up the garden t' meet 'un. 'Im wunt like it if I don' meet 'un."

"Theese don' wanna gow out there t'night, are Mam. It be bitter cold out thare. Thou'll be better off 'ere at wome in vront of thick vire."

This briefly caused Mother Harding some consternation, but she soon recovered and hastened to reassure her worried second son. "Oh, it be all right, are Bill. I did get 'un a liddle coat when I wuz in Blakeney with Mrs Marfell. I bought it special, like. I know 'im d' feel the cold. I did buy 'un some gloves fur 'iz little 'ands uz well, 'im don' need no boots. I aa still got 'ims boots."

This peroration went on and on and gradually became more and more fragmented and disjointed, so that Bill could only comprehend snatches of it.

"Come 'ere y' little worrit. Let me do yer 'air. Doesn't thou wunt zum sweeties afore thou goes out t' plaiy? Don' taike no notice of thy faither. 'Im wunt taike 'iz belt off t' thee! Zeven nines iz sixty-dree. Iz that what thee zaid? 'Oo's a clever little 'un, then? Rev'rend Toomer, 'e d' think a lot of thou; coz 'uh wouldn't be a'gwowin' to let thee sing a zolo in the church, would 'u?"

Bill feverishly mopped up his gravy with some of his mother's home-made bread and put his cutlery together. He arose from the table and made for the back door, lifting the latch and taking his aged donkey jacket from its customary hook. He turned to face his mother.

"Oi be just gowin' up t' ex Mr Marfell about zummat, are Mam," he said. "Thee finish yuttin' thy vood and staiy 'ere. Oi doesn't want thee gowin' out on a night like this. Art thou listenin', are Mam?" He turned up the collar of his donkey jacket and repeated his admonishment.

"Jem'll be 'ere zoon, bless 'im."

Bill became more insistent. "Listen now. Oi wunt be long. Kip thick vire byuilt up 'n' sit by 'un. And doesn't thee be gowin' nowhere whilst Oi be gone!"

"Them be nice curls thee 'ave got, Jem. T'yunt vair fur a boy t' 'ave preddy curls like that."

"Shan' be long, Mam!" Bill opened the door and caught his breath as an icy blast howled round the cottage and all but consumed him. It began to snow in the wind and by the time he had climbed the path and the bank to the Marfell's cottage some half mile above the road, it was beginning to stick.

The Marfells expressed concern and immediately offered Bill the phone to call the doctor. Unfortunately, there appeared to be something wrong with it. Bill silently cursed and returned the receiver to its cradle. The line had probably come down in the wind, which had gained in momentum to become a blizzard and the kindly Mr Marfell suggested taking Bill to fetch the doctor from Blakeney by car. Mr Marfell had both a phone and a car which, in those days, not many people could afford.

Bill thanked the couple in his monosyllabic way and stated that it could wait until morning. He bid them goodnight and hunched his shoulders for the return journey. He negotiated the bank from the Marfell's homestead without too much difficulty, crossed the now snow-laden road below it and began descending the path to his home. Halfway down he stumbled and fell heavily to the ground. He tried to rise, and a searing pain afflicted his ankle. He began to crawl forward slowly and painfully. His knees soon became sodden and, at a point more precipitous than elsewhere, he lost control completely and slid into a small culvert at the side of the path. The water's icy propensity made him catch his breath and for some minutes he struggled in vain to climb out. Fortuitously and to his relief, a torch beam licked the top of the path and began to move nearer. It flickered on unerringly and soon Bill could discern the person carrying it. The beam lingered for a second over him and then, disastrously, made to continue on its way. Bill cried out and after a slight pause, the light returned, and the dark figure of Mr Marfell stood looking down at him.

"Bill, be that thou, ol' butt?"

Worried about Mother Harding, Mr Marfell had decided to follow Bill home in the hope he could do something to help, and not without some difficulty, succeeded in hoisting his young neighbour from the culvert. He was a strong man and putting an arm round the shivering Bill's shoulder and aided by his heavily studded ex-Gloucestershire regiment footwear, he lugged him down to the garden gate.

Bill had been away an hour and how long his mother had been lying there, he could not imagine. He became frantic. "Oi did tell 'er not to gow out. Oi did tell 'er! Iz thick bloody Jem, 'tiz! 'er reckoned uz 'im were comin' wome t'night. But 'er 'ad t' gow 'n' meet 'un. Oi told 'er not to, but 'er wunt listen t' I, would 'er? Oi told 'er t' stop indoors …"

Whilst Bill continued ranting, sobbing and holding on to the gate, his neighbour assumed a 'miner's squat' and examined Mother Harding with his torch.

He seemed satisfied and stood up, hands on hips. " 'er's breathin' all right, any rowd. Stay where thee bist, Bill. I'll come back for thou. I must zee t' yer mam virst." A powerful man, he bent his back and picked up the slight frame of Mother Harding without effort. She had diminished in size over the years through both ageing and unreliable appetite. He carried her to the cottage without difficulty and once inside, placed her gently in the rocking chair. He returned to assist Bill and having them now both safely indoors, made up the fire and put the kettle on. He hoped hypothermia would not set in and somehow found fresh clothes for them both to put on. Despite Mother Harding's slight protests, his experience as an army batman helped him in persuading her to change and he performed the same service for Bill, whose tremors indicated that the whole experience had been almost too much for him. The good neighbour made hot drinks and decided not to disturb the old lady, who now appeared to be slumbering peacefully. He went to the back door, opening it slightly to look at the weather and noted that the blizzard appeared to have abated. It was still snowing lightly, but the wind had dropped, and Mr Marfell decided to go and fetch his wife who was also ex-army and a pretty strong character who would be a great help in the present situation. He apprised Bill of his intentions, but Bill appeared too bemused to comprehend. He began to revile the memory of Jem, cursing his mother and denigrating the illusion which she had cherished all those anguished years.

The next day Mrs Marfell sat with the Hardings until the ambulance came and transported Mother Harding to hospital in Gloucester.

Mother Harding did not last long after that, but when she was going, she had regained consciousness just long enough to utter the words "Jem's boots," to Bill who, with chilling indifference, took no notice and waited patiently for his mother to decline into oblivion.

*

A month or two later, when the bluebells and anemones proliferated in the woods, Bill alighted from the work bus and made his way down the path to the cottage. Before entering, he stood to contemplate his vegetable garden which showed every sign of embryonic activity. He went indoors and began to prepare his tea; a simple task these days when you only had one person for whom to cater. It didn't take long, tea for one, and he ate it quickly before doing what little washing up there was to do. He lit a cigarette, a habit he'd adopted since his mother had died and slumped into the rocking chair. One of the cats attempted to claim his lap, but he would have none of it and sat staring vacantly at the fireplace. Sunlight streamed remorselessly through the window and glistened momentarily on Jem's boots, with Jem's photograph still evident below.

Angrily, Bill arose and snatched the boots from their hallowed resting place. He removed the photo and crushed the fading likeness until it became beyond repair. Turning round slowly, he walked out of the room into the hall and went through the front door to the garden.

A spade stood where he had left it the previous evening on the completion of some other job and removing it, he began to dig up a small flower bed that his mother had laboriously toiled to begat. He dug down to a depth of two and a half feet and carefully placed the boots, left and right, in asymmetrical order. Then, deliberately and with obvious relish, he filled the hole and stood looking at it with undisguised satisfaction. After a while spent leaning on the spade, he forsook it and strolled over to the garden gate. He clenched the top slat until his knuckles became deathly white and began to speak in a soft, hesitant undertone.

"Mam? Bist thou there, are Mam? It yunt Jem, Mam. I's Bill. When y' comin' wome, Mam? When bist comin' wome?"

Daddy's Girl
1988, slightly revised 2019

From the elegant drawing room of her parents' restored Georgian pile, Natasha could look back over the centuries to where stood the neglected and rapidly decaying tithe barn.

Once used by the Church to collect Harland's assurance of heaven – the universal tithe of wheat and root crops – it now housed a few rusting farm implements, some superfluous bales and a prodigious number of mice. Unspectacular outside, with plain walls and stolid buttresses, it had an impressive cruck frame of pedunculate oak within and had somehow escaped the notice of local historians, the authorities, conservationists, and any other parties who may have taken it into their respective heads to take more than a passing interest.

On several evenings in succession during her accustomed peregrinations round the village, Natasha had noticed a lone barn owl taking off from the tower of Hartland's imposing twelfth-century church and had assumed that its destination would be the old barn. It kept making forays in that direction and despite slight parental concern, she had often stopped out after dark to catch a glimpse of it in the moonlight. Not that much harm could befall her in Hartland. Hartland was a haven for the elderly, some of whom, Natasha facetiously maintained, had been around when the village was still a pocket borough and sent a chinless aristocrat off to help misrule the nation. One of the king Georges, who had a penchant for hunting, had bestowed upon Hartland this exalted status, but not particularly benefiting from his patronage, the place had tended to decline ever since. Not helped by the closure of the village school and a lack of council housing, children were almost as scarce as hen's teeth and the village pub, which dated back to the thirteenth century, kept going largely through the needs of tourists who were persuaded that Hartland was an essential ingredient in any visit to the Forest of Dean.

Very much a child of the eighties, Natasha had a mother who collected Capodimonte china and a father who commuted over the Severn Bridge to Bristol every day. Her mother also ran a gift shop in nearby Monmouth and this activity tended to explain the lady's lack of discernment when it came to furnishing her own home. Most of it, alas, consisted of reproduction prints thought daringly modern though in reality, marooned in the sixties. These passé examples of questionable art uneasily adorned the walls and added to the tacky modern furniture which, in Natasha's opinion, flagrantly proved what an abundance of money could do when not allied to a modicum of good taste.

At present on vacation from university, Natasha had been assigned the onerous task of waiting for the central heating engineer to arrive on his annual visit to service the boiler. She had also to attend her father, who was off work and in bed with one of his increasingly regular migraines. It was a source of concern to his sensitive daughter but not, ostensibly, to the local doctor, whose dilatory attitude irritated Natasha and caused her to display not the best aspects of her normally tolerant and charismatic character. Natasha thought Daddy should see a specialist, but Daddy could be obdurate and so was Dr Bowen. She had made sure that the doctor had received one of her black looks before leaving and after filling her father with paracetamol, had driven his Saab into Coleford with little faith to collect a prescription.

Whilst she awaited the central heating engineer, she sat listlessly in a reproduction Chippendale chair and played patience on a nondescript contemporary table. A good-looking girl aged nineteen, Natasha possessed her father's broad forehead and his glittering, sometimes quizzical blue eyes. From her mother she had inherited a luxurious growth of long, auburn hair; a petite, slightly retroussé nose and a figure which would attract a considerable number of male admirers.

The central heating engineer came in a lather of protesting brakes and a flurry of displaced gravel and, by any standards, could not be classified as an Adonis. Short, squat and sporting spiked highlighted hair; his eyes sat well back in their sockets and fluttered nervously when confronted with Natasha, He held a large, adjustable spanner in one hand and a metal tool case in the other and could not have been more than twenty years old.

Natasha smiled encouragingly at him. "The boiler?" she said.

A slight leer displaced the nervousness.

"S'right."

"I'll show you up. It's in the bathroom." Glad of her jeans, Natasha conducted the young man up the stairs and left him to it.

She entered her parents' room and studied her father who lay, propped on his pillows in a fitful sleep. His face the colour of pumice powder, had lined alarmingly in the last year and Natasha could not make anyone realise it. Purblind, her mother concerned herself almost exclusively with her sordid shop and tended to treat the man in her life as just another appendage: in much the same way that she treated the cat and dog and even, to some extent, Natasha herself.

Daddy opened his eyes and extended an arm; patting the bedclothes and inviting her to sit down.

" 'Tasha, dear. I feel a little better now. Who was that at the door? I thought I heard a car?"

Natasha plopped herself down and took the proffered hand.

"You did. Alas, it was only the gorgeous heating engineer. All of four foot eleven, a lascivious grin, piggy eyes, heavily cultivated hair and a clapped-out minivan."

Daddy's eyes twinkled. "For all his sartorial, physical and material shortcomings, I imagine the lad would not refuse a cup of coffee and neither would I, if you please, sweetheart?"

Natasha produced a nail file and began to ply it in leisurely fashion. Her father pulled himself up on his right elbow and stared at her acutely.

"You wouldn't be thinking of playing your usual trick on that hapless individual, I suppose?"

There followed an interval to enable Natasha to consider and try on new perfume from amongst the expensive clutter on her mother's dressing table.

" 'Tasha!"

"What's that? Ah, yes – I mean, no!" The girl assumed her most virginal expression. "As if I would! Him? I think I've a bit more nous than that!"

Satisfied, her father lay down again. "And the coffee?"

Natasha arose in a flurry of facetious animation. "The coffee. Yes, the coffee. A woman's work is never done. To the kitchen with you, girl! I shall not be long, o lord and master!"

As she ground the coffee, Natasha contemplated the scenery framed idyllically by the kitchen window. Beyond the garden, the almshouses – now correctly restored to their original brown and white – huddled beneath the towering mass of All Saints' and a covey of bent old ladies stood gossiping by the alleyway that led to this locally designated 'Cathedral of the Forest'. Natasha knew that her beloved barn owl would be somewhere around it and when consulted, the rector had commented wryly that the best place to breed would probably be the font, where no baby had been baptised for five years.

Natasha poured the coffee and took it upstairs. The callow heating engineer eyed her uncertainly as she handed him the steaming mug and leant provocatively on the sink.

"D' you live round here?" she enquired in her huskiest voice.

The flustered young man shuffled his feet, sat down on the toilet, realised what he'd done and stood up again. That part of his neck that had declined to accommodate the acne present elsewhere went a revealing shade of pink, and this discomposure spread rapidly upwards until it reached his cheeks.

"No," he said. "Drybrook." The second syllable coming out as a short 'u' sound.

"Oh, well, you can't help that," remarked the girl unkindly. "I suppose there are more insalubrious places to live, although I can't think where. Anyway, Daddy, who's in bed with a migraine, says that if you're going to seduce me, would you do it quietly, please?"

An instant temptress, Natasha sat down cross-legged on the bathroom floor and poker faced, challenged the demolished youth with her devastating eyes.

The adjustable spanner fell to the carpet with a dull thud and the boy's mouth fell open a thousand feet to reveal a surprisingly presentable set of gleaming teeth which, Natasha mused, was a small something in his favour.

" 'Tasha!" The girl had forgotten the bedroom door and her father had keen hearing. "Can I have my coffee please?"

Daddy delivered his customary mock admonition and smiling to herself, Natasha light heartedly returned to the kitchen to find the terrified young heating engineer had left a note. He had fled and could be heard creating great furrows in the driveway in his frantic hurry to escape.

Natasha crumpled up the note, tossed it in the waste bin and went into the drawing room. With slight apprehension overcoming her, she noticed that the scene from the window had changed for the worst. A man with a tripod and an unnecessarily expensive camera stood in the paddock taking photos of the old barn and she wondered what he was up to. She left the house by the solid front door and walked over to the peripheral hedge where, halfway along, a small gate gave access into the paddock.

The photographer, a decidedly worn middle-aged individual sporting both pinstripes and a prominent beer paunch, continued with his work and was only startled when after a stealthy approach, Natasha robustly accosted him.

"D' you mind telling me what exactly you are doing please?"

The man quickly regained his composure. "If it's any business of yours, Miss, what does it look like?"

Natasha bestowed one of her dark looks on him and the man gave up. From his wallet he produced an estate agent's card and assumed an air of instant obsequiousness.

"Up for auction," he said.

"Not the barn?" The question came out as a venomous hiss.

"Sure, Miss, why not the barn?"

"But surely, it's a listed building? Mr Cowmeadow can't just sell it off just like that?!" Curse him, thought Natasha, curse old man Cowmeadow and all his forebears!

The estate agent produced a packet of Sobranie Black Russians and offered it to Natasha. The girl pulled a face and watched him struggle to light up in the faint, but inconvenient breeze. This task accomplished, he inhaled deeply and tried to explain.

"If something isn't done to this old heap soon, sweetie, it'll collapse and under the law, that can't happen. And, moreover, some of these conversions can be quite attractive, you know. You shouldn't condemn the whole thing out of hand merely because it's become a habit to see it as it is."

"You mean to say, we could have people living over there?"

"Very likely. It has planning permission for a dwelling and why not? Isn't it better it should be put to some use, rather than be left to rot?"

"But it is used!"

"You could have fooled me!" The estate agent shrugged his shoulders. "Apart from some misuse by the old farmer, I don't see what purpose it serves at the moment."

Natasha tried to combat what she saw as the man's intrinsic insensitivity. "Don't you know what a bat is or a barn owl? If you people had your way, there wouldn't be any wildlife left. You'd destroy all the natural habitat by flinging down concrete and tarmac over everything. You'd rip up all the hedges and having destroyed vast areas of the country, you'd patronisingly allow some right-minded but feeble ecological organisation to use your spare window for display purposes. Then you'd go on to build hundreds of your hideous boxes on greenfield sites all over the land!"

The estate agent put his hands together and gave her a sarcastic round of applause.

"A pretty speech, sweetie. But people have to live somewhere, and the fact remains that if something isn't done about that old ruin soon, it'll fall down and bang goes your barn and your idealism in one fell swoop! It's Hobson's choice if you ask me." He began to dismember his tripod and concluded by inserting his Japanese 'wondercamera' into its plush leather case. "Tell you what, sweetie," he muttered with his back to Natasha, "The Flamingo's still open. How about you and me having a cosy chat and a drink in the lounge to discuss the matter? What's your poison? G&T? Or are you a lager addict?"

"Get lost!" snorted Natasha, turning in disgust towards the house. "I'm sure your probably long-suffering wife would just love that!" She hastily traversed the field, angrily flung the gate open, ran across the well-manicured lawn and disappeared into the house.

*

From the seclusion of an all-embracing yew tree, Natasha delighted in the sight of a fat young owlet trying to depart from an arrow slit in All Saints' tower. She swept her binoculars forty-five degrees to the left and downwards and watched its mother trying to convey encouragement from a vertical tombstone some twenty yards away and then switched back to her original target.

The convivial rector had acquainted her with the whereabouts of the brood. He had stumbled upon them by accident when mounting the tower to examine the church clock and had pinpointed the position with commendable accuracy. Natasha had watched the tower and on three successive evenings in the gathering twilight been lucky enough to witness the male bird toing and froing with abundant prey for his voracious offspring. But this was something new. A tentative step into the unknown. As Natasha held her breath, the emergent young owlet teetered on the brink and finally took the plunge; landing a few yards short of his mother's perch. Thirty-one days in the egg, a few weeks dependent on parental care and a barn owl could take to the outside world. Natasha considered it made the human race look pretty bilious. And why were these fascinating creatures with their startling eyes and dove-white undercarriage, associated in the human mind with death? True, they inhabited graveyards and other eerie places, but where better to catch the odd mouse or any other unsuspecting rodent?

Another young owlet emerged and after a perfunctory flight which went full circle, joined its mother on the tombstone with comparative ease. Natasha remained engrossed with this performance until complete darkness closed in and she went home to supper.

Her parents sat one each end of the pine table and her mother crabbily expressed disapproval of Natasha's late arrival. Natasha tried to explain about the owls, but met with little response from either and Daddy, she thought, by his increasingly unhealthy pallor, desperately needed respite and more medical help than he was receiving from Dr Bowen. She broached the subject warily and her mother looked mildly irritated.

"You fuss too much, 'Tasha. Your father's eaten quite well this evening, haven't you, dear? I'm sure Dr Bowen knows what he's doing. It can't be anything serious or he'd have done something about it by now."

Natasha mentioned a holiday and her mother – invariably inclined to disagree – habitually demurred again.

"You know I can't leave the shop, dear. It's our busiest time. Besides, I think your father's too busy as well. We can't all afford long vacations …"

"Precisely," rejoined her daughter curtly, "and that is why, my stubborn parental mentor, I could mind the shop whilst you and Daddy swan off to the Algarve or Dubrovnik or some other exotic paradise. Do not cite lack of loot as an excuse. I know you've got plenty. You shouldn't leave your bank book lying around, Mother …"

" 'Tasha!"

"You know I don't go back to uni till October, so what's stopping you? Are you frightened of what I might get up to when you're away? Jesus Christ, Mother dear; what in the hell could a body get up to in a geriatric dormitory like Hartland?"

Daddy smiled wanly. " 'S enough 'Tasha," he said. "I really don't feel like a verbal battle between you and your mother tonight. Let's leave things as they are, shall we?"

*

Exactly one year later, the young man came in a brand-new van to service the central heating again. Natasha noticed the spikes and the highlights had gone and so had most of the acne.

He seemed very assured and swaggered up the stairs darting covert glances at Natasha's shapely backside as he went. She made coffee and invited him to come down and drink it in the kitchen. She supposed she owed the poor lad a little hospitality after the enigmatic teasing he'd had to endure twelve months previously, but she certainly wasn't going to take his drink up to the bathroom this time. He came down and sat opposite Natasha and she tried valiantly to start a dialogue with him. She began to tell him about last year's owls and their regrettable absence this year. He seemed interested.

" An' you yunt zin 'em this year, at all, then? Vunny, yunt it?"

Natasha refrained from remarking that that was what she'd just said and pointed out that it could be the barn conversion that was to blame.

The young man shook his head in agreement. "Ye', Oi d' reckon it'd soon get rid of all thaiy rats 'n' mice. Mind, I can't say uz 'ow Oi d' care fur all thaiy bats, flyin' aroun' ut night 'n' landin' in yer 'air! It'd give Oi the creeps zummat vairish!" He made no effort to disguise his ripe dialect and seemed to think it complemented his new macho image. "Mind," he went on, "they byunt bad people over at the barn. Oi just bin thair 'un thaiy give Oi a tip. Mr and Mrs Billericay; come from up London zomewhere. 'Im's an arte-tec an 'im designed a lot of it 'izzelf. Made a nice job o'nt!"

Why he should think Natasha had not made the acquaintance of these new neighbours, she could not imagine. Although she'd not approved of the conversion, she was not that unneighbourly and, as he said, found them perfectly friendly and amenable.

She did not comment and poured herself another coffee. Her mind wandered. You have a garrulous tongue my boy, she thought, and I suspect I know what you're getting round to saying next. But go, hang yourself and get it over with. Will I ever get over it, though? That and the departed owls. Hartland, heart-shaped birds, unremitting heartache; a play on words. The newly emancipated engineer prattled on and Natasha poured coffee into a third, fresh cup. She placed it on the cooker and tried to be interested in what he was saying.

"Oi d' kip birds, thou knows. Oi d' belong t' the Gloucestershire Pigeon Fanciers. We d' zumtimes park are big 'artic' in that laiyby at Brierley 'n' let 'un gow vrum thaire. Mine d' allus come back."

"Really?" interjected Natasha hopefully and wished he'd take himself back upstairs to the boiler. This rustic patter was far removed from the mostly droll repartee she had to endure at uni and refreshing though it was to start with, it palled after a while.

"Wunt your faither's coffee get cold?" He pointed to the cup on the cooker, which remained untouched and offered to take it upstairs, making a wrong assumption.

"That's for Mr Beard," retorted Natasha abruptly. "He'll be here in a minute. I ought to call him really."

"Mr Beard?"

"The part-time gardener."

"Yunt yer faither 'ere t'daiy, then?"

"You could say that."

At this, the engineer stood up and winked suggestively at Natasha. "Well," he said, "if yer faither's not at wome t'day, 'ow about thou repeatin' what thou zaid t' me last year. 'Cos Oi might jus' take thee up on't this 'un ..." He concluded by placing a hand on Natasha's shoulder and she surveyed him coldly.

All men except Daddy. Her eyes filled with tears. She brushed aside the oppressive hand and arose. She was several inches taller than her would-be defiler, and this gave her courage.

"I think you'd better be off before I slap your positively ugly face!"

The engineer looked askance. " 'Ave Oi offended thee? Oi be zorry. Oi didn't mean to. I'z just that thou's very attractive 'n' thee did lead Oi t' think ..."

"I led you to think nothing!" Natasha crossed to the kitchen door, opened it and stood, stamping her foot frenetically.

The startled young man tried appeasement. "But what about thick boiler? Oi a gotta service 'n' now Oi've come. It 'as to be serviced!"

Natasha exploded, "Fuck the effing boiler! I don't care if it blows up and takes the whole bloody house and me with it! Just get your arse into that van of yours and piss off!"

"Thaire be no need t' use language like that ..." He had gone a deathly white and made a feeble attempt at protest.

"For Christ's sake, get out!" screamed the girl. "Just leave me alone and get out!"

"Your faither; 'im woun't like t' 'ear thee talk to no one like that, Oi d' reckon ..."

"Will you please go!"

"Nor your mam; 'ow bist your dad, by the way?"

She quietened down and told him and mortified, he turned tail, slammed the door and vanished from her existence like an unwelcome wraith. The noise of his van gradually receded as she slumped down on the table, put her head on her arms and sobbed uncontrollably.

A moment later Mr Beard, the gardener, walked in to rest from his exertions and to refresh himself with a drink which he knew Natasha would have ready. A dependable soul, Mr Beard had tended the garden since Daddy had died and, not far off being an octogenarian and therefore not overly concerned with the material things of this world, took very little in the way of payment.

Very concerned, he came over and took one of Natasha's hands in his own.

"Whatever be the matter, my love?"

Natasha explained and the old gentleman produced a capacious man's handkerchief with which he gently dried her eyes. His coffee was cold, so he helped himself to another one and sat down.

"Any rowd, my dear," he said, "Oi'uv got zum good news fur thou. Dost want t' 'ear it?"

At this Natasha visibly revived and sat with her chin in her hands.

"Good news? Is there such a thing?"

"Well," said the old gardener ponderously, "Oi sin thick owl uf thine. 'Im flew right across Toby Sprout's top medda when Oi wuz goin' wome last night!"

Elation replaced dejection. Natasha flung her arms around the startled old man and planted a large kiss on his stubbly cheek.

"Jesus," she said. "I don't believe it!"

*

The day before she returned to university, Natasha put a large bunch of freesias on her father's grave. Leaves scudded aimlessly round All Saints' churchyard and on the telegraph wires, the birds were already gathering to make a winter migration. In the half-light, Natasha stood and cast her gaze upon the looming tower.

Turning to go, she noticed the shimmering yellow eyes; just behind and complementing the freesias. Then, in a superb ascent of celestially inspired co-ordination, the owl climbed heavenwards and was lost in the gathering gloom.

Boars

2021

Invasive porcine they were. Not from another planet, but still hell-bent on destroying your garden and any other vegetation that took their fancy. Their young were delightful, though preferably not to be encountered in the company of their mother. When minded, mother could be a little aggressive and when approaching a group or 'sunder' of these animals, it paid to proceed with caution.

In its questionable wisdom, the Forestry Commission had instigated a cull and rangers were now employed to implement it. A law had been introduced which prohibited private citizens from helping themselves to this new porcine largesse, but as in the case of the Royal deer, it did not prevent a certain amount of it ending up in freezers throughout the Forest. Poaching was a way of life for some and even 'ship' (sheep) were not immune to 'ship rustling'.

You could pay for the new meat from the culled beasts which the Commission sold to butchers, but who cared to do that when it could be obtained in a free, though admittedly risky way?

Which explained why young Aaron Meek had taken the latter option, shot one of these invaders and was now wondering how to manage its transportation, as promised, to the Queen's Head in Coleford. He and his fellow imbibers had been well oiled when the manager of the hotel had challenged Aaron to do it, not a thing to be undertaken lightly, and it took a while for the young man to accede to his request. But the manager brushed all Aaron's objections aside. He was confident Aaron could do the job and had no qualms about putting boar on the menu or anyone questioning his source of supply.

The Forest was akin to the neighbouring Marches in the

Middle Ages. It was still sturdily independent and even if you were a hardened criminal on the run, you would probably be able to survive in the depths of it for some time.

At first emboldened by the amount of alcohol they had consumed, Aaron's mates had agreed to accompany him, but had 'chickened out' and here he was, mission accomplished, but with no means of moving the lifeless great beast.

The prospect of felling the animal had made Aaron very nervous, but a full moon made things very easy. He'd spotted the king-size boar foraging in a clearing and having sobered up, soon made short work of him. Some remorse invaded the young man's mind, but the thought of the renumeration he would receive for fulfilling his objective, helped to quell his misgivings.

A sudden rustling in the undergrowth could be a 'ship' in passing, but an appalling thought, it might well be the stricken boar's partner, aroused by the gunshot and bent on vengeance! His apprehension proved unfounded as a sheep broke cover and trotted across the clearing in the moonlight, then disappeared into the bracken and trees beyond. Eerie in their repetitive exclamations, the hidden and mystical owls were probably bent on snaring the unseen rodents that inhabited and scurried along the woodland plateau. Occasional light gusts of wind animated the leaves on the trees and to Aaron's consternation, another more recognisable sound started quietly and became louder as it drew nearer. Crunching footfalls and the brushing aside of impeding branches. Someone was approaching and Aaron decided to abandon his recumbent trophy. He made for the undergrowth and crouched, listening and hoping no one had 'welched' on him.

"Aaron?" A female voice. "Aaron, you there? Come on out. I can see what you've done, poor thing. The poor pig. You're a cruel bastard!" An educated female voice.

Fiona. He knew it was her. Former Cheltenham Ladies' College and not from 'round 'ere'. He'd taken the same path with her from Coalway early on Friday evening, before it was dark. It led to Cannop Ponds and on the way they'd walked into a one-man mine to indulge in an activity to which the exquisite girl was, for all her good breeding, not exactly adverse.

With a certain amount of trepidation, Aaron re-emerged

hesitatingly into the clearing and they both contemplated the dead boar.

" 'Ow did thou know I wuz 'ere?" Of a younger generation, Aaron did not speak broad 'Forest', but the odd archaic word crept in when he was nervous or carousing with his mates.

This induced a rapid response.

"Huh! We had a date, don't you remember? I sometimes ask myself why I bother with you? In case you've forgotten, we arranged to meet in the Queen's after the rugby with all those despicable friends of yours and I was to come along later. We were going to the cinema."

"I'm sorry ..."

"No, you're not. You're lucky I didn't go off with one of the others. It's extremely fortunate for you that they are such hideous examples of manhood, else I might have!"

He could not quite discern her flashing eyes and her show of belligerence and sought to remedy things by moving closer. She half resisted his attempted embrace, but not before he'd noticed how aroused she'd become. This only enhanced her attraction and he mentally chastised himself for a fool. He'd always suffered from impetuosity and what other sane male would prefer hunting a pig for gain to consorting with this highly desirable female? She'd now resorted to standing hands on hips whilst glowering at him at him in a harrowing and determinedly unforgiving manner.

"And what are you going to do with the poor bloody pig now you've shot it? You numpty!"

"The manager of the ..."

"Oh, I know all about that. Lot of brave heroes your almighty rugby-playing plebs are! So, how are you proposing to get this creature through the back door of the Queen's without someone seeing you? Always supposing you can get it that far in the first place ..."

"Didn't think o' that, did y', ol' butt?"

They hadn't noticed him. A master of stealth. Standing the other side of the clearing in his hand-knit sweater and black jeans and his jaunty hat.

A ranger, and perhaps where they were concerned, a fortunate one. Fiona's uncle was a ranger, something Aaron had forgotten.

Everybody had said that Fiona's Aunt Stephanie had married beneath herself. The couple were chalk and cheese, this apparently accounting for the fact that they'd stayed together for twenty years. The local sages had undoubtedly been wrong. Rough diamond that he was, Fiona adored her uncle, and the feeling was mutual. Having no children of his own, he'd spoilt her rotten and even helped pay for her education. Her parents were eternally grateful, for though reckoned locally to be 'a bit u' class' and 'nice with it, mind,' they had little to spare, and could never have afforded their girl's public-school education without help.

A very bright girl, Fiona was destined for Oxford, and it was a source of concern that she seemed hopelessly attracted to the rustic Aaron. As a supposedly sagacious native had spitefully observed, " 'Er bist a'gwowin th' zame waiy uz thick aunt of 'ern an' I daim (imagine) 'er might not be zo lucky!"

A well-padded and rugged individual, Uncle Martin bounded across the clearing in economical strides and confronted the anxious swine hunter. He had a severe expression on his face and stood over the culprit who, if it is possible for them both to co-exist, was experiencing both anxiety and relief. The first part of this unenviable state was dispelled however, when the ranger turned to his unconcerned niece, and she could just make out his smile in the moonlight.

"Lucky lad, this one. Wouldn't 'u bin if owld 'enry ud caught 'un! 'Im would 'u prob'ly bin taiken down t' thick pliss staition! I 'a gotta 'and it to 'un, though. 'Im en' a bad shot! Got this owld porker vair un' square!"

Aaron remained mute and Fiona turned on the charm.

"You won't report him, Uncle Martin, will you? You could pretend you shot the boar and get it moved for the Forestry to sell, couldn't you?"

His face still fixed in a stern expression, Uncle Martin took his time in replying and Aaron waited with bated breath.

"I could zertainly do that, my love, but dost thou think I should?"

But he couldn't resist her. He shrugged and confronted the hapless Aaron again. He gave him a severe dressing-down, included a warning as to what would happen if the young man ever erred again, and concluded the admonishment by telling them both to 'bugger off wome' and not use their 'vern tickets' on the 'waiy'.

*

The manager of the Queen's did not exactly expect the goods to arrive in broad daylight with a ranger in attendance. On the other hand, he did think some news might be forthcoming as to the success or failure of Aaron's solitary boar hunt. He just had to carry on with everyday life and hope something might transpire after dark. Unfortunately, he'd already been approached by Al Teague, the somewhat curmudgeonly butcher over the road who had perfectly legal boar meat in stock. Al had purchased it from the Forestry and was attempting to sell it at a vastly inflated price. Anticipating a much cheaper source of supply, the manager had turned down the offer and hoped it would not be a decision he lived to regret. Coleford was a small town and had an often highly injurious 'bush telegraph'. Seldom did anything go on in the parish that was not noted and converted into burgeoning gossip, malicious or otherwise and if, for instance, a diner conveyed his or her satisfaction of a meal with boar as the staple ingredient, it might come to the ears of Al Teague and the manager would be in trouble. He'd just have to take the risk. Business was not exactly booming and any good deals, dubious or not, had to be accepted in order to keep the place solvent.

Today, however, trade had been reasonably good and at about seven thirty, just as twilight was merging into darkness, ranger Martin Blanche walked into the bar. He nodded at a few familiar topers and asked if the manager had a minute to spare.

The manager raised his eyebrows, looking puzzled.

"Wunt kip thee a minute."

The manager assented and called the girl from reception to mind the bar. Uncle Martin motioned the manager out into the old coaching yard and opened the back of his minivan.

"Interested?"

The manager was taken aback, and Uncle Martin quickly shut the door again. A deal was agreed, the manager went to fetch the chef, and the contents of Uncle Martin's van were soon deposited in the outer kitchen of the Queen's Head. Banknotes were produced and business concluded, and Uncle Martin was soon ensconced on a bar stool making short work of a pint of Miner's Best, the local brew that only men with hairs on the inside of their chests could drink! Uncle Martin was a wily old bird and the Forestry Commission, he averred, could have the next one. It helped the finances to do 'a bit on the side', especially as he hadn't had to shoot the beast himself.

At about ten o'clock the same evening, Fiona and Aaron walked into the hotel, expecting to find the manager slightly irate at Aaron's lack of success in providing boar meat. Aaron just told the manager that he'd thought better of it and to his surprise, the manager accepted this and even gave them a drink on the house.

Author's Note

As previously pointed out elsewhere in this collection, a 'vern' or 'fern ticket' is a licence to gambol in the undergrowth for what Shakespeare called a 'hick and hack'!

The Almond

2014

He joined the singles club and became just another tentative optimist amongst the rest assembled in the old-fashioned ballroom. Here you could sample pricey drinks, cringe at the passé Cole's wallpaper, tolerate the downtrodden staff and possibly become myopic through enduring the subdued lighting.

Even the uninspired middle-aged disc jockey was scruffy and hire suited. His beard was overdue for a trim and his moustache, seeding downwards over his bottom lip, a ready depository for the clinging froth from the strong ale he was intermittently quaffing between banal utterances. Slightly apologetically, he played an indiscriminate mix from the sixties to the eighties and this, it seemed, went with the slightly pathetic territory which induced the somewhat desperate punters to attend, for the women present were mostly comb-overs and the men unashamedly balding.

Sebastian sat with his untouched pint of Guinness and tried to ignore the curious, though not particularly promising glances he was receiving. This, he reluctantly acknowledged, was a sad state of affairs. A clutching of straws; a last-chance saloon. Before leaving home, he'd surveyed the post-Christmas nut bowl. Inevitably, all that it now contained were almonds. The ones that even the hefty nutcracker spurned. Only attempted when all the more tempting varieties were gone. He had avariciously devoured the woody walnuts, challenged his teeth on the exotic Brazils; added too much salt to the dry hazelnuts and utterly failed to resist the high-cholesterol-inducing cashews. Best of all he'd enjoyed the roasted chestnuts, and these were done before an open fire on an old brass toasting fork bequeathed to him by a long-deceased grandmother. Which, of course, left only the almost inaccessible and usually unwanted almonds.

He currently felt like a discarded almond; unloved and irrelevant; the dross of late middle age. When he thought about it, there appeared to be little hope. At one time he'd almost become a misogynist, but after girding his loins and pulling himself together, he'd embarked upon a determined quest to end his lone state. When his second, albeit bigamous marriage to a polygamous Irish girl had foundered thirteen years previously, he'd eschewed thoughts of the opposite sex for a while, but sheer loneliness had become his lot, and he was now desperately hoping to assuage the terrible feelings of utter desolation which frequently overcame him like angry waves accosting the seashore.

There had been females who appeared to find him presentable, but their attitudes were to his experienced eye, sometimes incomprehensible and often enigmatic. Promisingly, they seemed to desire a man, but at the same time nearly always stressed that they valued their independence. You were welcome to visit, but not too often. An early one behaved like a latter-day middle-aged nymphomaniac; then cruelly withdrew her services after a month. Another would meet for coffee, preach Jesus at you and offer nothing else; a vixen in a nun's habit; enticing, but frustratingly unobtainable.

An expensive dating agency had produced positive ogres of the species, all of whom appeared to want only 'companions' and some of whom took you for an expensive meal. Some were chic, but most were ugly and distinctly unbeddable and others were simply control freaks. Another was a bizarre kleptomaniac who paid for nothing. Some could not cook and nearly all evinced paranoia for foreign holidays and this was a desire he most definitely did not share. He had experienced balmy Brazil and Ireland had captivated him, but he had no desire to travel elsewhere.

To him, where he resided in the Forest of Dean was incomparable. Nowhere, surely, could the seasons change with such breathtaking beauty? The Forest was virtually a different country. A land of the Queen's deer, pig rustling, hordes of roaming sheep and a people of sturdy independence, unfortunately being slowly usurped by an influx of wealthy incomers who were inclined to want to change everything. A recent incursion of alien wild boars was not helping the balance of things and their fecund breeding was a cause of great concern So much so that calls for a cull were being posited from various quarters.

He realised his thoughts had wandered. He had not noticed the relatively young woman who now stood at the table in the corner of the ballroom where he had placed his person with a perverse, self-denigrating reserve. Thankfully he awakened from his reverie and smiled nervously at the newcomer. He felt strangely uneasy at her intrusion. She was not more than five feet in height, her hair shimmering, soft and lustrous, and she had two mellow, light-brown eyes which unashamedly engaged his. Her expression was quizzical, her figure well-kept and her breasts firm and ample. She held a glass in one hand and what was probably a genuine leather handbag in the other. Her jewellery, mostly silver and unfussy, nicely complemented her rich, burgundy-hued attire; the skirt of which was not too modest and allowed more than a glimpse of two well shaped, but not very long legs.

Uncertain, she momentarily hesitated. The place had become very busy. Most of the tables were taken and mainly presided over by the ageing hunters. These were the lacklustre almonds; all perhaps plying well-worn chat-up lines and timeless clichés. The partially bibulous DJ was haranguing the punters, attempting to get them to take to the floor. He tried a waltz and was spurned, but the mercurial Tom Jones did the trick and an elderly Lothario with rotten teeth and two drinks disentangled himself before proceeding to a table where a stone-faced fat woman sat regretting her impetuous encouragement.

"Would you mind?"

"Please do ..." He couldn't believe his luck and smiled assuredly as the girl literally melted into the chair opposite him. Without realising it, he had this habit of traversing his face from top to bottom with his hand before he spoke.

"Are you new to this place?" He resisted the question that he'd liked to have asked. "What is a gorgeous young thing doing here amongst such a decrepit load of old farts?"

"Yes, and yourself?"

Don't be too direct, he chastised himself. Don't be too

egotistical or imposing. But he could hardly help himself. What a stroke of luck! The best-looking woman in the ghastly place had chosen to approach him! Take it easy, man, take it easy. This was not to be handled clumsily.

She fumbled in her capacious handbag and produced a comb.

"Hardly necessary," he oozed and instantly regretted it.

A mirror followed and she gave him another ravishing smile.

"Didn't have much time, you know. And your name is?" This was accompanied by a slight contraction of the corners of the mouth and those eyes were beguiling him in a frank and highly irresistible manner. He was taken aback by her candour. There seemed to be nothing devious about her. She was a rare breed of woman. One that did not dissimulate. Not playing a man like a hapless piscatorial species on the end of a reel. Was it possible?

Where she was concerned, he must curb his cynicism over the distaff half of humanity. He really could not comprehend what she was doing here. She was undeniably not an almond!

He leant forward in what he thought might be an agreeable pose, trying desperately not to mishandle things.

"The name's Sebastian. Seb for short." He proffered a hand and immediately realised what a crass gesture this was. He hadn't been prepared for how delicate her hand would be and mindlessly held on to it a little more than he should have.

This time he received more of a mischievous grin. "Mine's Jonquil and your surname wouldn't be Bach by any chance?"

He could be droll if he chose and countered this with no expression whatsoever. Obviously a cultured girlie as well as a good-looking one, he wondered if she'd get the point.

"I'm actually the Forest Bach."

She didn't comprehend and he explained. "You know there was the old man, J.S. and J.C., the English Bach and W.F. and all his other sons, cousins, sisters and maybe, his aunts. If I may quote W. S. Gilbert ...?"

She became all animated. "Ah, now I see what you mean. I love the Brandenburg Concertos. Especially No. 2 with that fantastic trumpet! One of Bach's trumpet players was said to have dropped dead playing it!" She took a breath and a sip from her glass, pulling a face at the same time.

"Is that port?"

"Yes, and not a very good one."

Here was an opportunity. "Can I get you something else?"

She shrugged and tried again. "No thanks. Perhaps I'm mistaken. It's not that bad. Now tell me about yourself. What brings you to this pseudo high class, but decidedly geriatric meat market?"

This directness of hers was very disarming, though highly promising, and he opted to continue his cautious approach.

"I could ask you the same question?"

At this, she lowered her eyebrows and shrugged again. She seemed suddenly burdened and a little distressed. And why, he conjectured, should he feel contrite? But he did and tried to clumsily make amends.

"I'm sorry, I appear to have ..."

She quickly recovered and her eyes twinkled once more. "Tell you what. How about we ask our sprightly DJ to play some Bach?"

He laughed, more with empathy than anything else; this hardly audible over the sterling sounds of 'YMCA.', an old chestnut that succeeded at last in filling the floor. His hand frantically clawed his face in rapid fashion.

"And what, pray, would you dance to the Brandenburgs?"

The smile was wicked now, the eyes almost jumping out of their sockets.

"Oh, Sebastian, your namesake has been credited with almost inventing jazz. He really swings on occasions! And who says you can't dance to jazz? People always did. It's only the present generation that can't or won't." A pause before she frowned and resumed, tactlessly, her verbal assault. "And why, if I may ask, do you preface all your remarks with that nervous gesture with your hand?"

"Now boys and girls. That's got you goin' and here's a smooch. Get to know someone better." The DJ sounded like a cross between ancient Tony Blackburn and frantic Chris Evans.

This drowned Sebastian's reply and she doggedly persisted with her questioning.

"Tell you what. Are you particularly enamoured of this place?"

He shrugged in what he thought was an apologetic manner.

"Needs must and I can't answer your other question."

"I'm sorry. I had no right to taunt you."

"No, you're right. I don't realise I'm doing it half the time." Take a risk, damn it, she sounded like she wanted out of this bluestone mausoleum. "Am I being a little presumptuous, or do I sense you wouldn't be averse to going elsewhere?"

This obviously appealed to her and she adopted an attitude that was quite flippant. She hoisted her handbag on to her shoulder and stood up. She stretched a short arm over the tabletop, clasped his hand and attempted to bring him to his feet. The revelation of her twin appendages during this process made him feel anything but avuncular and he hastened to co-operate.

They zigzagged across the ballroom, dexterously avoiding the writhing throng and it was not until they exited the imposing front portico that he managed slightly breathlessly to say, "Where are we going?"

She halted and deftly lit a cigarette.

"D' you smoke?"

A minus Brownie point, he thought.

"No thanks."

She laughed; more of a chuckle, but something to complement the pungent night air, the rustling of leaves and the clatter of cloven hooves as a small patrol of sheep crossed the road. There seemed little in the way of traffic to impede their progress at this time of night.

"You have a car?"

"Yes," he affirmed. "But how did you get here?"

It hadn't apparently been a problem.

"A friend dropped me off." He couldn't see her provocative look but guessed by the tone of voice what she implied. "And I imagine I won't want for a lift back, will I?"

It was his turn for forced laughter. Not in his case a particularly pleasant sound. Emanating more from the nasal passages and emerging as a high-pitched snigger. "I don't doubt that, but where d' you want to go now?"

She hesitated; uncertain and running her hand through her now billowing hair. Obviously, she didn't know the area very well.

He came to the rescue.

"Have you eaten?"

"Sort of …"

"What does that mean?"

"Well, I sort of had breakfast …"

"And what time was that? Several days ago?"

"Well …"

He ushered her into the car, an Audi with nice lines and a potent motor.

"We'll go to Dale's Club." He was surprised by his own assertiveness.

She failed to be impressed. "Bit of a flash machine for an old far—, well, a guy of your, well … sorry, I didn't mean …" The hole was well and truly dug, but it only served to amuse him further. He gunned the Audi down the steep hill and to her consternation, did not slow down at the dog-legged crossroads at the bottom. He took the ascent on the other side effortlessly and after a series of complicated left and right turns, brought the car into the car park of Dale's Club, a rather nondescript building which declared itself to be a haven for golf and sundry other activities. He switched the ignition off and turned to face her.

She looked disconcerted. "Are you a member?"

"No," he said, "but they know me. The restaurant is open to anybody, and they do very good food here."

She took his arm and they sauntered inside, receiving unabashed glances from the imbibers in the Ikea like bar with its spartan straight-edged surfaces and glass-topped tables. Was this, they speculated, a niece, or the recipient of a sugar-daddy's largesse? Or maybe the old guy had just struck lucky.

Sebastian was right about the food and wondered if she would offer to help financially. He always had more time for females who offered to cough up their share. He, of course, never accepted and persuaded her to have the Loin of Venison. This was an exotic dish devised by the resident German chef. It included a choice of sauces and either black or white pepper.

Tasting it, her eyebrows rose and her physiognomy became delightfully lugubrious. She paused; noodles poised precariously on her fork.

"Hmm. If I'm not mistaken, there's something like vermouth, garlic and a host of herbs impregnating this." Her features relaxed. "D' you think the chef would let me have the recipe?"

He shook his head. "I would think not. Strangely for this part of the world, he's a German and a somewhat reticent example of the species at that."

The wine, a bland and immature Commonwealth red, displeased him. He sniffed it and took a tentative drop, hastily planting it back on the table with obvious disapproval.

"Don't know why we had this. Still, better leave it now. I don't know the chef that well and if I did get to talk to him, he'd probably only give me an accented discourse on the merits of sausages in German cuisine!"

She looked blank. "Why sausages?"

This caused him even more amusement. "My dear, are you not aware that – if you are not careful – everything in a German dish comes with sausages of one sort or another and what we are consuming now is due solely to a plentiful supply of deer in Her Majesty's Royal Forest of Dean. I don't think Kurt has twigged that there are also hordes of wild boar now roaming through the trees but give him time and they'll all be made into sausages!"

She didn't seem particularly interested in this, but was still adroit with her replies.

"Well, I'm afraid national cuisines are not a strong point with me. I was always interested in my Aunt Rachel's cottage pie."

For a while they ate in silence, until he suddenly said, "What about almonds, d' you have an opinion about those?"

"Almonds? Why on earth should you ask that?" She frowned, perplexed by the question.

"Yes, you know. The nuts that get left over after Christmas. The ones you can't crack even if you assault them with a sledgehammer."

Her laughter rippled delightfully round the room and terminated in an almost musically acceptable cadence. "Don't know that I have an opinion. Don't think that I do almonds!" She paused to take another mouthful, swallowed it quickly and then continued, "What an odd chat-up line!"

He persisted. "I just think that the people we left behind at the singles club are like rejected almonds. Nobody really wants them. When it boils down to it, they are just so much human dross."

A sudden sea change came over her and this time her laughter was not accompanied by the expansive smile. Her eyes became cold and restless and something within him presaged a warning.

She put down her cutlery with a clatter and sat back. He offered her more wine, which she accepted with a cursory nod and noticed she did not demur when he filled her glass to the brim.

He thought he ought to ask. "You won't be driving, of course ...?"

"A friend was to pick me up ..."

"As I told you. You don't need to worry about that ..."

She finished the last remnants of her meal and relaxed; replete and restored to her disarmingly attractive best.

"So these almonds of yours in this dish. Do they wait until the household is abed and then at midnight come out of their shells to cavort and ultimately mate with one another?"

That wretched mannerism of his. He cursed and reviled it, but could not constrain it. Acutely, she was quick on the uptake.

"There you go again. I suppose I shouldn't tease you, but don't you think you've left the nut bowl by now?" She contemplated him coolly, her eyes again transformed to a frozen neutral. A changed and almost sinister stance he could not fathom.

He took a deep breath and floundered for an appropriate original reply; the romantic punchline that would be just advanced enough not to be a turn off.

"Maybe not I'm afraid. How about you?"

"That depends."

Suddenly bile rose in his throat, and he began to sweat heavily. His hands were moist and unbearably clammy. Horrified, he tried to convince himself that what he had just glimpsed was a figment of his imagination. But alarmingly, he knew he was not mistaken. In shrugging, a thing she indulged in a lot, the lady had caused her shoulder strap to drop, revealing a dark skin blemish shaped something like a fleur-de-lys. A disfigurement that undoubtedly revealed her true identity. She was Maria, a girl sprung from his own loins. His daughter: the infant he'd abandoned through straitened circumstances, adorned with the distinctive inherited birthmark of her wayward mother.

There was a slight chink; an unsteady hand as the second bottle jarred against the wine glass. With driving in mind, he'd only had one glass and here she was helping herself with abandon. This indicated that she was stressed, and quickly brought him back to life. She had re-adjusted her shoulder strap, but not quickly enough. She realised this and her eyes narrowed. Her whole demeanour changed utterly, and she became visibly antagonistic.

"What a pity. That was unfortunate, wasn't it, dear Daddy? I was going to reveal myself in good time. You are a complete bastard and you cannot imagine what it means to me to have at last tracked you down!"

If he'd had culpable feelings about this child over the years, they were nothing to what he felt now. He was at a loss as to how to cope with the situation. Desperately, he stood and spread his arms, almost in despair. He was firmly enmeshed within the deadly web of this beautiful young arachnid an encounter he'd dreaded for years. Leaving her mother; her fey and acerbic mother, had not been easy; but a financial implosion had caused him to flee. He fled to Brazil, the usual safe haven for monetary swindlers and Nazi criminals. There he changed his name and a few years later moved back across the water to Southern Ireland. Although so adjacent to the UK, nobody enquired much about you providing you kept your nose clean and he eventually returned to the country of his birth and former misdoings with a doctored identity and an assumed name: Sebastian O'Neill, citizen of the Irish Republic. He now ran an insurance business in the former industrial township of Cinderford. Not the most picturesque of places, Cinderford's most prominent feature was perhaps a proliferation of sheep droppings; a circumstance which offended incomers, but not locals, who contended that 'thick ship 'ad bin there fur 'undreds a' years; which is more 'n thou 'az, ol' butt!'

And the same phoney Sebastian O'Neill had sedulously assumed the role of local councillor and earned grudging respect from the phlegmatic Foresters for his efforts, even though ' 'im were a furrener!'

Alas, it now seemed that his carefully constructed maze of deceit was in imminent danger of being exposed. He had to think quickly. Agitated and uncertain, he shoved his chair unnecessarily heavily under the table. There were a few other couples in the dining room and the waiter, an elderly Croatian of very few words, awakened from his slumber by the kitchen door and came across.

"Do you not want a sweet, sir?" Like most of his kind, he spoke very good English.

Maria answered for Sebastian. She smiled effusively at the waiter and motioned her dazed parent to sit down. This he did laboriously; his mind working overtime. Hopefully, she had just wanted to make contact. Surely this is what any child would want to do? It did not mean she was bent on any sort of revenge. It cannot have been very easy for her; not knowing all these years. Perhaps for certain considerations she could be persuaded to keep quiet. On the other hand, he had abandoned her, and she might deem that unforgivable. She'd hardly shown a desire for affection or even been the tearful, emotional offspring that others may have become when confronted with a long-lost parent.

They ate the second course in almost uncanny silence, with only the soft murmur of the rest of the diners for accompaniment. Having consumed it with difficulty, a rather insipid ice cream-based concoction which he slowly devoured in almost a trance, he found himself uttering quite inanely, "Coffee?"

Maria declined. Calm, unperturbed; possibly awaiting some show of contriteness on his part. He decided to try a frank, direct approach.

"How did you find me?"

Irritatingly, she played with a table mat; nothing very inviting about her now.

"Quite by accident. I was in The New Inn, Gloucester when you walked in with what I assumed was a friend or client. You haven't changed much from the photos mother showed me. My boyfriend and I followed you to the Forest and I have been stalking you – if you can stalk your own father – for quite a while."

"And tonight?"

"You have a garrulous neighbour. She knew all your movements. I just said I had an appointment and that you'd probably forgotten. That was a mistake, though it appears she also forgot to tell you."

He made a wry face. "That is very unlike her. Probably her ancient and blatantly spoilt feline friend chose to pass away at that precise moment. The old witch lived for that animal. Nothing else could have distracted her!"

Practically unnoticed, the aged waiter had approached their table with stealth and obvious intent. "Your bill, sir."

That was the last thing the beleaguered Sebastian wanted at this moment, but he acknowledged it with good grace.

Maria regarded him reproachfully; an attitude which was accusingly censorious. She brushed her hair from her ravishing eyes and stood up with an air of impatience.

"I think we should talk. Can we go back to your place?"

Relief flooded through him. He escorted her to reception, paid the bill and noticed she did not take his arm as they proceeded across the car park to the car. An almost full moon hung in the cloudless sky and an eerie silence prevailed; punctuated by the odd noisy internal-combustion engine as vehicles laboured up the steep incline from the town.

He opened the passenger door and she clambered in. He settled into the driving seat, shoved the ignition key in and before he could turn it to fire the Audi, felt the cold steel on the back of his neck.

"Don't try anything and drive where I tell you!" A deep, growling baritone; ominous and not of a timbre that suggested dissent would be tolerated.

Maria sat next to him, exuding silent hostility. She fixed his seat belt with a degree of roughness and with a sort of ghoulish inanity and he thought this a ludicrous gesture towards a man whose life might imminently be imperilled.

He took a deep breath. "And if I don't?"

"Then I blow your head off. It's quite simple." Quite like the baddy in a James Bond movie, thought Sebastian. It was strange that this 'Sword of Damocles' scenario had not completely unnerved him. He probably owed this to his seedy sojourn in the underworld of São Paulo, Brazil's second city. His life had been endangered a couple of times, but he had survived. Maybe he could this time.

"Where d' you want to go?"

"Out of here and up the hill and don't think I won't know where you're going. I have an intimate knowledge of this area."

It did appear that the unknown assailant was fully aware of where he was going, for he took a complicated route, culminating in a rough ride down a barely negotiable forest track which terminated at an old, disused mineshaft; picked out by the Audi's bright headlights.

Deftly, Maria unfastened him and he was conscious of the gun, now placed in the small of his back, which followed him out of the car. The unrevealed accomplice had somehow switched the car headlights out before alighting and Maria produced a small torch which she shone at the mineshaft head, now derelict and surmounted by trees. Sebastian wondered about the stature of her partner; not a thing you usually risked finding out when your entrails were within a trigger-happy second of being blown out of your churning insides without further notice. For the first time he felt real terror and overwhelming panic.

"What the fucking hell are you doing and why have you brought me here?"

In a fit of unrestrained belligerence, Maria placed herself before him, swung her arm and slapped his face; a surprisingly savage blow which nearly toppled him over. She grabbed bunches of his shirt and hissed at him through almost clamped teeth.

"You fucking bastard. Thanks to you I nearly grew up wholly unnurtured. Mother died an alcoholic and I had it all. Drugs, prostitution, the fucking lot and it was only Leo's dad, the father of this man who has the power to blast you to hell, who dragged me out of it and saw to my education. Something you should have done, dearest Daddy!" Here she gave a hideous, repetitive laugh. "And what an old pervert you are! You really thought you'd struck lucky tonight. How sick!"

Momentarily uncertain, she released her hold, and the boyfriend became impatient. Sebastian could sense that he had an unsteady hand, and his bravura did not hide the fact that he'd probably not done anything like this before. The gun wandered carelessly, as if in the hands of an inexperienced practitioner and Sebastian sensed this would give him a chance. He'd have to pick the moment. Again, a similar situation had once been his in Rathmines, a not particularly salubrious part of Dublin. What had aided his escape then? He must concentrate and when he moved, move quickly.

The voice behind him became insistent. "Let's get this over, Maria. Walk towards the mineshaft, old man!"

"Why?"

"Because you're descending it, my friend. And unless I'm mistaken, descending it very quickly!"

Christ, he'd risk it! He flung his body forwards and kicked backwards, landing savage blows on his captor's legs, causing him to scream and stumble, letting off a shot that whistled harmlessly into the undergrowth. Sebastian praised God for his one-time association with the IRA and swivelling, quickly knocked his wavering assailant over, causing him to fall whilst dropping the gun in the process. Sebastian's size ten shoe firmly held the weapon hostage in the face of an onslaught from his screaming, hysterical daughter. He pushed her roughly aside and wondered what had happened to her compatriot, who had dropped out of the contest and was recumbent, either knocked out cold or dead.

He picked up the gun and pointed it at his now terrified offspring.

"Give me the torch!"

Her hand went limp, and he retrieved the torch from where it had dropped in a mound of horse dung, an entirely irrelevant observation being that this track was also a bridleway. Maria seemed incapable of any further action. She just stood in the pervading moonlight, weeping bitterly and no longer any sort of threat.

Just when the police car arrived or why it appeared in such a remote place, Sebastian only found out later, when they were at the police station. He'd handed over the weapon and was bundled into the police car with Maria. An ambulance collected the body of the boyfriend who, fortunately from Sebastian's viewpoint, was not dead; only concussed. The boyfriend turned out to be a known small-time criminal. Not that inexperienced, but just a little careless.

*

Prison did not suit Sebastian. But it was made bearable by the letters he was regularly receiving from his daughter, now ensconced in Holloway. A lot was revealed before and during her trial, including his faked identity, his sundry financial misdemeanours and his fiscal double-dealing. At his own, later trial, another judge took a more lenient view. He considered Sebastian could have suffered an horrendous fate. To be deposited down a mineshaft with very little hope of survival and no chance of rescue. To most likely suffer instant death or to lay there with agonising injuries until he either expired from them or starved. Allowing for these mitigating circumstances, the judge only imposed a two-year sentence, a lenient punishment which still did little to assuage Sebastian's mild agoraphobia.

Maria's latest missive was all contriteness and expressed a desire that they might meet again very soon, and he found to his gratification, that he could not wait for this to happen. Maybe with good conduct they would let him out in less than two years and in the meantime, he made sure that he replied to her letters promptly and with a fatherly affection he was beginning to feel quite strongly. He no longer felt an affinity with the despised almonds and to his roguish cellmate's bemusement, inserted Bach's Brandenburg No. 2 into the recently acquired black market music centre.

"What the hell's that crap?" questioned his musically tone-deaf companion, a former denizen of the Handsworth underworld and not particularly lauded for his taste and refinement.

"You wouldn't understand, my friend. You just would not understand."

Ignoring the protests, Sebastian lay back and took it all in. It made him feel infinitely better and he still marvelled at the way that a patrol car from the Gloucestershire police force had turned up out of the blue on that fateful day. They, it transpired, had been looking for deer poachers. He wondered whether venison would come his way in here; in Gloucester Prison. He thought it quite likely. You could get anything in here if you knew who to contact.

That frenetic first movement. The trumpet player must be traumatised. He closed his eyes as the evocative middle movement unfolded and even his cellmate had the decency to keep quiet.

He was awakened a little later by that same Midlands malcontent.

"Oi, Oiy thought yow was supposed to be listenin' to this, not snorin' threw it?"

Sebastian sat up abruptly, rubbing his eyes; his mind invaded by a sudden thought.

"Wayne, dear boy, d' you think you could get me some almonds?"

"What d' yow mean? Them sugar-coated sweets like?"

"Not exactly, but come to think of it, those would do very nicely."

"Oiy don' see why not. Oi'll ask Jemmy. 'Ave yow got a sweet tooth or somethink?"

Jemmy was the resident fence and Sebastian knew that with him, all things were possible. He patted Brummie Bernie on the shoulder and, before going back to sleep, wondered what Maria would make of it.

D' Stout

1962

Envisage an eighteen-stone lump of walking flesh, with a triangle for a stomach, sauntering ponderously down the main street of a small Irish town, a long, cherry pipe hinged beneath a stout-sodden moustache; the whole appearance offset with a fine, mulberry-coloured snout, the latter feature a fitting tribute to countless hours spent downing the 'black wine' of Dublin's famous brewery.

In an effort to combat the persistence of a lively sea breeze, this accident of the Almighty's design department clutched at his fading trilby, paused outside a door marked 'Surgery' and studied the brass plate which proclaimed the qualifications of a certain Dr Daniel Murphy, Medical Practitioner.

A squat little creature with glasses which did little to assist his myopia, Dr Murphy beckoned his heavyweight patient to a seat and wondered if he had not made a mistake in assigning the flimsy piece to withstand such a prodigious onslaught. The poor thing creaked ominously, and the doctor imagined he could perceive the four woodworm-ridden legs protesting and splaying out and praying for some sort of sustenance.

"An' what can I be doin' for you this mornin', Liam Duffy?"

The eighteen stones moved in unison and the trouser legs were hoisted to reveal a pair of socks held together with intricately worked holes.

"It's me poor ol' fit, Dr Murphy; dere all swelled up as y' can see. I had tought of cuttin' 'em off, but it occurred to me that if I was t' take such drastic action; I'd have nothin' to stand on. So I says t' meself I'll be goin' along to see what Dr Murphy has to say about the situation. Can youse be givin' me anyting for dem, doctor?"

The doctor scratched his right ear with a leadless pencil and followed this by absent-mindedly prodding his patient's mountainous frontage with the same useless object. Then, with an air of impending doom, he finally and gravely implied that before he could prescribe a possible aid to recovery, it would be advisable if Duffy removed his size thirteen boots, so that a closer inspection might be made.

This accomplished, not without much grunting and wheezy imprecations to Holy Mary; the doctor first held his nose and then bent down to examine the offending appendages with a cracked eyeglass. The removal of the shredded socks revealed two reddened, badly swollen feet and despite the camouflage of overriding dirt, it was clearly evident that something must be done to treat the afflicted 'plates' of this badly suffering man.

His inspection completed, Dr Murphy arose, walked unsteadily round the small surgery with his hands behind his back, eventually sat down again and after pulling a variety of faces, said, "And when did you last wash dose feet of yours, Liam Duffy?"

You could see the concentration on the patient's face, being replaced by something approaching wild panic and then relaxing into good owld Irish procrastination and hesitancy.

"I tink-I tink-uh- now yer askin' me. To be sure, I tink it'd be some whiles ago. Though it'd be no more than last Easter. An' doctor, it's not the walkin' that's difficult. It's the standin', if youse see what I mean? I can't be standin' for any length of time on deese fit. It's as if I've grown too heavy for dem, or somethin', by Jaisus, it does!"

Dr Murphy had another long think and while doing so, casually motioned the patient to replace his socks and boots, saying that he did not wish to open the window as the wind would 'play the divil with his fibrositis!'

"I think I'll be givin' you a diet sheet, some ointment and an exercise chart. No good giving you pills. Won't do any good. You'll have t' be stickin' to it. Dat's the only way. You can buy a bar of soap at the chemist while you're after getting the rest. An' perhaps a little less of the stout an' some more regular ablutions might help!"

Though not prescribed so much as a placebo, Duffy seemed

well content with the outcome of his visit to the doctor and not sensing the practitioner's wish to get rid of him, blithely voiced his approval.

"Dat's very good of y', doctor an' I tink I'll wash me fit before goin' to Mass on Sunday mornin'. It'll be pleasin' Father O'Donnell as well as yerself."

With difficulty, Liam pulled himself upright and watched, unconcerned, as his former resting place gave up the ghost, collapsing into near sawdust on the floor. Bidding the doctor farewell, he limped out into the street and made for the fraternal atmosphere of Dermot Hagan's bar, where even at half past eleven on a windblown Tuesday, good honest company could be sought and enjoyed. Those that mostly inhabited the alluring interior of Hagan's did so with solid conviction, united in the common belief that such an alien liquid as blood should not be allowed to permeate their respective stoutstreams. And in order to assist this worthy process, it was necessary to make an early start to proceedings and continuation of the libations throughout the day depended largely on the accessibility of one's work or the disposition of one's wife. If possible, neither of these things should be allowed to interfere with the more edifying activity of downing the 'black stuff' and the best insurance against such intrusion was preferably bachelorhood and a private income.

Liam Duffy had a private income – or so he told 'dose nosey tax people' and the fact that he was on equable terms with a leading Dublin turf accountant – his brother – did nothing to disparage this carefully nurtured image. He'd also had a wife who'd gone off to Limerick to see her sister ten years ago and sent him a card when it was Christmas or his birthday which, to all intents and purposes and in his opinion, sufficed to make him a single gentleman.

In Hagan's a man could spend many hours of stout-induced conviviality and entering the place, he was pleased to note that there were already two customers propping up the bar and presumably ready to engage in the usual banter, without which an Irish pub would be a soulless place.

The first of these early bird mortals was a thin, grey flannelled being with a prominent forehead and unkempt, slowly receding hair. His accidently stained tie hung loosely round his Adam's apple, which bobbed back and forth as he talked in a high, grumbling falsetto. But it appeared he was highly disposed to be amicable and greeted Liam Duffy in a cheerful enough manner.

"Hello dare, Liam an' how are youse dis mornin'?"

Duffy tried hard not to notice his interlocutor's empty pint glass and applied his considerable bulk to a hapless bar stool before replying.

"Aw, not so good, me boyo. Not so good. It's me fit. Dey won't stand what dey used too. I've just been along t' see Dr Murphy. He's sayin' I should be lookin' to take some of me fat off. He says it's not much use me havin' pills an' tings. I need to get me weight down. But that means drinkin' less an' I can't be doin' dat!"

There was a time when the barbers of medieval Europe were also called upon to act as primitive surgeons and medical sages and some of this historical nous must have been latent in Duffy's confidant, a hairdresser by trade, for he pushed his empty receptacle a little nearer the afflicted man and reeled off a string of supposedly certain remedies.

Duffy listened attentively to this panacea for troublesome feet until his own glass matched the barren aspect of his appointed counsellor's and with something approaching undisguised impertinence enquired – since he claimed to be in a state of near impecunity – whether his companion would pay for the drinks.

But Ferguson O'Neill – so named because of his Scots–Irish ancestry – quickly decided that he'd spotted one or two clients entering his premises over the road from Hagan's and apologising to Duffy, made off hastily to ply his scissors and to diminish the agonising feeling in his pocket. Fortunately, help was at hand in the person of Stationmaster Morrisey, the only other occupant of the drinking parlour, and awakening from a slumber caused by a too long association with Irish Railways, he offered to act as locum for the parsimonious headshaver.

"Dat man's a mean bugger," he said. "He's always doin' dat t' people. Bobbin' in an' out o' dis place like a bloody yo-yo! Is he not, Mick?"

"Sure," grunted Mick, the taciturn and unopinionated barman whilst drawing two fresh pints of the Guinness for his two remaining customers; an art in itself and not a process to be hurried. He'd been around when topping up glasses with jugs was common practice and lamented those days when the bar was a sea of black waiting to be tended by his skilled and loving hand.

Stationmaster Morrisey heaved his ample body on to the stool that the stingy O'Neill had vacated and lifted his glass to Duffy. Toasts having been exchanged, the stationmaster asked if his companion had thought of trying a chiropodist and was told quite adamantly that if Dr Murphy could not effect a cure, then he, Duffy, wasn't going all the way to Dublin to see 'one of dem fitbashers!'

Morrisey's eyes twinkled, and he suggested that Duffy, in the event of other remedies not working, he should 'try d' stout method'.

Duffy looked puzzled. "An' what would y' be meanin' by that, man? I already drink d' stuff in small quantities, though the doctor tinks I should be puttin' it down even less dan dat."

With a thespian inclination that would not have been out of place at the Abbey Theatre, Morrisey simulated sudden excitement and uttered his next advice with utter conviction and a touch of the dramatic.

"No, no, man! You don' understand my meanin'. Youse don't drink it. Youse put dem big, troublin' feet of yours in a bowl of d' stuff and let it course through dem and up through dose varicose veins. Dat'll fix dem in no time!"

"Ah, now, yer pullin' me leg?" Duffy demurred, though not without slight hesitation.

Stationmaster Morrisey was adamant. "Aw, I'm not doin' that, man. Where d' youse tink a man of my standin' would be if he took t' tellin' fancy stories like dat?"

The man with the sore feet still looked doubtful but was spared a further berating by the bar telephone which, at barman Mick's summons, took Morrisey off to answer it. The stationmaster stood, pen behind his ear; Irish Railways cap askew; whilst alternatively bellowing down the receiver and quaffing his stout.

"What's dat, y' say? D' Belfast–Dublin Express is comin' trou' an' y' want t' know if youse should change d' points?" Morrisey sighed, put down his glass and made a face at the receiver. The voice at the other end was adolescent and sounded frightened.

"Yes, Mr Morrisey, please, sir."

"Callaghan, which ways are d' bloody points pointin' now?"

"Uh-I tink, I tink ... let me see, now. I'll just be lookin' out d' winda ..." There was a considerable pause and then the voice returned.

"Mr Morrisey, sir?"

"I'm here, are youse dere?"

Another long pause and a deep breath from the railway station end of the line.

"Mr Morrisey, I tink d' points are ... just a minute, Mr Morrisey." The voice of the hapless Callaghan became almost hysterical, rising into the coloratura regions, whilst a noise like thunder and an ominous hooting drowned out any further conversation for about fifteen seconds.

When it was over, Stationmaster Morrisey hardly dared resume the phone conversation.

"Tell me, Liam, y' bloody spalpeen, was that the express an' did it get troo the station safely?"

There was a distinct pause, though maybe more of a lacuna and then the hapless Liam said in a very subdued and scarcely audible tone, "Yes, Mr Morrisey."

"So, you didn't change the points?"

"No, Stationmaster Morrisey."

"And where was Signalman O'Rourke during this near fuckin' calamity?"

"Well, he'd taken Tiger up the road t' the vet, Stationmaster Morrisey. Y' see, Tiger's been off his food fur some time ..."

"He took the fuckin' cat to the vet, the bloody useless creature! For sure, I don't why the fuckin' ting can't catch some of dem mice that plague the station, dat's why we got the bloody ting ... "

The voice on the other end brightened up. "Anyways, it was all right, Stationmaster Morrisey, for sure, he said he'd not be a minute and he'd changed the signal and the points, but I wasn't sure ..."

Stationmaster Morrisey could hardly believe this. "And has the man returned yet?"

"The man?"

"Jesus, Liam! Signalman O'Rourke, of course!"

"No sir, he said he might be callin' in for a swift one on the way back …"

Grinding his teeth, Morrisey gave the phone back to dour Mick and tried to control his rapidly becoming uncontrollable emotions. The overlord of the signal box would do well not to come in here for a sneaky one. A swift assassination would mean his intentions would promptly be aborted and if he had any sense he'd go into Dunne's Bar, another alehouse situated near the vet's surgery.

Morrisey took another plenteous quaff of the black stuff and turned his attentions back to the beleaguered Duffy. "Aw, man, now y' be listenin' to me. You be goin' back home and Mick here'll be deliverin' a small firkin of d' stout to youse when he has a minute …"

Abandoning his almost perpetual inscrutability, Mick the barman displayed a rare air of reluctance towards this unlikely proposal. An atypical example of his servile breed, he would never oppose a customer's wishes normally, but the thought of delivering a cumbersome barrel up the steep incline to Murphy's abode did not appeal to him one bit. Then there was the question of who was going to pay for it; a question he put to both his current imbibers who implied that the other 'fella' would oblige. But Stationmaster Morrisey was having none of it. "Aw, now. Not to worry yerself about dat, Michael. Youse can be borrowin' a sack truck from d' station and Liam will be payin' y' when you deliver it."

It was now Murphy's turn to exude doubts, but Stationmaster Morrisey having the sort of persona that would not brook dissent, the suffering man had to comply, and it was arranged that Mick would deliver the stout around teatime when help in the bar would enable him to do so.

*

Murphy became bored and his daily help, who came in twice a day to cook and do other things for him, could hardly contain her amusement. It was a strange sight, for Murphy sat most of the day watching the racing on television, ringing his brother for tips and placing bets with a variety of bookmakers. This to make sure they accepted his money, rather than sticking to just one who, if he continued his habit of winning most of the time, would not be very happy. The only time he removed his appendages from the alcoholic bath was when he wiped them to visit the loo or to go to bed, but it appeared the treatment was working. After a week or more, he'd visibly diminished in bulk and was rapidly coming to the conclusion that the overlord of the railway station had been right in his diagnosis. The only thing about it was the odour. Having now gone stale, the stout stunk. But there was now no temptation to drink the stuff as, overwhelmingly, there had been in the first place, and though he did not realise it, this was the reason he'd now lost so much weight. If it continued, he'd be able to get out and about again and the first place he'd visit would be O'Hagan's. He felt he owed Morrisey a pint and for the first time in living memory he would not resent having to prise apart the folds of his wallet to buy one.

*

The first person Duffy encountered when entering O'Hagan's was the scrawny and unprepossessing young buck from the railway station, Callaghan. The naïve youth evinced an aura of palpable uneasiness. With an eye for business, the taciturn Mick had ignored the lad's obvious underage status and supplied him with a manly pint. What would have happened if Callaghan's undeniable overlord, Stationmaster Morrisey, had chosen to make an unscheduled entry at this precise moment did not bear contemplation and with a twinkle in his eye, Duffy hailed the youngster warmly.

"You're l-l-lookin' better, Mr Duffy." Callaghan's reply was cautious and tentative.

"Dat I am, tanks t' yer man, y' know." Here he paused to accept a pint from the immediately attentive Mick, who knew where this return to the alcoholic fold would lead, but fully intended to keep his own counsel. Business was business and concern for Duffy's welfare should not be allowed to override a barman's main objective in life.

"Yer man? Who's dat?" Callaghan looked puzzled.

"I'm surprised y' don't know. It was dat man Morrisey that suggested the stout remedy. Did he not say anything to youse?"

Revealing that he was certainly not a candidate for the title of 'village eejit', the suddenly enlightened railway porter and dogsbody realised the extent of his master's perfidy. And here was an awakened knowledge which could be put to good use. He'd heard the rumours of Duffy's gullibility and did not wonder at Morrisey's lack of communication. The stationmaster spent most of his time berating the hapless Callaghan for mostly unfounded misdemeanours and probably thought that what the boy did not know, he could not broadcast to the world at large.

But the day of reckoning was nigh. Callaghan swiftly downed the rest of his pint, bid Duffy good day and made his now sprightly way over the road to the station.

"An' where have youse, been, boy?" Stationmaster Morrisey was in his usual slightly belligerent mood, but not prepared for what ensued.

"In the bar on my break," answered his normally subservient minion boldly.

"What did y' say!" Normally florid in complexion, the outraged railwayman turned an unhealthy shade of what could be described as apoplectic purple. He accompanied this with a deluge of profanities and concluded by stating the many ways he would punish the insubordinate Callaghan for drinking whilst on duty and furthermore, doing it underage.

Amazingly, none of this fazed the youngster.

"Mrs Sullivan," said Callaghan. A bald statement that saw the stationmaster immediately deflated and reduced to the defensive. Not a stance he'd experienced before. Mrs Sullivan was the attractive spouse of the local Church of Ireland minister and a vicious rumour had it that she and Morrisey were furtively cementing Anglo-Catholic relations from time to time and Callaghan knew this to be true. He'd recently taken a walk in the woods, which covered the hills inland from the small township, and seen what he'd seen. Even more amazingly, he now confronted the subdued stationmaster with his own knowledge of this flagrant infidelity, and garnished it by revealing that he was also aware of the duping of poor, soon-to-be corpulent-again, Duffy.

Even Mick the barman had his doubts. He had more than a notion why Morrisey was plying the youngster with drinks. He felt uneasy about it and only hoped the Garda would not put in an appearance. Anyway, it appeared that the gullible Duffy was quite happily imbibing again, and it would not be long before Mick, with Machiavellian cunning, could suggest a repeat dose of the stout remedy. Particularly as, with the connivance of his boss, Mick had siphoned off half the contents of the original firkin into another barrel and replaced it with water. He'd not felt guilty about it, for as a devout Catholic, he didn't have to have a conscience. He went to Mass and confession and providing the owld Father got his not inconsiderable amount of stout for free most of the time, all would be well.

Author's Note

A story inspired by my misspent youth in a small place not so far from Dublin. Possibly written around 1962, revised 2022.

Coffee Break

A whimsical tale written in 2017

It was said that Dolly had served coffee at the White Lion since Attila the Hun had roamed the planet imposing rape and pillage and with the inexorable passage of time, regulars had noticed a gradual decline in service. But not one of them would have done the unthinkable by registering a complaint. There was more than adequate compensation for this minor failing in that the beverage provided was French, vastly superior to anything served up by the High Street bistros and multiples and included gratis, one of Dolly's delicious home-made flapjacks.

The establishment attracted goodly custom every day of the week and although those that did not know took a while to accustom themselves to the lady's slightly diffident Herefordian manner, they soon came to realise that it hid a heart of gold. It was true that she had slowed up, but occasional non-intrusive sorties into the lounge at busy times by younger staff ensured things still ran smoothly and the atmosphere partook of one that might more readily be found in a family social club, rather than a prestigious hotel situated in the best street in town.

Dolly's 'station' and coffee-making facilities were near the lounge door and when entering, etiquette demanded that you did not blatantly park yourself in front of it in order to place an order. Instead, custom dictated that you proceeded to and enveloped your person within one of the exceedingly comfortable armchairs to await your turn with patience. Your presence would have been duly noted, for whilst her physical being was now a little impaired, her mind remained very acute and in due course, Dolly would wander over in her deliberate way to attend to your needs. It did not do to try and attract her attention with flagrant comments or inappropriate gestures and the most heinous crime was to click your fingers at her! This meant instant relegation to the back of the queue and if you really upset her, you'd be lucky to get bread and water before midnight. However, if you ticked the right boxes and as a result, met with her approval, she would eventually deem to furnish you with your order and with great deliberation, proceed to unload the contents of an elaborate silver salver on to your table. This consisted of a proper sugar bowl; some spotless serviettes; bone china cups; willow-patterned plates and if you preferred tea – a decorative teapot, equipped with a strainer to cope with the loose leaves. Teabags were anathema at the White Lion and the use of loose tea strictly mandatory.

No one knew how old Dolly was and nobody would have dared to ask. This did not deter speculation behind her back and the fact that she'd had a comb-over for at least twenty-five years made any attempt to determine the truth of the matter, wildly inaccurate.

Quite often, Dolly brought her son George in to help. George was around fifty, had learning difficulties and had never left home. Generally considered a sweetie, he had a very engaging nature and liked nothing better than to help his mother as she fussed – and depending on their amiability – sometimes overly cosseted her customers. Those who were not in this limited 'inner circle' strove avidly to be accepted into it and a begrudging smile from the less than effusive Dolly usually meant that they would soon be granted admittance.

Self-appointed cleaner of the tables, George was universally cherished by the punters and rarely had some ignorant soul got away with losing patience and been allowed to castigate him over his supposed shortcomings. Such instances were as rare as hen's teeth and when they did occur, the clientele would arise almost en masse in his defence. The inevitable result meant that the antagonist became *persona non grata* and was immediately barred from entering the hallowed portals of the White Lion again.

This state of affairs held good until a new manager arrived. With his arrival the status quo looked like it might be endangered and one or two of the more enlightened members of Dolly's 'supporters' club' were keen to ensure that it was preserved. One of these patrons and not particularly well-heeled persons was an eccentric semi-retired gentleman called Leonard Easton. A highly respected local solicitor, he refuted this assumed respectability by not conforming to type.

He sported an ancient bowler hat, which he always removed when entering the inner sanctum of the White Lion and assisted this perhaps manufactured characterisation by myopically viewing the world through a pair of half-moon glasses. A beak of a nose completed the picture and, to further confuse this carefully nurtured image, he was also somewhat surprisingly, a stalwart and lay preacher at the local Baptist church.

When appointments and disposition permitted, he religiously patronised the White Lion at 11 a.m. and was one of the few people who could cause the sometimes-flustered Dolly to pause in her in her endeavours to acknowledge his presence. She had no need to take an order from him as it never varied and it was usually the devoted George who was delegated to attend to the unconventional solicitor's needs. And, like most of the customers, Leonard looked upon Dolly's son with fondness and compassion. This usually resulted in a large tip being left and with childlike insouciance, George would dutifully take it to his mother, who invariably allowed him to keep it.

But this morning Leonard Easton seemed visibly disquieted and even agitated over something. He'd given his Telegraph only a perfunctory perusal, vigorously stirred his coffee and almost verbally accosted an old friend who had joined him at the table.

"Rumours, Clive, dear boy, I hear rumours …"

The inscrutable Clive, who'd retired from the firm through heart problems, yet still liked to keep in contact, sat forward and wondered if his indefatigable friend's rumours were the same ones he had heard. If so, something would most definitely have to be done about it. There was a buzz of conversation in the lounge, but he still took care to speak in undertones. It was said that walls have ears and so had the new manager.

"Not Dolly?"

"Yes, Dolly." Leonard was usually never anything other than purposeful, but he took to fiddling aimlessly with his bowler hat and hastily realising what he was doing, put it down and picked up his coffee. "And we can't allow that to happen, can we Clive?"

Nattily dressed in a bow tie, waistcoat and fashionable pink trousers, Clive concurred.

"They tell me he wants to make the lounge a sort of up-market Costa or Sundoes."

Leonard emitted a derisory snort.

"What d' you think then? Ageism? Wrongful dismissal?"

"Certainly, on both counts."

"Then we shall have to do something about it, shan't we?"

*

The young man had been perfectly affable, had willingly acceded to Leonard Easton's request for a few minutes of his time and it was arranged that they should meet in the dinner hour. The new manager's arrival in the hotel had caused a revolution to occur in the office. All the recently installed computers and other technological marvels looked state of the art and this did not augur well for what the solicitor had to say. Indeed, now the moment had come, the solicitor was not quite sure how he was going to say it. He cleared his throat several times and tried manfully to combat the frank, curious look he was getting from the manager.

"Uh, well, Mr Felton. You will probably think it's none of my business and I don't wish to assume my long-time patronage of the White Lion gives me the right to presume, but some of us are a little concerned ... and I hope you don't mind me asking ..."

Here he faltered and eagerly, Edmond Felton took the opportunity to butt in. "The name's Ed, by the way, and of course I'd like to know what concerns the customers about the place. If you don't get feedback from the punters, you can't put things right. Fire away! I'm all ears."

Leonard Easton did not like the 'call me by my Christian name bit', but noted the immaculately ironed shirt with approval, though disapproved of the lack of a necktie to go with it. Another pause occurred whilst he summoned up enough willpower to come to the point.

"Uh, well, it actually concerns Dolly."

"Dolly?" Amusement now showed on the young manager's face. "What about Dolly?"

Quite unnecessarily, the solicitor took his glasses off, addressed them with a none too clean handkerchief and put them back on again.

"Well, as you may be aware, a number of us have been coming here for years and we'd hate to think that any alteration to things might mean ..."

This received a strangely enigmatic reply.

"If changes are implemented here, Mr. Easton, I daresay all the staff will be considered and consulted. No more so than Dolly, who has a mind of her own and will doubtless put in her pennyworth. At least, she always has for as long as I've known her!"

The solicitor was puzzled. "You've known her long? That is, before you came here?"

The young man to whom this question was put was one of those lucky people who, when fully smiling, exuded an assurance which left the recipient of this bonhomie with no doubts as to his credibility. He appeared to be getting increasingly amused as the interview progressed.

"Certainly, and I'd go as far as to say she's had a considerable influence over my existence from a very early age."

"You've known her since childhood?"

"Of course, Mr Easton. She is actually my great aunt. And as everyone in the family knows, you cross Aunt Dolly at your peril! So, I'd say the fears you have about her are needless. True, the old hotel needs a lot of refurbishment, but I don't think your favourite barista needs to be affected, do you?"

*

At home with a port and lemon, Clive Mulholland was surprised to receive a call form Leonard Easton. He wanted to know something that could surely have been left until they met for coffee on the morrow. It was an odd request.

"Sorry to bother you at home, old man. D' you happen to

know who holds the deeds of the White Lion? I know that sounds like an impossible question. The place is probably owned by some big combine. It's always been shrouded in mystery. The deeds could be anywhere."

Clive took a hefty swig of his port and lemon. Why, he thought, was the old bugger pursuing this line of enquiry?

"As a matter of fact, I do know who has them. But before I answer that question, how d' you get on with the new young manager?"

Leonard quickly filled in his friend and what he had to say made Clive empty his glass in surprise and anticipation of a refill.

"Fancy that, and to answer your query re the deeds. I was filling in time just before I left the firm and in doing some filing of old papers in the basement, I recall coming quite by chance, a folder marked 'White Lion.' At the time I wasn't particularly interested, though the folder was on a shelf with others in alphabetical order and would be very easy to find. Why are you so eager to see them? I am intrigued."

The voice on the other end of the line became very animated. "So am I, dear boy, so am I."

*

And there it was. It had been put there even before either of them had joined the company and judging from the very musty smell emanating from it, not opened since. And there, indisputably, was her signature. Dorothy L. Heeton. Otherwise known as Dolly. At which unexpected revelation, they could not contain themselves. The boot was on the other foot and Edward Felton, poor boy, would have to watch his step! He certainly couldn't afford to risk the ire of Aunt Dolly, the latently discovered and most unlikely owner of the White Lion Hotel.

When they'd managed to stop laughing, the two crusty old solicitors decided to go for a tipple.

"Where shall we go?"

"There's only one place?"

"You mean the White Lion?"

"Not for coffee this time of night surely?"

"Good heavens, no," asserted nonconformist Leonard, "I think even my teetotal self is telling me that we need something stronger than that, and whilst we're at it, perhaps we can buy the management a drink, crafty young devil that he was …"

Child of the Harvest

A story of New Zealand, 1973

Grant Hickmott walked the familiar patch between the rows of heavily laden fruit trees. Stooping to pick an apple from a low branch, he shook it gently and confirmed what he had already suspected. No sign of a pip rattle meant no picking for a while and in his deliberate way, he surveyed the 'delicious' all round before concluding it would be another week before he could call upon his army of apple women. These good ladies would come to escape domesticity for a while, to expose themselves unwisely to the lethal rays of the Nelson sun and mostly to earn a few dollars: the last serving as a panacea for overstretched household budgets.

New Zealand was truly a land of plenty, and he'd often averred that because of this, everyone expected to have everything; a practical impossibility and a sure recipe for raising a nation of spoilt children.

To augment this flock of aspiring (and perspiring!) femininity, he was also hoping to recruit one or two Fijians who'd soon be finished with the tobacco harvest, and he hoped their very masculine charms would not be too much of a temptation for the temporarily emancipated housewives.

Gazing across the shimmering waters of the bay, he cast his eyes on the city with its prominent marble cathedral and beyond that, to the looming mountains. These peaks were entwined in lingering mists and above them the imminent sunset promised another fine day tomorrow. The dairy men and cattle breeders were nearly on their knees for rain and though sympathising, Grant hoped it would come now rather than during the picking. The last time he recalled the heavens obliging with a downpour had been over the Christmas period and as yet, the drought showed no signs of abating. The province was undeniably living up to its 'sunshine' slogan this year and – as was usual in February – there would probably be a lot more to come.

Unravelling his near seven-foot length beneath a tree which displayed a bumper crop and adjusting his 'sunnies', Grant turned about to watch the sun drop behind the ravishing Moutre Hills. This would be his fifteenth year in apples. He had married when thirty, acquired this rolling, sloping property and the partnership had been successful except in the ability to produce children. Jean was a good wife and they'd considered adoption, but there always seemed too much to do about the place and now she was just approaching forty years, it all looked a little too late.

He sighed, lay back against the tree, sniffed the pure air and savoured the embracing twilight, listening to the gregarious cicadas' unremitting carousel. Some just seemed to click away in a repetitive monologue, others half whistled, and the whole chorus of them made a sound of which he never grew tired. Spectre-like, a broad-winged Australasian harrier zoomed across the darkening sky: a noble sight until you realised he had probably been picking at some dead opossum on the highway and was returning, gorged, to his lofty hideout in the southerly mountains.

The apple grower's eyes began to droop, but a new sound caught his ears. A high-pitched silvery sing-song, coming from somewhere behind him. Fighting his drowsy inclinations, he stirred himself to look round and, having done so, encountered a small, impish face surveying him from the lower boughs of a neighbouring tree. Two big brown eyes shone out, wondrous pools in a distinctly Maori visage: her hair black as night and her demeanour utterly irresistible. Beneath this, a slender body hid itself in a soft, leaf-green material and the whole effect of the young girl and her outfit were further enhanced by a pair of transparent, decorated slippers encasing two shapely feet. The child could not be more than ten years old and though startled by her appearance, Grant tried not to show it.

"G' day," he said, "and who might you be?"

The girl swung down from the branches and stood facing him, hands on hips, her expansive grin more evident than ever. She tossed her hair, smoothed her tunic down, and folding her arms in an unabashed and completely fearless gesture, stood looking at the recumbent giant in a provocative manner before deigning to answer.

"And why should I tell you?"

This was not the answer he'd been expecting. He arose, scratched his head in perplexity, tried hard to move the bone-dry earth with his left boot and failing, took a little while to reply.

"Well, since I just happen to be the owner of this property, I'd like to know what such a neat-looking young lady is doing in one of my fruit trees at this time of day?"

The girl laughed, ostensibly unfazed by the situation.

"You see," she replied, as if dealing with a particularly obtuse member of the human race and a Pakeha t' boot, "it's quite simple. If it wasn't for me fixing it every year, you might not grow anything like the crop you do!"

Not being used to the directness of children, the big man was taken aback again, but determined to be decisive and questioned the child further.

"Look, dear, I may be a simple joker, but don't you think you ought to be going home? D' you live around here? Won't your parents be worried about you? Besides, you shouldn't be pilfering. For one thing, the apples are not quite ripe and won't be doing you any good and for another, I don't like the idea of just any wee girl coming into my orchard and helping herself."

Ignoring this gentle upbraiding, the interloper skipped twenty yards away from her inquisitor, cheekily lolloped back and once more fixed him with her startling great orbs. She fragrantly ignored all his questions, began to sing again and despite his almost apologetic chiding, seemed lost in a world of her own.

He tried again. "I'm sorry, but if you won't tell me anything about yourself, I'm gonna hive (have) to take you home to my wife. It's getting on for eight and we can't have you shooting all over the place at this time of night. Won't you tell me where your people live?"

Awakened from her reverie, the girl stopped singing, and smiling far more whimsically than before, at last deigned to reply.

"Well, if you must know, I don't have people. I'm called Mirimar and I work for Rongo, god of fruits and the harvest. I try to make sure you have a big, healthy crop and don't you think

I've done so this year? I'm not supposed to be seen, but you looked like a nice man, and I get tired of being on my own. My job can be very lonely."

The orchardist thought the youngster had a vivid imagination. Obviously very sensitive, she was unlike his havoc-wrecking nephew who visited at sporadic intervals. Nevertheless, he recognised the child's fantasy and decided the best thing to do was to take the delightful creature home to his wife. Jean might even know her and if she did not, would almost certainly be able to glean the required information about the child's background without too much trouble. Jean had a good way with children which, though he tried not to dwell on it, saddened him even more. Hesitating no longer, he addressed the girl in a firm manner.

"I think you'd better come down to the house with me, young Mirimar, if that's what you're really called," he said positively, at the same time smiling inwardly to himself. He was aware that a goodly number of females in New Zealand were called Mirimar, only he imagined most of them would not harbour grand delusions of Maori gods, particularly of this Rongo, who as the supposed overseer of all things fertile, still had a number of native disciples.

"Of course it is. I just told you!"

Whilst obviously irritated by Grant's doubts over her name, she put a small trusting hand in his and seemed willing to acquiesce. "I'd like to git (get) a look at a house. I've never been in one. What are they like inside?"

She appeared excited at the prospect and skipped happily by his side as they made their way down the slope through the orchard.

"Suppose you wait and see," said the relieved orchardist. "I'll git my wife to fix you some tucker and then perhaps you can tell me more about yourself?"

It was almost dark as the big man and his nymph-like companion reached the brightly painted homestead at the bottom of the incline. Not that visible in the fading light, the Hickmott's home could still be described as more functional than aesthetic. Half an internal-combustion engine did little to enhance the back lawn, an empty dog kennel rotted on the all-round verandah and an old piano languished in the timber-littered lean-to nearby. Old beer bottles, long since bereft of their liquid contents, waited to be disposed of and cats of sundry varieties sat about in various poses of indolence. A boat, which the owner had been trying to build since – his wife sardonically observed – the dawn of time, occupied most of the front lawn and behind this blissful but cluttered habitat, the grading and packing house stood ready for the fray.

"Hallo, who's this then?"

An attractive woman who did not look anything like her thirty-eight years, Jean Hickmott looked up from some intricate crochet work which, amidst the countless tasks of housework and helping her husband on the acreage, provided balm at the end of a long working day. She displayed little consternation at the newcomer's arrival. She was used to people arriving out of the blue. Sometimes they would be lost and ask to use the phone and Kiwi etiquette demanded that you never refused, and quite often complete strangers would be invited to sit down for tea and cakes. An excuse for such a repast was never needed in New Zealand's country areas, since they didn't see that many people and quite often as a result of these casual meetings, firm friendships were established and lasted for many years.

Grant sat down and gave his wife what could only be described as a quizzical look.

"As far as I can make out this is Mirimar. Found her way up in the orchard." Grant arose again and gingerly helped the girl on to a chair at a large pinewood table he'd made some years earlier in anticipation of the large brood who had failed to materialise. From there she sat regarding the lady of the house with her large serious eyes.

With a lump in her throat, Jean Hickmott smiled and thought how beautiful the child was. If only … but it was no use fretting over her apparent barrenness. It hadn't happened and the more time elapsed, the less likely it was to do so. She put down her crochet and got to her feet.

"Would you like some tucker, dear? Then perhaps I'll git Grant to run you home." Jean thought the child looked hungry and wondered how long it was since she'd had a square meal. And the girl now seemed eager to convey some more information.

"No, you can't take me home, thank you. I don't live round here. I live a long way over the mountains. I just happened to be sent here this time. I'm very glad, because it's very lovely. You don't have children, do you?"

The winning smile bestowed itself on Jean this time and trying not to succumb to her feelings, Grant's wife hurried off to the kitchen, leaving her husband to entertain their charming little guest. The girl chattered away to him without a trace of self-consciousness and now appeared wholly at home in the unfamiliar surroundings.

It was not long before the mouth-watering aromas wafting from the kitchen materialised into a fine impromptu meal consisting of corn on the cob, a large kumara, a hogget chop, fresh anchovies and for afters, a slice of left-over pavlova from the fridge.

During the consumption of this hastily contrived meal, the slight stranger failed to volunteer anything else about herself or her background, save that she'd been 'sent' and after considerable hesitation, and beckoning him out of earshot, Jean suggested her husband contact the police. With reluctance inscribed all over his weathered face, Grant picked up the receiver and it wasn't long before a patrol car from down the road in Richmond arrived. The patrolmen were well known to the Hickmotts and very friendly toward the bubbling Mirimar.

Due to her initial lack of response, they questioned her with difficulty and tried not to disparage her preposterous claim that she worked for the scarcely credible Maori god, Rongo. It was fortunate that one of them happened to be half-Maori and was prepared to give some credence to the old ways. He tried to temper his colleague's more forthright approach with a little caution, but despite his efforts, the supposed waif was taken to Nelson in tears, protesting vigorously and insisting she had no earthly attachments.

Though highly implausible to those of no spiritual conception, this seemed almost to be the truth and after several months of fruitless enquiries, during which the Hickmotts visited her in a local children's home, the police kept the matter in hand, but hoped someone would eventually come forward to claim the child. An appeal had been launched on TV and in newspapers, but as the days passed and no one came forward to claim her, Mirimar ceased to be the engaging, charismatic child of the orchards. She stuck to her story and, incarcerated in a world she didn't understand and surrounded by children with very worldly demands, withdrew into herself, became morose and was finally taken to hospital with an illness for which the medics were unable to provide a prognosis.

The end came with the Hickmotts at her bedside. They had put in a request to adopt her, but the obdurate authorities were insistent that until her natural parents or relatives were located, this was not legally possible. She passed on with Grant holding her hand, the stricken girl offering a supplication to Rongo and taking her natural gifts with her and a year later, all the fruit trees in Nelson province bore no apples whatsoever, struck by a mysterious blight.

Devastated, the orchardist once more sat in his domain amongst the stunted, ravaged trees. He was not one for literature or anything too cultured but knew enough to know that the great English Bard had been right. The Maoris would surely not have believed in what they believed without good reason. In Rangi and Papa and the whole dynasty of gods and their functions and purposes. Thus, to him, the gregarious cicadas now clicked a curious requiem for poor little Mirimar, a sad victim of man's blatant disbelief and as William Shakespeare had said, 'There are more things in heaven and earth, Horatio, than are dreamt of in your philosophy.'

Author's Note

Set in the early seventies when I was in New Zealand, it is likely things have changed radically since then. I suspect housewives no longer apple pick, though if Nelson province isn't still the most beautiful place in the world – along with my own blessed May Hill – then I'd like to see the place that is!

Feeding the Ducks

A long, short story – 2019

He could never understand why Christianity had survived two thousand years until someone told him about the emperor. In his infinite wisdom, Constantine had declared that Christianity would be the new all-embracing religion of the Roman Empire and his virtual omnipotence was enough to guarantee that it would supersede all other beliefs.

You had time to consider these things when, in your reduced circumstances, you inhabited a tent situated within the bushes that fringe the city's picturesque duck pond. For company he had two similarly 'housed' neighbours with whom he regularly tried to engage in philosophical discussion – something of an uphill struggle due to their somewhat limited mental capacity – but thankfully, providing they all lived in relative harmony, the council did not feel it incumbent as the local authority to do anything other than 'let sleeping dogs lie'.

Where their welfare was concerned, the trio regularly took breakfast at one or other of the charitable churches in the city; the food bank was another option and, if all else failed, supermarket skips were another source of possible sustenance. Winter often meant resorting to St Bartholomew's night shelter and on inclement days during that bleak season they often took to huddling round one of the big stoves that attempted, with limited success, to heat the vast interior of the city's ancient cathedral. Sometimes they were requested to move on by one of the edifice's not particularly charitable clerics, but the humane exception to this mild form of harassment came in the form of the pleasant and avuncular dean, who displayed a truly Christian attitude to their presence. Seemingly immune to their not particularly hygienic condition, he would often conduct them to the cloisters to drink tea in one of the side rooms off it.

The leader of the trio, Calvin, had soon revealed himself to be something of a thwarted intellectual which his reticence when confronted by members of the unsympathetic world at large, labelled him unfairly as 'just another scrounger'. It is usually wrong to 'judge a book by its cover' and in the past Calvin had regaled the slightly amused dean with his emphatic and contrary views on Christianity. He maintained that the ancient and pre-Roman Etruscans carried and wore croziers and mitres long before the Christians allegedly brought them into being. He suggested that the building of churches on pagan sites was another example of the 'old ways' still permeating Christianity and the dean did not deny it. Regardless of the dean's sensitivity, he opined that Christ did not direct his followers to go forth and build great new temples in his name and that the Roman and Protestant liturgies were a complete distortion of His original teachings. From whence, he protested, did Mass and Eucharist come from and how did 'when two or three of you are gathered together' evolve into a contrived and contentious ceremony? And how could the modern 'high priests' possibly claim to be the successors of Christ's humble fishermen?

Not one to shun a confrontation, the dean defended himself and his calling well. He alluded to St Peter's demise in Rome and justified the building of the magnificent cathedrals as an act of assured faith and a symbol of man's great ability to appease the aesthete within. He implied that it mattered not which way you worshipped as long as you did so, and even promoted his liberal beliefs by stating that there were assuredly good things in other religions which it did not do to dismiss lightly.

The dogged Calvin had no opinions on this but suspected that most of the Norman building was achieved with the considerable assistance of Saxon slave labour. He pointed out that William the Conqueror's followers could probably be counted in mere thousands and could not see how so many of these incredible structures could have possibly been erected in such a short time without coercing the natives. At which juncture the dean had had to bid them farewell. He'd been requested to attend the marriage clinic. Two members of the regular congregation had been at loggerheads, and they'd wanted spiritual as well as practical guidance.

He had to admit that sometimes the city and its often-ignorant inhabitants depressed him. In their seemingly inbuilt misapprehension, they were often under the impression that the imposing Bishop's Palace just housed the bishop. They thought he lived there with his family in a comparatively opulent state not enjoyed by the rest of the allegedly great unwashed proletariat. But, in reality, the mild-mannered prelate just inhabited a flat somewhere in the rear of the place and did his best to exude a common touch which was slowly gaining him a reputation as 'Bishop John, the People's Bishop'. Apart from the diocesan office itself and amongst rooms ceded to other worthwhile organisations, the Church used one to conduct its own marriage guidance service. On his way to this worthy dispensary of hopefully helpful advice, the dean had time to contemplate the situation vis-à-vis the cathedral's not always welcome trio of wayfaring visitors. He trusted them – Calvin in particular – and it grieved him that the rest of the chapter, with the odd exception, did not share his charitable view. He knew they would take the teacups back to the 'matriarch' of the cathedral kitchens – the imposing Mrs Bendlove – and after they'd gone the good lady would voice her disapproval of them to her sidekick, the aptly named Mrs Panworthy. The 'effluvia' of the gentlemen offended and 'what was the dean thinking of?': another example which demonstrated that the cathedral sometimes had very little to do with Jesus Christ and Christian charity.

The dean did not look forward to marriage guidance interviews but resolved to do his best where this one was concerned. The couple in question were almost glutinously obsequious towards him; an attitude starkly at odds with their attitude to one another. His reverence suspected that there was not much love left between them and he felt sorry for Mr Trenchard, the beleaguered marriage guidance counsellor who had so far failed to settle their differences. They had ostensibly reached an impasse and the situation was unusually exacerbated by their respective beliefs. Although in an attempt to preserve domestic harmony, the husband attended the cathedral, he was really an avid Roman Catholic and did not partake of communion there. His true allegiance was to St Francis's, a stone's throw away and he went to Mass there on Saturday evenings and other holy occasions. This arrangement would have operated reasonably well had the couple not been endowed with children: a boy and a girl. True disciple of Rome that he was, he wanted both siblings brought up eventually to be members of the 'one, true faith' and his wife's stout resistance to this process had caused what appeared to be an irreparable rift in their marriage. Whilst he would appease her by attending the cathedral occasionally, she would not humour him by going to his church and more and more, the hapless children were involved in an unsavoury tug-of-war; perhaps calculated to turn them against religion of any sort for ever. He constantly reminded her that divorce was not an option where his faith was concerned and she, spawned from a background where her mother was a 'rough diamond' and her father had been incarcerated more than once, unceremoniously informed him that he could place his faith within his 'anal passage'. She was not having her children sullied by 'that hypocritical bunch of unmitigated perverts' and that old Father O'Donnell could look elsewhere for his gullible converts. To better herself some years ago, she had joined the C. of E. and as her accent and status improved because of it, she had no intention of giving way on the subject. That the established Church was not entirely blameless when it came to the question of perverted activities, she conveniently ignored, and her stance often made anything remotely related to reason a non-starter.

It was obvious that the bespectacled and moithered Mr Trenchard had had enough. He politely pointed out that as the main issue was a religious one, then perhaps the dean would be of more use and hastily proffered this as an excuse to leave the room.

*

Summer duly arrived and with it the long school holiday. Helen and Joseph were feeding the ducks and back in his tent, Calvin could see them through the open flap. He loved children and it was a source of grief that he'd not been allowed to know his daughter's. Drink, drugs and a financial scam had landed him inside at the time they were born within a year of one another, and when he was released he was not allowed anywhere near them. He surmised that these two, perhaps aged about ten and eleven, would be more or less the same age as his grandchildren. They both had blond mops and the girl was slightly taller than the boy, not an unusual circumstance at their age.

Having apparently sated the ducks, the boy began to kick a football about and was joined, a trifle reluctantly, by the girl. One hefty kick from the boy landed the ball in the bushes and rather than risk an invasion, Calvin emerged from the undergrowth with it: causing visible consternation to both children. He could not resist offering them a smile, though his appearance was less than reassuring. He still wore an overcoat – it was cool within the bushes – his ill-fitting trousers were in sore need of a wash and his unkempt beard did not inspire confidence in what lay behind it. He threw the ball back and received a brief and awkward nod of thanks. Obviously nervous, the children were still intrigued, not knowing from where he had sprung and hoping he would not accost them. He would like to have engaged them in conversation, but decided it would be sanguine to leave them to their own devices; a resolution which, through more inaccurate football, was soon broken.

He discovered that the boy, whose sensitive face seemed familiar, was a bird-lover and the girl had ballet lessons. And then with a matter-of-fact statement that made the vagrant's whole being shudder, the boy calmly informed him "She's Helen and I'm Jo."

Could it be? Not uncommon names, but they were the right age. He'd never seen so much as a photograph, but it was quite possible. Evidently, the parents both worked, mistakenly thinking the children could legitimately be left to amuse themselves during the holidays. It seemed that although there was this constant and at times heated bickering over religious matters – mainly about confirmation into the Roman Catholic church – not too much care was taken over their everyday earthly needs. The fact that leaving children under a certain age on their own for hours was unlawful did not seem to concern the parents. Helen and Joseph were 'pretty sensible'. This was stressed to their paternal grandmother who had gladly minded them before she became infirm. She was naturally concerned but was assured they would be 'perfectly alright on their own' and told that there really was nothing to worry about.

As time progressed, Calvin found it difficult. Either unaware of or choosing to ignore his reduced circumstances, the children paid further visits to the duck pond and it even got to the stage where he could introduce his similarly impecunious 'neighbours' from the tents on either side.

Alas, fate decreed that this odd, but amiable friendship was soon to be terminated. Bored with standing around High Town and answering difficult questions directed at him from tourists and idle yokels, a member of Her Majesty's Constabulary, PC Alun Davis, decided to take a stroll elsewhere and his footsteps took him in the direction of the duck pond. He set out with the intention of checking up on those lads who inhabited the bushes. He knew that providing they did not make too much mess, the council would tolerate them, but it would do no harm to pay them an unscheduled visit.

Unfortunately, upon arrival, he found that what they were doing failed to meet with his approval. None of these three 'street merchants' had ever given the slightest impression that they were perverted in any way, but you could never quite be sure. At first, he addressed the vagrants and Calvin protested and explained about the football, at the same time stating that it was not a crime merely to talk to children. Did not he, PC Davis, recall the time Calvin had brought a little lost boy into the police station? As it happened the police officer did, but he still instructed the trio to retire to their respective tents whilst he interviewed the children.

The policeman had a loud voice and his questioning easily reached Calvin's ears. That address they gave. It was his daughter's! He'd never been allowed near, but he knew it through a small drugs dealer and acquaintance that lived nearby, over the other side of the city. With a justifiable frisson of excitement, he realised that these youngsters must be his grandchildren. He could now hear PC Davis remonstrating with them; asking them if their parents knew where they were, and their shrill young voices explaining that their mother and father both worked. They were trusted to behave and could look after themselves; not an explanation that satisfied the concerned police officer, who summoned a police car to take them home. He then rang a phone number the boy had produced and gave the lad's mother an official roasting. He informed her he would be travelling with the patrol car and bluntly advised her to get home as soon as possible. He summoned Calvin from his bosky surroundings and to the vagrant's relief, attached no blame to him or his laissez-faire colleagues. He nevertheless intimated that it might be a good idea for persons of their drug related and cider consuming habits not to consort with vulnerable children and took himself off with his charges in the police car which had taken little time to arrive.

All of which made Calvin's heart plummet. Now convinced that they were unquestionably his kin, he could see that little had changed. No chance had he, a stinking drop-out with a criminal record, of seeing them again, let alone forming some sort of relationship. That is, until one of his mates, Geraint, came up with a surprising suggestion. Generally reckoned to be 'tuppence short of a shilling' by almost all those that knew him, the allegedly half-witted Welshman was a dark horse that in Calvin's opinion was much maligned. To some, he had an incomprehensible sense of humour, an obsession with oddly related things and his sometimes disjointed and often unfinished sentences were hard to comprehend, but what was he saying now?

"The d-dean-the dean-you knows; the d-dean at the cathe-cathedral ..."

"The dean? What about the dean?" Calvin was mystified, though remaining tolerant.

Geraint struggled to convey his meaning. "These little 'uns. You says their yourn. Go see 'im, Tell 'im. 'E might 'elp."

Geraint had just endorsed his friend's faith in him, and Calvin felt a small amount of optimism overriding the black depression which had begun to descend. It might work. He thought the dean a good man, but would it be unlikely that such an exalted figure would deign to help? He didn't see the distinguished clergyman a lot in the summer months, and would it be wise to try and contact him over such an extraneous matter? And what, in the event of Calvin deciding to do so, would be the best way to approach him?

However, this did not seem to trouble the straightforward Geraint. To him it was not a problem. A simple matter. Calvin should simply apply the heavy brass knocker to the sturdy deanery door. In Geraint's view, a logical thing to do.

Calvin, of course, knew where the deanery stood bordering the cloisters. An aesthetically pleasing Georgian pile, smothered in ivy and housing the dean and his young family. But would he have the temerity to call upon the dean without warning? If he did, he'd have to do something about his appearance. The swimming baths had showers, one of which he stealthily 'appropriated' occasionally and a troll round the charity shops would most likely provide fresh apparel. He would have to resurrect his recorder – which he played badly – and do some busking. The local populace was quite tolerant; they knew him and although he had a limited repertoire, at least he did not use an invasive backing tape. This euphemistically questionable musical activity might furnish him with a little of the 'necessary' and he might also be able to afford a much-needed haircut.

Good for old Geraint, he thought, and offered this unexpected fount of advice a roll-up. They all three smoked roll-ups and it was fortunate that PC Davis had not chosen to inspect their domicile behind the bushes. The local force did little to combat the soft drugs scene in the city – a man needed a substance a bit more satisfying than tobacco in his fag paper – and the stuff wasn't difficult to obtain if you knew where to look for it.

The dean tried not to show his surprise at the transformed being that currently stood on his doorstep. Handily, service as a curate in a not particularly salubrious part of Mancunian Moss Side had equipped him for most scenarios and implanted a tolerance not evident in his early years. He'd even sampled the 'weed' at Lampeter College – not all potential servants of God are opposed to a minimal use of cannabis – and had sensed Calvin was an advocate of this so-called 'recreational' drug.

"Calvin? Nice to see you. Do come in. Is there something I can do for you?"

The visitor was hesitant; reluctant to step over the threshold.

From what he could see, without being luxurious, the deanery had a degree of comfort far removed from that of a rudimentary tent concealed in the bushes behind a duck pond. He began to wish he hadn't come, but the dean was insistent and behind him, a pleasant looking lady – presumably his wife – smiled a welcome.

"Please do come in." Not taking no for an answer, the dean ushered the reluctant Calvin through the high-ceilinged hall into a small study and momentarily turning to his wife said, "Moyra, this is Calvin and d' you think some coffee might be possible, my dear? How d' you take it, Calvin? White with sugar?" Not a question when hidden in the undergrowth the feasibly reformed tramp would normally have to answer. Although he did have a small Primus stove and a large bottle of Camp Coffee. He also possessed a saucepan and a large demijohn. A tap oddly located outside the nearby community centre provided water and three tin mugs enabled him, Geraint and the deliberately indolent Ernest to modestly indulge. Faced with the dilemma as to how he partook of the dean's prime French beverage – they were never offered anything other than tea in the cloisters – Calvin played safe and still slightly bemused said, "That would be fine, please."

Decorated with photos of the dean's four fresh-faced, attractive children, the study was decidedly functional. A dated laptop sat on an antique escritoire, and a printer kept it company. Having just spewed out notices for a forthcoming service, the latter was now silent and resting. The dean found a hard chair and with a courteous gesture, invited his unusual guest to sit on the much more comfortable floral-patterned settee opposite.

"So, what can I do for you?" The dean's manner was very reassuring and Calvin felt able to confide in him without misgivings. He leant forward in a gesture of complete confidence.

"Well, i'z like this, sir ..." He explained about the names and the incident with the police officer and the children's address. He wanted to make contact with them on a normal basis and did he not have a statutory right to do so? The policeman, he said, had probably put the 'kibosh' on this, but surely his criminal record could not be held against him forever?

Recent publicity in the press establishing that grandparents had virtually no rights over their grandchildren, did not augur well for any future relationship, although the dean thought some legal action could be taken; a costly exercise well beyond 'a gentleman of the road'.

A tap on the study door signalled the arrival of the dean's wife with the coffee and this interruption gave the senior clergyman a sudden moment of inspiration. He gave the lady a broad smile.

"Thank you, Moyra, my dear. D' you think Deaconess Lydia might be at home just now? I'd rather like to ask her something."

The dean's wife beamed back at him, giving the impression that she bestowed this beatific expression on him most of the time. She loved this generous man of hers and they made a formidable team.

"As a matter of fact, I encountered her in the cloisters earlier this morning. It's her day off. She laughingly said her place is a tip and she was dashing off to do some terribly overdue housework. Something, I suspect, that occurs but rarely."

Vivacious Deaconess Lydia was the most recent addition to the cathedral clergy. Very sincere, very young and delightfully scatty. Politely summoned by that most intrusive of modern inventions, her mobile phone, Lydia hastened to the deanery. To her mind, anything beat cleaning the toilet or doing the week's washing and besides, she could not resist the dean's wife, who had quickly become one of her favourite people. Whilst awaiting her arrival, the dean had apprised his visitor of his idea and though dubious, Calvin knew what to expect when the slightly plump, but pretty deaconess arrived.

*

Margaret Gray had luxurious blonde hair, not complemented by her almost permanently creased forehead. Added to this, her reddening freckles and a current bout of almost overwhelming vitriol threatened to damage even further the steadily foundering relationship between her and her startled husband, Peter.

"That's fucking preposterous! As if I could leave the kids with that old reprobate! You say this dog-collared cleric – a female one no less – rang you and before you say it, no, she's not coming to discuss it. What a bloody cheek! You'll just have to take the time off until we can make some arrangement. I earn more than you do, anyway, so that's the way it'll have to be!"

"What about Gran?"

"Don't be so damn stupid. You know Gran has to have carers herself and she can't have the kids round there moithering her half the time!"

"Well, then, we'll just have to go on the way we were."

"Jesus Christ! I despair of you sometimes. You know what that copper said. They could check up on us at any time and then there's the bloody neighbours! They'd love to get us into trouble. We can't even just leave the kids at home and in any case, we wouldn't know if they went out or not."

"Well, could we not just try what that young lady suggested? She did say your dad had spruced himself up and it might work ..."

His wife emitted a sound which could be interpreted as an indeterminate cross between a snort and a sigh of extreme exasperation.

"Oh yes and where would he take them, I wonder? It would be so humiliating if their friends found out that 'Grandad' dossed down in a tatty tent by the duck pond!"

From somewhere her husband found a latent degree of assertiveness.

"You know what the deaconess also told me. Calvin has really landed on his feet. They've offered him a part-time job and one of those nice little places in the cloisters."

His pumped-up adversary allowed herself a hollow laugh and returned to the fray.

"And can you really see that coming off? Besides, that would take the children even further away from becoming captives of your unholy Catholics and anyway ..." She paused, unsure how to go on.

"Anyway, what? Can't you see? It would only be until the end of the holidays. Another four weeks or so."

With a look of unremitting determination on her face, his wife chose to ignore this. She wrung her hands in a gesture which suggested that what she was about to say next had afforded her more than a few misgivings.

"I've made up my mind. I'm going for a divorce. Then we'll have to split up and the children will be in the same position as a lot of their friends. It's not fair on them, I know, but I can't help it. It's caused mainly by you insisting, among other things, that they become followers of the 'one, true' fucking religion!"

Tentatively, he offered a restraining hand. It almost looked like he was going to have to combat a physical assault.

"I keep telling you. The Catholic Church does not recognise divorce. You can't do that."

"Oh yes I can, and I bloody well will."

The subject of her ire had a sudden thought. "Where are the children, anyway?"

She calmed down a little before responding. "They were upstairs in their rooms. They're probably on the stairs now, God help us, listening to all that's going on." Coming to an irrelevant decision, the irate mother suddenly said, "I want a drink," and slouched off into the faded lounge where a gin bottle and a glass would possibly help to improve – or not – her present disposition.

A solid door shut off the cottage's tumblehome stairway from the hall and opening it, he discovered that his offspring were not, as anticipated, eavesdropping. He called up the stairs, assuming they must be in their respective bedrooms.

"Helen! Jo!"

"Yes Dad!" Two high voices replied in unison.

"D' you fancy a walk?"

Two bedroom doors opened and slammed shut and two pairs of bright eyes were soon surveying him from the top of the stairs.

"Can we go down the pub, Dad?"

The pub stood by one of the city's pleasant and recently cleaned up streams and a nearby outlet contained a different sort of wildfowl, quirky moorhens.

His mind in turmoil, their father gave them something akin to a wry grin and tried not to think of his fractious wife and what might be their uncertain future.

"I don't see why not," he assented.

Calvin still went to see his friends, though their reciprocating visits did not meet with the approval of all the personnel at the imposing cathedral.

Bedfellows in conspiritual gossip, Mesdames Bedlove and Panworthy expressed unreserved disapproval.

" 'T'ent right," essayed the senior and tubbier damsel of the intolerant duo. "Afore you knows it they'll be 'avin a kip an' dossin' down in there. I reckons it 'ent right!"

This pearl of rustic wisdom was accompanied by the waving in the air of a mixing spoon which caused a portion of the mixture to just miss her colleague's person: the pastry apparently ending any of its aspirations regarding being included in the embryonic pie by landing unceremoniously on the kitchen floor.

Not even fazed a trifle by her near besmirching, the redoubtable Dame Panworthy bent her lower appendages as much as her afflicting arthritis would allow and scooping it up with hitherto unsuspected athleticism, consigned the unfortunate pastry to a convenient waste bin. This achieved, she settled herself heavily on a kitchen chair and proclaimed with slightly malicious enthusiasm "Uz no good would come of it 'n' what wuz the dean thinkin' of?"

Calvin, who was enjoying his new responsibilities as a part-time odd-job man, could not believe his luck in obtaining his new abode – he'd moved in within a matter of days – and was further bemused to receive a visit from Helen and Jo, accompanied by their father, Peter. Not very optimistically, the latter was hoping this unscheduled visit might just provide a solution to the childcare problem. He had not deigned to consult his wife over it. She remained adamant that in no way would she approve of assigning the care of the children to their allegedly 'reformed' grandad. Peter knew he was taking a risk but having to take too much time off or paying for childcare, could not be a long-term solution. Poor Gran, bless her, had done her stint in the past, was even now assisting financially, but could not be expected to stump up indefinitely. Another three weeks of summer holidays would stretch him to the limit and choosing mostly to ignore the situation, his mercurial wife became utterly selfish in her attitude. Her job as manageress of a prestigious store in town had, in her opinion, to take priority and nothing would persuade her that she might give it up and work part-time for a while. This, she adamantly stated, was the age of equality and the children would have to accept it.

An easy-going Catholic in some respects – save for his insistence that the children must be brought up in the faith – Peter sometimes thought that his spouse and some women of the twenty-first century were rapidly reaching a stage in their development where they practically suffered from a 'superiority' complex. Certainly, hundreds of years of subjection were being reversed with a vengeance; not an opinion he dared to elaborate on in public.

A jarring sound assaulted his ears, and he wondered why on earth – no pun intended – he'd chosen to select 'Mars' from *The Planets* as his dialling tone.

"Is that Mr Peter Eddery?" A sombre voice.

"Speaking."

"Sergeant Wills, City Police Station here. We don't want to alarm you, but we have to inform you that your wife collapsed in High Town and has just been taken to the County Hospital. We found your number on her mobile phone. Also her credit card gave us her name. Fortunately, one of our officers was within yards of her when she collapsed. He called the ambulance. The medics revived her, but we suggest you get to the hospital right away."

He switched the phone off and contemplated the two small anxious faces looking up at him. They'd obviously overheard the police sergeant's rather stentorian voice. Calvin's face, too, was a mixture of enquiry and anxiety.

"Bad news?" he said.

Peter sat on his heels and put an arm round each of the children. He addressed them gently. "I don't suppose it's a lot to worry about, but your mum fainted in town and is in hospital for a check-up." He gave Calvin an appealing look. A look that conveyed 'needs must'. An ill wind it was that turned out to be purely negative.

Calvin did not need asking. "I'll look after 'em. You get yerself to the 'ospital."

Peter hesitated, unsure, but possessed of the feeling that he had no alternative.

This time he appealed to the children. "Would you stay with your-your-uh-grandad, that is, until I can pick you up? I don't suppose your mother is that ill. Sometimes people faint for no apparent reason. I shouldn't be long."

Although they were now well aware who he was, this was the first time they had heard Calvin referred to as 'Grandad' in his presence. And Grandad was not slow in taking advantage of his newly acquired status.

"We'll 'ave pizzas – pizzas and chips. I got an advance on my first pay, so there's plenty in the fridge." Calvin almost lasered his engagingly lopsided smile to the children. It was extraordinary how life was looking up. For the first time in years, he'd actually been able to do some legitimate shopping and it would be very satisfying to eschew food that was past its sell-by date or cooked up by those well-meaning though not necessarily adept chefs at the various church kitchens.

"You sure you don't mind?" Peter asked anxiously. "You haven't a phone, have you? The children aren't allowed one yet."

Full of solicitude, Calvin suggested he relayed any news to the 'office'.

"Office?"

"There's an office in the Bishop's Palace."

"Of course. I am a dumbo. You mean the diocesan office?" Recalling his visits for marriage counselling, Peter was fully aware of it. The young secretary was always very obliging. The cloisters were close by, and it would not take long to deliver a message. Peter bent to kiss the top of the children's heads.

"Look, this is very good of you," he assured Calvin, "and I must go. I'll call in for the office phone number on the way."

It transpired that the ill wind turned out to be a malignant one. A tumour on the brain. Nevertheless, it was operable, and there was an even chance of survival. What price divorce now? Where to the feisty woman, now very sick and transported to the Queen Elizabeth Hospital, Birmingham. How ironic. Separation now seemed inconceivable, yet he might be powerless to stop it.

*

Peter found himself more and more dependent on Calvin and thanks to a compassionate stance taken by his employers, which enabled him to make daytime visits to the hospital; he would catch an early train and when not taking them with him, pick the children up around teatime. They soon became part of the scenery around the cloisters and once the novelty of the train trip ceased to appeal, Peter suspected they far preferred to be under Calvin's supervision. Their mother's operation did not appear to be happening for a while and playing with the plentiful juvenile company that existed round the cathedral appealed more than answering her questions about clean underwear and other boring things. Calvin kept a keen eye on them, and he was grateful for the kind help of various other people who took it upon themselves to assist. They were often taken for walks or perhaps to the shops or library by off-duty clergy and Deaconess Lydia unobtrusively 'mothered' them: a tower of strength and young enough to fantasise with them and laugh at their feeble jokes. They loved visiting her shambolic flat where they were often given unhealthy chips-with-everything; eaten on a small, cluttered kitchen table covered with dust and, surprisingly, fashion magazines you wouldn't expect a female member of the clergy to read. Even those sages of culinary expertise and malicious gossip, Mesdames Bedlove and Panworthy were eventually captivated, and it was not an unusual sight to witness the two siblings seated within the ladies' inner sanctum, bent upon acquiring one or two delicious handouts. Sometimes they were given the remnants of a mixing bowl or simply consumed what was on offer with their newfound friends, the dean's children; in whose idyllic garden they were often invited to play.

To say Calvin basked in his improved status would be to understate things and Peter gradually came to realise that whatever happened where their mother was concerned, the relationship with him could never revert to what it was. The surgeons had informed him that they could operate, but it would be a very tricky process and while they were pretty confident of success, Margaret's chances of survival were dependent on the entire tumour being removed. There was a real chance of failure, but on balance they were confident it would be best to proceed.

Daunted by the stark possibility that there was a good chance she might not survive the lady in question had almost become a changed character. Her previous concerns over her marital situation had now become largely irrelevant. And did it matter a damn if her children were snaffled by the bloody Catholics? Mischievously, she thought they could always defect later on in life, and it might be an idea to accede to their father's viewpoint on the matter. Embroiled in what she now realised had been a somewhat selfish attitude, she had almost disregarded Peter's good points and although not entirely reconciled to his newfound role, she had to admit that 'Grandad' Calvin had become a godsend. Still disturbed by his reprehensible past, she only hoped he would continue his stoic path to stay on the straight and narrow.

The headaches were never far away and when the day came for the operation, it engendered relief rather than apprehension. The previous time Peter had brought the children to visit, she sensed she had surprised them. Her emotional reaction when they arrived – an uncharacteristically tearful hug – was almost unprecedented. Not a particularly tactile person, her emotional greeting brought muted response. She could tell they felt awkward and resolved that if she survived, things between them must surely change. Gone was her slight intolerance and often overbearing insistence that she have her own way. Unconsciously, her reign as a control freak had ended and to Peter's obvious surprise, she broached the subject of the children's eventual acceptance into the Catholic Church. It now seemed to her that it didn't matter a jot where they worshipped and, in her turn, she was taken aback when he concurred. He'd had, he said, plenty of time to consider things and the help he'd received from the cathedral had served to convince him that the stricture that there was only 'one, true faith' was utter nonsense. Had Jesus been a Catholic and was Mass not just a convenient human invention to keep the proletariat in subjection? He even went further and posited the idea that the children, when older, might choose what path they were to take themselves.

And divorce? Not an issue any more, unless he desired it which, of course, he did not. Did he think she intended to come out of the operation only to continue as they were and if she failed to recover … if she were to …

He endeavoured to reassure her and pointed out how supportive Calvin, Deaconess Lydia and the people at the cathedral had been. Of the female cleric she expressed approval, but he could tell it might take some time for her to become reconciled to the former inhabitant of a tent pitched amongst the foliage behind the duck pond.

*

Calvin's two 'obbos' continued to live a flawed existence in their respective tents by this same aquatic sanctuary and occasionally, would call on their old friend; though being firmly entrenched 'gentlemen of the road', they were never comfortable with a roof over their heads. They had been offered accommodation by the local authority, but were unable to cope and soon reverted, it seemed from choice, to their former homelessness.

August elapsed and with the onset of darker nights, the children of all hues and classes returned to school. With the operation on Margaret an unqualified success, she was now recuperating in the local hospital, and this made life easier for everyone concerned. Calvin conducted his grandchildren to school and duly fetched them at the appropriate time. They either stayed with him in the evening whilst their father went to the hospital or they went along, until sometime later, their mother was allowed home.

Deaconess Lydia, who had become an unofficial aunt, frequently visited and with Peter quite adept in the kitchen, the children became noticeably less dependent by the day and the only fly in the ointment was Margaret's obvious reluctance to fully approve visits from the willing Calvin. Unjustly, she hardly acknowledged him, and the relationship was further blighted when, without her knowledge, Peter invited him to Sunday dinner. Her otherwise newly found charisma and benevolence extended to everyone but her father and nothing her husband could do, served to alter the situation.

*

With the onset of autumn, hobos Geraint and Ernest, basically insouciant souls, abandoned their tents and quit the duck pond. The weather still relatively mild, they hied to an empty store doorway and staked it out with their meagre possessions. These included two less than pristine duvets, several moth-eaten blankets and some slightly pathetic items of a more personal nature.

"Ah, now,'oo 'ave we 'ere?" The near giant figure stood looking down at them, made more daunting by the streetlight which somehow accentuated his grim features.

'Fearful' Francis was not a person to be cultivated or crossed and his unexpected appearance caused them a great deal of trepidation. He must have been recently released from jail, thought Ernest and his look of despair left no doubt that the big man's presence was very unwelcome.

"An' where's yer other 'obo?"

"What other 'ob-'obo?" replied Geraint, knowing full well who the intruder meant. He played the innocent and seated on his duvet soon had to endure 'Fearful' placing a foot on his leg while at the same time pressing down hard to inflict pain. Geraint winced but resisted an almost irresistible urge to cry out or protest. Clenching his teeth, he nevertheless managed to mutter, "I don' know 'oo you means."

The giant changed tack. He sat down and his eyes bored into his victim's. "Don' y' try it on with me, sonny boy. You know 'oo I means. Where's that Calvin?"

"Calvin?"

"Yes, Calvin. I bin 'earin' things about 'im. I understands 'e 'ave gone up in the world lately."

Probably motivated by sheer terror, Ernest interjected. " 'E lives in the—"

"Tha's enough, Ern." This from an alarmed and loyal Geraint.

The oppressor caught hold of Geraint's arm and twisted it. "Let 'im finish!"

In trying to spare his friend further distress, Ernest continued. " 'E lives in the cathedral."

"What d' y' mean? They wouldn't let 'im doss down in there."

" 'E don't. 'E lives in that square of 'ouses be'ind it. Can't think what it's called."

It dawned on his interlocutor.

"Oh, now that's interestin'. You means the cloisters. Now what number might 'e be livin' in I wonders?" For good measure, he gave Geraint's arm another tweak and despite his distress he managed to cry out "Don' tell 'im! WE don' want 'im goin' round there!"

But it was to no avail and sometime later Calvin was aroused from a semi-slumber by a heavy hand on the door. In the dim light his reaction contained elements of both shock and dismay. He hadn't heard the heavy footfalls on the cloister flagstones and Peter and the children had long gone, so he knew that it would not be them returning.

And here was Fearful Francis come to call; an undesirable legend he'd thought more or less permanently incarcerated. Except that he obviously wasn't and his jail sentence must have either been shortened or more time had elapsed than Calvin realised.

"Well, well, well. Nice place you 'ave 'ere."

"You better come in." Why had he said that? What a foolish invitation! Although it would have been no good to have demurred. Perhaps if he offered the giant a meal he would go away, but knowing Francis, extortion would probably be the name of the game.

Another knock, lighter and almost apologetic. The dean. "Ah, Calvin. Just came to see how you were settling in. Don't seem to have had a chance before." Startled, he observed the towering visitor. "Oh, I'm sorry; momentarily I didn't realise you had company."

Calvin quickly seized the opportunity. "I's all right, sir. This is Francis, 'e's just goin'.'"

Taken aback, feeling decidedly uncomfortable and cursing to himself, the unkempt and truculent visitor gave the clergyman a curt nod; lumbering away in a decidedly belligerent fashion and not deigning to bid farewell as he slammed the door heavily behind him.

The dean gave Calvin a candid look. "Do I sense trouble? Not a visitor you particularly wanted to see?"

Calvin invited the dean to sit and proceeded to describe something of the notorious Francis's history.

"I don' s'pose 'e'll come back. 'Iz bark's worse than 'iz bite, I reckons. I shall be all right ..."

The dean did not agree and making Calvin promise to lock his door at all times, he resolved to visit the police station. For a moment he thought he might be 'judging a book by its cover'. This was something he was not prone to do normally, but in this instance, he had an uneasy feeling that, for once, appearances were not deceptive.

The police were no help. What crime had the newly released Francis committed other than paying an old acquaintance a visit?

The dean tried to convey Calvin's unspoken but obvious misgivings and they promised to keep an eye on things.

This was a promise unfulfilled when a few days later, in the early hours; Calvin was discovered recumbent and unconscious in one of the secluded alleyways that led from the cathedral. His not overfilled wallet had been taken and there was, of course, no sign of his assailant or any clue as to whom he might be. The police hauled in the obvious suspect but could not prove anything as Calvin had been surprised from behind and they otherwise had little to go on. Francis avowed that on the night in question he'd been staying with an 'associate' – albeit a dubious one – in the country and having his alibi confirmed, insisted he be released. They let him go pending further enquiries and warned him to keep out of trouble. This was an admonition they knew would be ignored and they were fully aware that it would not be long before they would again be 'entertaining' his obnoxious person for some misdeed or other. A leopard does not change its spots and Francis was a classic example of the species.

After an overnight stay, Calvin was accompanied home in a hospital car by Peter and found to his astonishment that someone had deposited a splendid display of flowers in an expensive vase on his small lounge table.

A succession of visitors followed, headed at first by the dean, then Deaconess Lydia, the cathedral steward and various other clergy and even those portly ladies Bedlove and Panworthy bearing succulent gifts from the kitchen. After school came Helen and Jo who, for the very first time, indulged him with heartfelt and very big hugs.

Although some brought small gifts like grapes and chocolates, none of them confessed to being responsible for the splendid floral display. The only other person with a key, Peter, was questioned by Calvin over this and flatly denied any involvement. The children displayed understandable consternation at Calvin's bruised appearance, but he assured them of his well-being and with a start, something dawned on him. Peter was certainly the only other person with a key to Calvin's apartment and it was very possible that Peter had left it hanging amongst others on a convenient hook in his own home. In which case, his wife could have been the donor of the surprising bouquet.

And so it proved. Another ill wind had struck and sometime later, Calvin became a baptised and confirmed member of the Church of England as did his grandchildren, Helen and Joseph.

Inevitably, the nefarious Francis ended up back in jail, incarcerated for some other serious crime and as for Geraint and Ernest – despite the now converted Calvin's best efforts, old canines and new tricks came to mind. The Father didn't like it, but even though his newfound broad-mindedness had morphed him into a borderline agnostic, Peter continued to attend both the Catholic church and the cathedral. He just didn't get the transformation of bread and wine bit, but kept this revelation strictly to himself. He had almost come to think that it was the company of like-minded people that enabled organised religion to survive, not a faith in God, who most of the time didn't seem to be interested.

"Can't remember," said an ebullient Calvin, brandishing the kettle and addressing his current guest. "Is it one or two sugars?"

"None," replied his daughter. "Thought you would have known that by now."

True, she had now fully accepted him, but it might take a while for the slight asperity in her voice to absent itself permanently.

Author's Note

Readers of my other fiction are doubtless aware that I usually give Christianity a hard time. This is probably because I was brought up in a household where to speak against it was tantamount to blasphemy. My father had an indestructible faith which was all right in theory but did not seem to work in practice. We were always in debt, lost a couple of homes and did not have an easy existence. This largely accounts for what could be termed my cynicism and my 'descent' into agnosticism. I think atheists – particularly when I look at the mind-blowing universe – are equally misguided and believe no one has the truth and to claim to do so is sheer folly. However, in this story I have redressed the balance and toed the Christian line which, of course, may or may not be one route to immortality.

A Hat for all Seasons

(A fantasy for James)

ONE

Retired old farts came to Bellminster because it was mostly flat, and they could happily stagger round its small shopping centre before they declined and eventually expired. Some spent a good deal of their waking hours hurtling around on scooters trying to maim those of the innocent general populace who were not sprightly enough to evade their Formula One like antics and if a collision occurred, the police did not usually prosecute. A ninety-three-year-old speed merchant with dementia had little to fear from them and any dispute that arose from these geriatric high-speed activities was usually assigned to 'Bloody-minded Brenda'.

A civil enforcement officer, Brenda came over from the city to Bellminster twice a week and despite her draconian reputation, could sometimes be bribed with a pastry or two purchased from the excellent patisserie in the square. She accepted these offerings without an iota of guilt and unobserved by her bosses when in Bellminster, spent a lot of time 'chopsin' to all and sundry in a conducive coffee bar next to the library.

Everybody in Bellminster knew mercurial Brenda, including Nathan, who didn't have to concern himself overly with the invasive lady, as he hadn't a car. He therefore remained immune from her one overwhelming and assiduous passion: that of harassing the poor motorists who had the impudence to flout Bellminster's rigorous parking restrictions. Nathan didn't live on the flat, but in an avenue off the main road which led up to the vast Earl's Court Estate, a rabbit warren with a high percentage of the unemployed. It had a rife drug culture and harboured quite a number of the socially ill-disposed; partially leavened by a long-suffering minority of honest citizens, all of whom were supplied with the essentials of life from an adjacent supermarket.

Right now, Nathan was experiencing a dilemma. He couldn't decide what to wear on his head. A fine spring morning did not warrant the furtive donning of his all-embracing balaclava, and the fact that summer was some way off, made his Texan look – achieved with a Stetson specially imported from the longhorn state – a no-brainer. The fez acquired when on holiday in Marrakesh was an option but, as he hesitated at the idea of being labelled the only Muslim in Bellminster apart from the charming people at the Bangladeshi restaurant, he settled on his Breton beret. It would be no trouble to buy a string of onions in town and if he vaped whilst wearing them, he'd be able to tolerate the smell.

Armed with his partner's essential shopping list, he walked up to the main road and set off down the hill. He passed the large house that in Victorian times had housed accommodation for those of the opposite sex who were denoted on its exterior as 'decrepit ladies' – what was a decrepit lady? – and came to the crossroads and the traffic lights. Here heavy traffic made for the north and the Shropshire foothills: that largely unspoilt landscape of the poet Housman and the young English composer George Butterworth, slain in the First World War. Friday was market day, and he did not take long to reach Cob Square, where the traders did their best to make a bob or two in a not very healthy retail climate. The square contained a Wetherspoons tastefully functioning from the former GPO building and next door, imbibers lounged around, languorously sampling cask beers from a premises which bizarrely doubled as a tourist office. Hopefully, this dual purpose did not deter any teetotal visitors who merely wished to enquire about the whereabouts of the nearest toilet and perhaps a little optimistically, how they could get to the riverbank?

That any stranger should know of the river's existence was quite unlikely, but Bellminster did have a watercourse with which even some locals were not familiar. It flowed unobtrusively under a concrete bridge and remained remarkably undistinguished until it reached the outskirts of the town. Passing the back of the railway station, it became transformed, making its unhurried way through Hanboroughshire's gentle pastures, until it eventually arrived at Bodlingham, a place of man-made lakes that attracted an abundance of both indigenous and migrating wildfowl.

To reach his destination, Bellminster's imposing abbey, Nathan took a path near the banks of the oddly named River Plugwort and whereas on another occasion he might have paused a while to contemplate its depths, today he was in a hurry. He was anxious not to be late for his therapeutic ride on the great church's inherited ducking stool and, increasing his stride, arrived to see that a queue had formed in front of it.

Ducking stool rides were the brainchild of the vicar, the Reverend Oswald Stridlutt, and Nathan found his weekly participation in this practice soothingly satisfying. And today, after having his own ride, he had agreed to relieve the Reverend Oswald and to do some ducking himself.

Sometime in the days ahead, the vicar hoped to revive the process of 'dipping' people into the Plugwort, something that had been done to prove the innocence or guilt of 'witches' in the sixteenth century. The good clerk in holy orders anticipated that this proposed renaissance of 'people dipping' could be reinvented as a form of baptism. It would be retribution for the heinous use to which the ducking stool had been put in former days.

Meanwhile, the enterprising clergyman charged a guinea a time for the up and down rides which could be paid for by cash, card and contactless payments. This was a welcome boost for church funds – and for an extra fifty pence, depending on your taste, the organist would play either 'The Birdie Song' or a piece by Stockhausen to entertain you whilst you were in motion.

People came from far and wide to be 'ducked' and this popular pastime had not escaped the notice of St Edfrith, founder of an earlier monastery that had existed centuries before the abbey had come into being.

Silent, but attentive, yet not discernible to the human eye, St Edfrith was awaiting the sudden appearance of his friend and fellow apparition, St Botolph; a medieval missionary monk, who had visited and healed the sick and suffering of the parish for over a thousand years. St Edfrith hailed from the holy site of Lindisfarne and knew that Botolph would hit town pretty soon.

All the signs were there. Most significant of all, he'd seen a cruttock sitting on a fence post near Dinmore the other day and as cruttocks did not usually venture much further south than Bellminster, it was definitely an omen. The two-beaked, five-winged, cross-eyed cruttock was a rarity in these parts and its recent visit could only mean one thing: Botolph was not far off, and his apparition could materialise at any moment.

Two

Fed up with waiting and irritated by the constant squeaking of the ducking stool, Edfrith decided he would wait a further five minutes, then head off to the other place Botolph had been known to appear: the Duke's Head in Etnam Street. Botolph liked his pint and his revelation as an apparition in this worthy alehouse would not faze the punters who, either through engaging in quaffing vast amounts of ale or taking advantage of the considerable drugs scene in Bellminster, were quite used to being spaced out and could easily accept his presence with otherworldly equanimity.

Without bothering to open it, Edfrith left the abbey through the great door and wafted across the Grange, a square of manicured green where once cricket had been played. But cricket in such a constricted area had resulted in too many injuries and the park-like enclosure's former pavilion – an elegant black and white structure – now housed a café where the geriatrics and the mothers and toddlers who mostly inhabited the place, could sojourn for vittles and coffee at a reasonable price.

As he traversed the couple of quaint alleyways that led to Etnam Street, Edfrith was slightly overcome with nostalgia. He'd once played cricket in no-man's-land between heaven and hell. He'd turned out for the saints against the demons and realised the demons were not all bad. They'd stood their round in the Celestial Tavern afterwards and Jesus and St Peter had been umpires. Jesus confirmed that God was, indeed, a bearded white Englishman who invented the game, but at the same time, expressed his frustration that his Catholic and C. of E. followers practiced Mass and Eucharist. And not as black as theology has painted him, the

Devil was inclined to agree. Tired of being held responsible for perpetuating all the evil that, in reality, mankind caused on earth, he yearned for a peaceful life; free of the reputation which, in his opinion, he did not deserve.

Mulling things over as he entered the Duke's Head, and now openly visible, Edfrith encountered the apparition of Botolph propping up the bar. Various of the pub's regulars had no qualms in greeting him and he was not surprised to see his saintly friend, a halo hovering above him, talking in conducive fashion to the rosy-cheeked landlady.

On one of the brass-topped tables, a cruttock perched, and with what could be termed alternate eating habits, devoured a packet of tripe and treacle crisps. The bird had tried marijuana and prune flavoured and other sorts, but conveying his preference in alarmingly strident tones, had persuaded the startled landlady to supply packets of his preferred brand without dissent or requesting renumeration. The lateral movement of his head from left to right and back when feeding was caused by him having two beaks; a brace of throats and dual stomachs and favouring one side over the other would have caused severe digestive problems. He had similar difficulties with his five wings and tended to fly round in circles rather than in a straight line.

"What y' havin'?" Botolph enquired of his old friend. They hadn't had a good session for a long time, and he always enjoyed visiting Bellminster for the beer. Butty was an excellent real ale produced by the famous Wye Valley Brewery and given the opportunity, he would drink nothing else. His real mission was to cure the sick and feeble, but as the National Health Service did such a good job these days, he usually contented himself with dispensing a few heavenly placebos to the town's late-night drunks and left it at that.

Bending his elbow, Botolph said, "May the divine liquid enhance you and those that get pissed with you," and took a large gulp of the life-invigorating beverage.

"Cheers," replied Edfrith and winced as the cruttock, whose interest in the beer had been aroused, suddenly abandoned his repast and clumsily flew over to alight on the local saint's shoulder.

THREE

A kindly man, the Reverend Oswald Stridlutt was somewhat exhausted from manipulating the ducking school, and hanging a note on it saying, 'Back in an hour', he invited Nathan to join him for bacon and eggs at the café on the Grange. He had not yet revealed an ulterior motive for this generosity but knew that what he had to propose would probably be acceptable to his lunchtime companion. His intention to instigate baptism in the River Plugwort by immersing candidates with the aid of the ducking stool, would be unique, probably attract the faithful from near and far and was not something he could achieve without a good deal of help. He was sure the amiable and slightly eccentric Nathan would be interested, and the fact that the intelligent and highly gifted mortal had to the reverend's knowledge, no particular religious propensities, would not detract from his suitability.

In the Reverend Oswald's eyes, the main purpose of baptism was to ensure that the Church of England continued to survive. In common with most clergy attached to that flaky organisation (including the women who became ordained because it was a cushy job that didn't require childcare), he didn't believe in the Virgin Birth or the Resurrection but didn't want to be out of a job. So he evangelised and tried to perpetuate the Gospels to the best of his ability. That is not to say that he neglected the pragmatic side of Christ's teachings. He would help anyone that needed it and as a result, was very popular. He was married to a jolly lady who had recently joined the Jehovah's Witnesses. He did not find this a handicap yet longed for the day when an injury meant she'd have to accept or refuse a blood transfusion. He'd even allowed her to place copies of *The Watchtower* in the abbey; safe in the knowledge that most of his congregation would not be corrupted and would end up taking the scurrilous magazine home to hang in the toilet: judging from the abbey's meagre collections that some of them were possibly too mean to purchase toilet paper.

Nathan agreed to help with the baptisms and tentatively asked if he'd be allowed to wear the second-hand bishop's mitre he'd acquired from a pawn shop in Ludlow. The startled vicar wasn't sure about this and said he'd like to know more of its origins. Some time ago, the neighbouring Bishop of Crudshire had been defrocked, banished from his see and reduced to penury. He had been convicted of an unhealthy interest in the cathedral choirboys and though without proof, Reverend Oswald suspected that Nathan's mitre had been pawned by this same disgraced bishop and it might be irregular for a member of the nominal laity to wear it at a baptism.

After a brief lacuna when both parties resorted to sampling their coffees, the clergyman made up his mind. He would assent to Nathan wearing his mitre at the riverside service and if his own bishop got to hear of it, he could always maintain that Nathan was slightly deranged, had to be humoured, and that his services were so willing as to be indispensable.

FOUR

"You've heard of this ducking stool baptism idea, then?" said Edfrith. They were on about their fourth pint and his words came out a little slurred. Before replying, Botolph felt the need to sit on a tall bar stool.

"Certainly, we learn all the gossip up there, you know. Daft idea if you ask me."

"You're right and what does J.B. think of it? You've been there more recently than me; what does the old gypsy have to say?"

"John the Baptist? That old fart? Afraid he's lost it. He's too busy tryin' to find his head and even though relations are better with his nibs down below, no one can seem to locate it and he wanders around headless, muttering to himself and scaring the shit out of those with a nervous disposition."

"But surely our boss can sort that out? He always has the last word …"

He was bluntly interrupted by Botolph. "Ah, but it's that bloody Salome, she won't let on where she's put it, bloody whore that she is."

At this Edfrith displayed lascivious interest. "I have to say I did enjoy that old video of the dance she did. Nice pair of kno—"

Just then the bar door opened, and Nathan walked in. He seemed taken aback to discover the two saints propping up the bar and chatting in a convivial manner but was not alarmed when the cruttock suddenly transferred itself to his shoulder.

The bird uttered a cry that sounded as if he had sandpaper in his throat and Botolph hastened to make Nathan acquainted with the outlandish creature. Politely brought up, Nathan offered an effusive "How d' you do," and with a malevolent gleam in one of his three eyes, the cruttock proceeded to voice his probable disapproval by emitting a repetitious 'ORK, ORK, ORK!' frightening even the pub's spaced-out patrons who almost, but not quite, took refuge under the tables.

"What's your poison, lad, and what's this business about baptism by immersion in the Plugwort?"

Though playing the courteous host, Edfrith was keen to find out what exactly was happening from the horse's mouth, but before Nathan could say anything, in his forceful manner, Botolph butted in.

"Why's that old buffer doing it anyway? I thought the C. of E. and the Catholics were opposed to baptism by immersion and as for this nonsense with a ducking school ..."

Fortified by a goodly amount of his pint, Nathan felt it incumbent on him to explain. He thought baptism was a load of old cobblers and was just interested in the prospect of working the ducking stool. He would particularly enjoy the first candidate who, according to the vicar would be the newly converted and possibly politically expedient chairman of the county council. He was an extremely unpopular figure and with a bit of connivance and a substantial bribe, could be ducked down but not brought up from the river very quickly.

This underhand proposal had already been made to Nathan, who just happened to bump into the council's leader of the opposition as he left the abbey and made his way to the Duke's Head. The treacherous local politician had also suggested other fellow councillors he'd like to suffer the same fate, but after accepting an envelope to ensure the chairman's prolonged immersion, Nathan had politely declined this further offer and continued to the public house.

During all this discussion, Rosie the landlady had kept quiet, busying herself with pulling pints and unashamedly flaunting her cleavage; a prominent part of her anatomy blatantly admired by the two saints and other drinkers; the latter destined almost certainly to have unfulfilled desires in that direction. Neither of the holy men suffered from brewer's droop and it soon became obvious that they had other fish to fry. Still encumbered by the potentially hostile cruttock, Nathan deserted them to make conversation with an old friend, a sniffer of dubious solvents who'd once lent him a quid in order to relieve a past state of impecunity. Blessed with keen hearing, a genetic thing probably inherited from his crazy piano-tuning father, he tried not to eavesdrop on the talk now taking place at the bar in which the ravishing Rosie now seemed to be involved. He hadn't believed his partner when she'd firmly averred that Rosie had once dispensed her favours to all and sundry in the Earl's Cross red-light district and, dressed in his beret and onions, felt guilty to be drinking in such a den of iniquity. He was aware that Rosie's husband, 'creaking gate Kevin', was something of a damp squib – twenty years older and not providing enough to satisfy his wife's appetite – but the conversation coming from the bar profoundly shocked him.

Just then, the pub door opened and Avril, the part-time barmaid and general skivvy entered. She was a little wisp of a thing who apologised for her apparent lateness and more importantly, released Rosie to go upstairs with one of the apparitions: leaving Nathan to conjecture whether the other saint would be prepared to wait his turn.

FIVE

It was all over the *Bellminster Chronicle*. Front page news. People still bought this small-town newspaper to read about all the mundane misdemeanors you couldn't garner online. Funerals were especially something to savour and the fact that the deceased had more than likely been a complete bastard, did not deter half the townsfolk from attending his or her interment. Drug offences were common news and most recently, the populace had been convulsed when learning that a nonagenarian couple, Mr and Mrs Erasmus Splott of Concubine Way, had been 'busted' for growing 'weed' in the back garden of a council house situated in one of those sparsely populated villages on the back road to Ludlow. Most weeks, however, the *Chronicle* could only run to parking offences, sexual misconduct and badly written sports reports, but the front page of the current edition was nothing short of sensational.

It featured civil enforcement officer Bloody-minded Brenda, who'd been poking her nose in where she perhaps shouldn't and as a result, suffered an unprovoked attack by an extraordinary creature of the avian variety. She'd been severely traumatised and to the relief and amusement of Bellminster's harassed vehicle-owning fraternity, had fled back to the city to recuperate.

The initial object of her downfall had been a little yellow Fiat with bald tyres, parked outside the Duke's Head, and like a red rag to a bull the sight of it had persuaded her to enter the hostelry: her intention being to find the vehicle's owner and to call the police to make an arrest.

But what she encountered inside terrified her. Two sexually sated apparitions stood at the bar, whilst stoned and legless topers observed her with beatific expressions on their faces, and the only sober person appeared to be a relatively young man who, on his head, sported a Breton beret; this in turn complementing the string of onions which encircled his neck. To add to this, the small waif of a barmaid was conversing with the apparitions, and the buxom but dishevelled-looking landlady had returned from upstairs and was placing money in the till, which had definitely not been received from the sale of alcohol.

Bloody-minded Brenda only just had time to enquire whether anyone in the pub owned the offending motor, before the acutely prescient and savage cruttock was upon her. It appeared that the bird owned the little car and in his role of sacred harbinger, had travelled down to Bellminster a week ago to presage the imminent appearance of St Botolph. He came from a cruttock reservation in Wigan and with his inherent intellect, had passed his driving test, and emancipated from the slow process of flying round in small circles, had made short work of the journey. He'd immediately comprehended what Brenda was about as she walked through the door and his vicious attack took her completely by surprise. Circling behind her, he managed to gouge her left buttock with his left beak and the right one with the other; all the while emitting a series of raucous 'ORK, ORK, ORKs.' This bemused the already hornswoggled patrons and made them wholly incapable of rendering assistance to the by now, uncivil enforcement officer, who left in an undignified hurry: fleeing down the street to escape in her own car.

SIX

The police were entirely unsuccessful in their search for the two apparitions and the cruttock, and were currently interviewing Nathan Klavier, the well-known local pianist and artist who still sat in the interview room wearing his beret. He claimed to have been a mere spectator at the alleged public house fracas, and the only one sober and able to help them with their enquiries. They overlooked the beret and onions, aware that most artistic people in Bellminster suffered from similar idiosyncrasies and in any case, they didn't think what he had to reveal was anything more than a figment of his imagination.

Notified of Bloody-minded Brenda's flight by a passing pedestrian who'd been in Etnam Street at the time and who'd also expressed his astonishment at the soon-after departure from the pub of the two apparitions, he'd also informed them of an exotic bird who to his surprise made off in a small yellow Fiat.

It did not seem likely that both Nathan and the pedestrian were deranged, but even though their accounts of what happened were preposterous, the police had gone to the Duke's Head to check on what the landlady made of the unlikely happening. They arrived to find the pub deserted save for landlady Rosie and her tame little barmaid. The clientele had somehow sensed the arrival of the patrol car even before it entered Etnam Street and though hampered by their excessive indulgence in things debilitating, managed to scatter with remarkable alacrity.

Rosie, the landlady, denied the whole thing. Alerted on the grapevine that the boys in blue were imminent, she'd applied strong air freshener everywhere, supplied them with refreshment when they arrived and after answering a few perfunctory questions, watched them quickly depart. They said they had enough to occupy them without having to deal with apparitions and odd birds and since Brenda wouldn't show the city police the bites on her bum, the evidence was only circumstantial, and they couldn't be arsed to do anything about it.

They thanked Nathan for his co-operation, let him go and watched as he left the station. He was bound for the leisure centre where he sometimes played the piano in the lunch hour; an impromptu recital that gave pleasure to the staff and any nearby workers who came in to eat their midday sandwiches. During a break in his playing, he thought about the two cash-filled envelopes he now had stashed away in a box in the toilet. The one he'd got for assenting to prolong the recently converted chairman of the council's forthcoming baptismal ducking and the other acquired from the Chronicle for information supplied just recently for his basically true, but glamourised version of the goings-on in the Duke's Head. As it happened, the pedestrian who had notified the police over the incident was a friend he'd bumped into shortly afterwards in town, and a certain amount of collaboration had gone into the supposedly accurate account they'd given to the local rag. This was not an action which, if they had known, would have endeared them to the police who now had to pretend they were investigating it further. This thoroughly pissed off the inspector, a lazy sod who reiterated constantly that he too couldn't be arsed.

Arising from his piano stool, Nathan received a smattering of applause and nodding at a few acquaintances, made his way out of the leisure centre with the object of calling in at a small shop in Southern Avenue. The proprietors of this dubious retail unit, an Anglo-Chinese couple called Ho and Chee Ponsoby-Smith, had come to Bellminster to open a Chinese restaurant, but found that selling opium and similar products under the counter and owning one of several brothels in the Earl's Cross red-light district, to be a far more profitable enterprise.

After purchasing a toilet roll, a busby (ex-Irish guards' type), two Mars bars and some manure for the back garden, and resisting the temptation to buy any of the Anglo-Chinese couple's more questionable products, Nathan headed for the other end of town where he had arranged to meet the well-known musician, Aaron Rumple, at the Leonine Ballroom.

SEVEN

A slick and expeditious operator despite his benign façade, the Reverend Oswald had already signed up Aaron Rumple to provide music at the baptism service. Nathan was to attend a rehearsal of Pandemonium, a collection of amateur musicians that had been gathered by Bellminster's downtown musician. This eclectic ensemble included shawms, rebecs, lutes, an electric guitar, sundry out-of-tune recorders, a seven-string mandolin (the player couldn't afford eight), an ophicleide, a tea chest bass and a mighty four-manualled bloddlesplonge: the latter to be played by Nathan when released from operating the ducking stool or adjusting his mitre.

Arriving at his destination, Nathan was effusively greeted by Aaron, who was attired in his usual all-year-round garb of sandals and socks; a sartorial faux pas that nobody had the heart to point out to him. Its one redeeming aspect was that it did provide employment for a local chiropodist in the winter whose wife was a financial liability and fishaholic, with an addiction for fish fingers. She ate nothing else and this, allied to her penchant for consuming two bottles of vodka per day, meant the chiropodist was glad of the money.

The rehearsal went well, and once Nathan had solved the mystery of the row of stops above the keyboard that shot out at intervals of their own volition, he enjoyed playing the raucous bloddlesplonge at full volume. He soon discovered that the stops were being activated by large Icelandic beetles called addlenots that had been transported to Bellminster via ship and rail to replace a shortage of Liechtenstein prawns. They had escaped the freezer to colonise the enclosed wind chest of the bloddlesplonge, finding it a warmer habitat than their accustomed home at the bottom of an ice-covered lake. When approached by Nathan to reconsider their interference, they were quite amicable and simply furnishing them with join-the-dots kindergarten books as an alternative, kept them happy while he was performing,

EIGHT

Brenda's bum hadn't healed that well, but gallantly returning to work, she was having to sit on her left buttock. The chair she sat on had a cushion provided by the kind proprietors of the café next to the library, and presently she would have to shift her not inconsiderable weight to her right buttock. But even though this was causing her much discomfort, she had other things to worry about.

Unbeknown to her employers she had taken to carrying a small pistol. She kept it secreted in a pocket of her knickers with the intention of shooting the infernal bird that had molested her backside should she ever encounter it again. But there had been no sign of the cruttock since the incident, and as they had a habit of doing, both saintly apparitions had vanished.

Not that familiar with firearms, Beryl hoped she'd put the safety catch on the pistol which was positioned dangerously near a vital part of her frontal anatomy and hoped it wouldn't discharge a bullet by accident. Another concern was the Reverend Oswald's intention to hold a big baptism service down by the footbridge which spanned the River Plugwort. She gravely questioned the decision to trundle the ducking stool down there to assist in this sacred ceremony and wondered if it was within her remit to interfere. She didn't imagine that anyone had served a parking ticket on a ducking stool before, and thought the notoriety earned from doing so, could make her the most hated civil enforcement officer in the county. She would be proud to achieve this exalted status and drinking up her heavily impregnated coffee (the proprietors laced it liberally with gin; this serving to ensure their Robin Reliant remained ticketless) she set out once more to terrorise the town's hapless motorists. Carrying a gun in her underwear gave her a sense of impregnability and if she received any protests from her victims, she'd not hesitate to use it.

NINE

The bishop sent his apologies. He didn't really approve of baptism by immersion. He preferred christening and later confirmation, but he wished them well and hoped none of those subjecting themselves to a ducking would end up drowning: something the Reverend Oswald assured him would not happen.

With the bishop not attending, Nathan was free to wear the mitre. He surveyed himself in a mirror inherited from a great aunt and seemed satisfied. Great Aunt Pegatha had expired from consorting too much with certain members of an underground Catholic men's society who were employed sticking pins into the products of a condom-manufacturing factory: thus ensuring the Catholic Church of future congregations, but also contributing to a number of furtive abortions. This was unfortunate and Nathan had considered trying to trace what must be Pegatha's variously sired offspring, but since a good percentage of them were likely to be in need, he thought better of it and reverted to adjusting his attire and inciting his partner not to make a fuss. His partner thought the whole thing sheer nonsense, yet encouraged his participation whilst shrewdly keeping out of it and thinking herself lucky to be able to concentrate on her own normal interests.

TEN

Nathan took his usual route to the Plugwort and was thankful it was a fine day. It could equally have been bloody awful with 'urine' descending remorselessly and for this reason, he did not fully accept the notion of an omnipotent deity. He'd undoubtedly experienced the apparitions that were Botolph and Edfrith, but without conversing with them in depth and putting their emotive opinions under scrutiny and taking into account what he now thought of their 'hypocritical sexual deviance', he was inclined to keep his own counsel: adding a pinch of salt and concentrating on a more temporal existence.

He passed the house of 'decrepit' women and – want to tally the number of times he'd acknowledge a greeting from someone on the way – felt that Bellminster wasn't such a bad place, and that there was no real explanation as to why some people were well disposed to others, and others not. He wondered if in future the medical profession would be enabled to transplant mental attitudes, eradicate 'badness' and, going one up on the supposed God, implant a sunny disposition and an honest demeanour into the incorruptible mind of every soul that inhabited the earth.

Still very early, he noted that the sky had changed into hues of bruising blacks, yellows and purples and he hoped that the great orb that lay behind this expanse would soon reveal itself again and that a raging tempest would not break and ruin the day. He promised the Reverend Oswald he'd arrive early and this he did; finding the ducking stool already in place by the footbridge: a somewhat alien sight that had not been seen for some four hundred years. He understood that before the ducking ceremony could begin, the vicar would bless this archaic machine and even though not of any particular religious persuasion or an advocate of superstition, Nathan had mildly inherent doubts about using the thing for a holy experience and was glad the clergyman had seen fit to consecrate it.

Only one thing marred this pending use of the ducking stool for religious purposes. A parking ticket had been stuck on the side of it, denoting that the notorious Bloody-minded Brenda had walked this way. Nathan hoped she'd keep clear of the immersions. He hadn't seen evidence of the cruttock being in the vicinity and she'd be best to stay out of the way. With the Reverend Oswald's approval, he tore the offending ticket off the ducking stool and tossed it into a temporarily sited waste bin nearby. What could only be described as a rustically home-made stage had been constructed in the pasture on the other side of the river and Nathan was pleased to note that with it taking centre stage, someone had thoughtfully covered the bloddlesplonge with polythene sheeting. Another improvement was an absence of all the flotsam and jetsam that normally besmirched the Plugwort. The usual selection of Coca-Cola cans, takeaway cartons, face masks and condoms were conspicuous by their absence, and an old pram which to Nathan's knowledge had been there for at least five years, had also been removed. Having emigrated downstream, the ducks were now returned, and the river displayed a purity not seen for many years. The scene was set and in a slow trickle, people and performers began to arrive.

ELEVEN

Even before the cruttock flew into the branches of the willow, he sensed their presence. He stood under the nearby alder and acknowledged the poor, deluded folk as they came along the footpath, and he could not help but feel a smidgeon of empathy for them. They greeted him in passing and he'd never forgotten he'd once been an important member of the holy host himself and tried to temper his interference with a little compassion and understanding. To look at him you would not know, and he'd only decided to pay a visitation out of curiosity. He could have sent a minion, but as there was no record of ducking stools being revived and used for such contrary ceremonies until now, it intrigued him to know what would transpire.

He watched as the Reverend Oswald began the first duckings by shaking hands, then nodding at Nathan, raised his hands in the air; this inciting the excited gathering to indulge in a succession of triumphant 'Hallelujahs.' The eminent visitor had known and tempted the ducking stool operator over the years, admired his taste in head gear and wondered if he was aware that the mitre and bishop's crook were the inventions of the Etruscans and possibly before them, the Greeks. They were pre-Roman and pagan in their beliefs and that the formal churches had declared bishops to be the descendants of the Apostles was sheer fabrication and probably just another falsehood that had served to keep the people in awe and subjection.

Glancing at the cruttock in the willow, he sensed it was regarding him with its triple beady eyes, but it surely knew better than to tangle with such an eminent representative of the underworld.

The sun had deigned to disperse the ominous black clouds, and all was progressing well, save rather than appearing elated and 'born anew', the first candidate came up half-drowned as predetermined and not very happy. The stranger knew this to be the chairman of the council and thought it served the bastard right. Good for Nathan who, after the first few duckings, handed over to the Reverend Oswald's rather lovely female curate and crossed the footbridge to take his place at the imposing bloddlesplonge. Standing there, attired in a deerstalker and a tweed suit, the stranger lit his pipe and was faintly amused when, led by the enthusiastic Aaron Rumple, the musically polyglot ensemble launched in to 'I do Like to be Beside the Seaside' in an unholy selection of disparate keys.

Fortunately, the competent bloddlesplonge player succeeded in drowning his fellow performers, and as the piece came to a ragged conclusion, he promptly sounded the opening bars of Bach's famous *Toccata and Fugue in D minor*, which vanquished the other instrumentalists, who weren't quite up to it. Whether Johann Sebastian would have approved of this, the pipe-smoking observer did not know, but as far as he was concerned, the bloddlesplonge made a great sound and he'd have to persuade its player to bring it with him when he eventually left 'this mortal coil'. For he was sure the lad would almost certainly be descending into his neck of the woods. He would surely not opt for that other celestial destination and as a further incentive, could be offered the prized deerstalker. Added to that, who would turn down an eternal scenario of loose women, plenteous alcohol and as a musician, the chance to fraternise with all those composers like Debussy and Schubert who had arrived there allegedly through prematurely acquired sexual diseases. Contrary to Christian teaching, when passing away, people were given a choice as to where they spent eternity and where 'he' ruled, they had the lot. Christians, Muslims, Hindus, Sikhs, Jews; all of whom upon death had been surprised to find out that their respective creeds were of no consequence: some of whom chose to ascend, and others descend. There wasn't much to choose between the bland life above the clouds and that in the very bowels of the universe, but in the lower domain, souls would not be chivvied over any so-called transgressions. Up there, you'd probably have to endure the constant censorship of God and Allah, although he had a lot of time for Jesus who'd always shown a good deal of compassion, but as for Muhammad...

A sudden shriek came from the sturdy young lady curate who was working the ducking stool and that could only mean one thing. With a candidate still immersed, she'd hastily let go and the Reverend Oswald had to step in and hoist the near-drowned convert to safety.

TWELVE

The young curate was being comforted by a matronly lady bedecked with what could be described as half a garden displayed on her hat and he knew that the poor young girl would have a job explaining what had happened and probably wouldn't be believed.

St Botolph again. He had a nasty habit of remaining invisible whilst molesting members of the opposite sex. He'd most likely fondled her where he shouldn't and how on earth could she claim it happened without anyone seeing?

And now things were really hotting up. Without warning, the apparition of St Edfrith appeared, closely followed by that of St Botolph, and the two of them were soon engaged in a furious verbal altercation with the Reverend Oswald Stridlutt who, despite his seemingly inoffensive manner, gave as good as he got. A multitude began to gather around them: a goodly number not sympathetic to baptism by immersion and mostly present with the sole intention of causing disruption to proceedings. They included the drunken old Catholic priest, Father Sheamus O'Guinness – a member of the famous family who'd been cast aside for drinking most of the profits – supported by his followers and aided by conspirators from the C. of E. who were utterly opposed to the vicar's innovative new ideas. In opposition, members of the charismatic churches had come along to lend support and a gradually increasing, an angry murmur arose from the simmering crowd.

It was not known who landed the first punch and soon mayhem broke out. All intentions of continuing with the immersions were abandoned and in the general melee, the ducking stool was cursed by the two saints and turned on its side in the Plugwort. The demonic cruttock left its perch in the willow and flew at the Reverend Oswald who, showing great defensive qualities, warded him off by whacking the ferocious creature with his crucifix; an action for which he would ask God's forgiveness and understanding later, as he was under extreme provocation at the time.

Someone summoned the authorities with a mobile phone and sirens could soon be heard, both ambulances and police cars making for the pastures on the opposite bank as there was no way they could attend the disturbance otherwise. They arrived to find the 'orchestra' in disarray: some of whom, too, were not pro-immersion and had turned on their fellow instrumentalists. This resulted in fractured recorders and holed drum vellums – not in the deerstalkered figure's later observation of the scene, a particularly unfortunate outcome!

With good fortune the bloddlesplonge and its player seemed to be inviolate and blessed with exceptional eyesight, the aloof observer noticed Nathan creeping over the pasture and away from the conflagration taking place. The watcher was glad of this. He considered the man to be his protégé and had long since given up tempting him. Let him go home to his placid and understanding partner, well out of all that was happening here. He only hoped that a longing to smoke again would not recur and taking advantage of his superior status in being able to do that which he recommended others should not do, he opened a pack of best Cuban cigars, pulled one out, lit it, and puffed away with sublime contentment.

The police came across the footbridge with almost murderous intent and were indiscriminate in the use of their batons. They were closely followed by the medics and this caused the unholy contest to soon subside. In cowardly fashion, the two apparitions dissolved and the cruttock, who had been dealt a mighty blow by the Reverend Oswald, retired to lick his wounds within the encompassing branches of a chestnut tree in full bloom.

Now might be a good time to go and see Rosie. She'd usually oblige, even if it would make a big hole in his wallet. So, with a high degree of anticipation, Lucifer made his way to the Duke's Head.

THIRTEEN

Nathan sat in the garden watching his Bohemian, dishevelled neighbour as he tried to start the ancient, unsightly and wholly rusted motorhome that had been parked outside their homes for the past ten years. Since the neighbour was comparatively harmless, it was something Nathan had come to accept, and now relieved to be ensconced in a deckchair, his mitre still mounted on his head, he was glad to have escaped the horrific confrontation on the Plugwort. Relieved to be home on this balmy evening, he'd been made a great cup of coffee by his understanding partner and had found amongst his vast collection of literature a book entitled The Ancient Etruscans: Their Civilisation and Their Spiritual Beliefs.

Intrigued, he settled down to read and did not notice a sudden fluttering, as something avian flew into the rowan tree nearby. This was closely followed by a raucous cry that shattered the still night air: 'ORK, ORK, ORK!'

He was further startled by a baritone hail from a female who now stood by the rusty motorhome; the owner of which had hastily retreated inside.

"This 'eap belong to you?"

The voice was unmistakable, and Nathan looked up from his book in time to see the alerted and savvy cruttock pursue the fleeing lady down the road, and after a brief, uneventful interval, a shot rang out. This was followed by a brief stentorian cry, and robbed of his victim, the cruttock continued on his ungainly way: down to where the bald-tyred Fiat was parked.

Silly bitch, thought the intelligent bird to himself. Must have forgotten to put the safety catch on.

Author's Note

My thanks to my son James who every so often sends me nonsensical texts to which I reply in kind, and – like a long rally in tennis – these exchanges can go on indefinitely, until one of us chooses to stop or expire from sheer exhaustion. However, 'it's an ill wind' and I hope this has enabled me to put our digital 'jousting' to good use by writing this farcical tale!